Toxic Airlines

Also distributed by DFT Enterprises Ltd on the aviation contaminated air issue:

DVD: Welcome Aboard Toxic Airlines - Documentary Film
Produced by Fact Not Fiction Films Ltd - 2007
EAN 5-060151-960009
(www.welcomeaboardtoxicairlines.com)

Aviation Contaminated Air Reference Manual
Editor: Susan Michaelis
ISBN 978 0 9555672 0 9
First edition published in April 2007
Published by Susan Michaelis
(www.susanmichaelis.com)

DVD: Contaminated Air - An Ongoing Health and Safety Issue
Educational Documentary produced by the non profit group
AOPIS for the Australian Federation of Air Pilots (AFAP) in
2003.
(www.aopis.org)

Toxic Airlines

Tristan Loraine

Edited by Katherine Gregor

DFT Enterprises Ltd 2007

Published by DFT Enterprises Ltd
www.dftenterprises.com

ISBN 978 0 9555437 1 5
First edition published in Great Britain in April 2007

A CIP catalogue record of this book is available from the British Library.

Printed and bound in England by Biddles Ltd.

This book is printed on paper made from fully managed and sustained forest sources.

FSC

TT-COC-002303

© 1996 Forest Stewardship Council A.C.

A copy of this book was donated to and available from the:

Bodleian Library (Oxford);
Cambridge University Library;
Ottawa Public Library;
Auckland City Libraries;
New York Public Library;
New South Wales State Library (Sydney);
Australian National Library.

Dedicated to all those individuals around the world who have suffered from exposure to contaminated air on commercial aircraft.

Chapter 1

Daylight is still a couple of hours away in Newcastle-upon-Tyne. The freezing Northumbrian temperatures are already affecting driving. This is the land of the short winter days, yet at the airport, located about six miles from the city centre, it is business as usual. Over six million passengers a year go through the Newcastle Airport and the weather will no more affect the hustle and bustle today than it has before.

Working in the control tower is the morning shift, made up of three air traffic controllers. They sit on the Western side of the airfield, overlooking the airport apron. The apron being the part of an airfield set aside for loading, unloading or maintaining aircraft. In a moment, several aircraft will be requesting start up clearances on the apron and the workload will increase significantly. A young controller walks up to the top floor carrying a tray with polystyrene cups of steaming tea.

Only two aircraft are currently inbound to the airport. Established on approach is JASP Flight 'JP303'. It is operated by an old Boeing 757 aircraft on the first flight of the day from London to Newcastle and is about six miles from touchdown. Some 10 miles behind JP303 is a cargo flight with the call sign 'Lift 212' – an equally old Airbus A300.

Heavy rain and a strong wind buffets the control tower windows. Another air traffic controller is looking through the heavy rain at the floodlit apron and the numerous aircraft being prepared for departure. The first ones are mostly charter flights with holiday makers bound for a selection of Mediterranean destinations.

He pushes the transmit switch. "JASP 303, clear to land two five, surface wind now three four zero degrees forty gusting fifty knots."

After a few seconds without reply, he transmits again. "JASP 303, clear to land two five, surface wind now three four zero degrees forty gusting fifty knots."

His colleague walks past him, slurping his tea. "Don't think they heard you. They will be earning their money today, in this weather!"

"You're right!" He tries again, "JASP 303, clear to land two five, surface wind now three four zero degrees forty gusting fifty knots."

A female voice finally replies, "Roger, cleared to land."

Two airport workers in a four wheel drive vehicle are carrying out a routine inspection of the airfield perimeter near the approach end of runway 25 as the Boeing 757 roars overhead. The man in the passenger seat looks out his side window and watches the aircraft as it rolls from side to side in the heavy gusts of wind. Condensation trails run off the wingtips and the red and white strobe lights on the aircraft fuselage and wing tips show the aircraft trajectory easily despite the heavy rain. The aircraft passes the usual touchdown point still airborne whilst pitching and rolling uncharacteristically, as though reluctant to return to hard ground.

In the distance, a light suddenly flashes from the right side of the aircraft. There is a deafening bang.

"Holy Shit!" shouts the man in the passenger seat.
The Boeing 757 has been seriously damaged and is engulfed in flames.

The 80,000 kilogram mass of the aircraft with the right undercarriage and nose gear collapsed moves rapidly away from the paved surface of the runway. Within seconds the aircraft has come to a halt amidst thick black smoke and scarlet flames.

One of the air traffic controllers has dropped his polystyrene cup on the carpet. Next to him, his colleague stares out of the window. "Please, no!"

Another man hits the 'crash' button and picks up the telephone. "Hello this is Newcastle tower, we've had a serious crash. JASP flight JP 303 has left the paved surface, broken into several pieces and is on fire. Airfield is closed. Please activate the emergency response plan."

The watch manager responds calmly. "At what time was the crash?"

"1 minute ago."

Flames and thick black smoke pour out of the crash site. The driver of the four wheel drive vehicle drives quickly towards the wreckage whilst his colleague transmits on the vehicle radio.

"Mayday, Mayday. Boeing 757 crashed on landing 200m left, left of runway centre line with fire and heavy smoke. Leader two en route."

Simultaneously, two Carmichael Cobra major foam tenders burst out of the airport fire station, heading for the crash site followed by a third appliance a short distance behind. With their sirens sounding and lights flashing they arrive quickly at the crash site. At 10,000 litres a minute the tenders quickly start to spray the fire, whilst several fire-fighters approach the burning aircraft.

The cockpit is seriously damaged. Straining to see through the smoke, Carol Parker, the co-pilot, turns her head slowly towards the Captain, Alan Jones. His head is slumped to the right, and blood is trickling down his forehead, over his closed eyelids.

Carol swallows a sob. She is in pain and her head is throbbing. Her right arm and legs are badly injured and she knows she could not move even if she tried. The cockpit is on its side. A bright torch beam shines into her face. The firefighter's voice sounds very far away. "Can you hear me? Can you hear me, Miss?"

The ringing in her ears fades, and the firefighter's face behind the torch grows blurred. Carol wants to speak but she cannot draw sufficient breath. Her eyelids weigh heavy over her eyes. She cannot see or hear anything.

"Miss, stay with me! Miss, look at me!"

The firefighter sees the young woman's head drop forward. The back of her blonde hair is covered in blood. He rushes to her and lifts up her chin. "Miss, open your eyes!"

He keeps shouting, hoping against hope.

Chapter 2

There are no spare seats at the Cathedral Church of St Nicholas in Newcastle. The cathedral is named for St Nicholas, the patron saint of sailors and boats. And pilots, thinks Jill Parker, as she glances around at the families and relatives of those attending the memorial service for those who lost their lives on JASP flight 303. Except that pilots did not exist when this church was built. St Nicholas was originally a parish church, built in 1091, but this was destroyed in a fire in 1216. It was rebuilt in 1359 and became a cathedral in 1882 when the diocese of Newcastle was created by Queen Victoria. Jill remembers the school trips but not the name of the Geordie teacher. "St Nicholas may not be in the same league as Durham Cathedral," he would say, "but it has had throughout the centuries equal impact on the lives of local people."

Family members occupy the front rows alongside the large group of management representatives of JASP who sit beside the aviation regulator and the local MP. Today, the Dean of Newcastle, the Very Reverend Christopher Young is addressing his flock. Jill thinks that his voice sounds almost metallic through the microphone pinned to his preaching scarf. He stands in the pulpit, his attention not just on the mourners but on the media cameras which now seem to be ever present at large scale tragedies. Events once kept for families to grieve over in peace but now broadcast to anyone who cares to watch.

Reverend Young's voice bounces off the stone walls, "I am asked why the Lord can take so many lives in such a tragic way and why he chooses to spare a small few. It is at moments like this that our faith in the Divine Plan is most tested."

Reverend Young turns the page of his prepared speech, "I am also asked how the Lord deals with blame. We have all seen the newspaper headlines and the question of blame yet again being placed upon the shoulders of those who are no longer with us to defend themselves. Our Lord Jesus teaches forgiveness and to love our neighbour. In these difficult times we should unite to share our grief and not seek to attribute blame. There is not a man or woman in this church who has not done wrong, however small, at some time in his or her life. And yet God forgives all."

What God? Jill knows she is doubting because of her anger. She does not seriously doubt. What God? My sister is dead. She was only twenty-four. She had dreams. Plans. Many terrorists and evil people are still alive. No. There is a God. There has to be. Life has to make some sort of sense, even if she cannot understand it right now.

Reverend Young's voice drones, "Love thy neighbour and learn forgiveness, the world has too much hatred and anger already. Our community needs to pull together and be strong through these testing moments. Finally, I would like to pay tribute to the heroic work of the emergency services and local hospitals which responded so professionally to this accident. I also ask you to pray for Paul Brown, the twenty year-old fireman who lost his life in trying to save others."

Twenty. That's even younger than her sister. Jill scans the neighbouring pews. She suddenly wants to see the face of his mother or his sister, if he has one. Her eyes well up. She swallows. She remembers that her mother, standing next to her, must not see her cry.

The congregation stand to sing the final hymn. Jill puts her right arm around her mother to comfort her. There are drops of water on her mother's New English Hymnal. They have already stood just like this. Six years ago, when Jill and Carol's father died in a military plane crash. The girls had stood on

6

either side of their mother. Today, Jill is alone with her arm around the thin, elderly frame. She cannot let go. Not yet. As they walk down the aisle several people offer their sympathy but they are but one of many families who have suffered. People they do not know and probably never will know. People with whom she and her mother will always have something in common now.

Outside the cathedral, the wind is hard and damp against Jill's face. "You stay here, my pet, I'll just go and get the car."

It is Margaret, Jill's mother's best friend. She hesitates, perhaps wondering if Jill has heard her. "Felicity, my love, Jill will look after you while I fetch the car. Don't go away."

And where would we go? Thinks Jill.

"Jill!"

"Are you cold, Mum?"

Felicity shakes her head.

"Jill!" The same man's voice through the crowd of dissipating congregation members. This time, he has put his hand on her shoulder.

Jill turns around. Gary. Gary from Junior school. Grown up. His soft face hardened by the grey shadow of a shaved beard. His unruly hair cropped up military style. The same cheeky blue eyes. All the girls in their form giggled when they talked of Gary's blue eyes.

"Gary! Good God – what are you –"

"My father was on the flight."

"Oh, Gary, I'm so sorry!"

"Yeah. He'd been down to watch Newcastle play West Ham in the cup tie with some mates. Retirement present the night before. We got beat 2-1 and he lost his life flying back on the first flight to do his last day at work. You got to hand it to the guy upstairs, he's got a sense of humour."

Gary always had a matter of fact attitude. Although he was close to his dad, Jill remembers his 'what will be' approach

7

to life from when they were younger. It was probably this characteristic that had seen Gary leave school at sixteen and join the Parachute Regiment. He must be at least six foot, Jill thinks, her eyes on his black suit as he turns his back to her and curves his shoulders to shake her mother's hand, offering his condolences. Felicity's face is trusting as she looks into his eyes, then turns inquisitively at her daughter. "This is Gary Bamford, Mum. We were at junior school together. Gary's dad was on Carol's flight."

Felicity holds Gary's hand for a moment, searching for something comforting to say. Words of wisdom from an older person to a young one. Instead, she tightens her lips as she grasps Gary's hand very tight. Her eyes glisten.

Gary puts his other hand on Felicity's, "I am very sorry about Carol, she was salt of the earth. I'll never forget those flights she took me on when she was building up her hours as a Private Pilot. Flying was her life. I thought she had gone to the Middle East to work so when I read her name in the paper yesterday when they finally disclosed the crew details, I couldn't believe it."

Mrs Parker nods, "Thank you, Gary. I am so sorry about your father."

Jill tells Gary that her sister decided not to take the Middle East job although it offered better pay and conditions because she wanted to stay in Newcastle, close to her family.

"Did Jill die on impact or later?"

Gary's directness takes Jill aback. If anyone else had been so inconsiderate, so soon... "The fireman did a great job," she says. "They found Carol still strapped to her seat very seriously injured. She died in A & E at the hospital."

Felicity's friend drives up to the curb and lowers the passenger window. Jill opens the back door, and helps her mother into the car.

"Have you seen the initial accident report?" Gary asks.

Jill is now angry with his questions. *What are you – a flipping journalist?* "No, I haven't. What will it change, anyway? Carol is gone."

As though that was an appropriate answer to her question, Gary takes his mobile phone out of his pocket. "I'm off to Canada on exercise, tomorrow. What's your number?"

He keys in the digits under Jill's dictation. She is sitting in the passenger seat, the rain lashing her face. Gary promises he will "pop by" when he is next home. She rolls up the window. Her face is suddenly burning. Margaret has switched on the heating inside the car.

Gary looks at the people huddling under their umbrellas. The rain is heavier now. Everyone has left the cathedral while he was talking to Jill. He searches in vain for a familiar face, then starts walking away. He tries to remember his mother's face. His father told him she had gone to be with the Angels. Gary was five then. He indulged in the hope that his parents may be together now. He shuddered in the cold air and found himself wishing Jill and her mother had invited him back for a cup of tea.

Chapter 3

The Vermont Hotel in Newcastle has an unrivalled setting next to the Castle overlooking the Tyne and Millennium Bridges and is very popular with holiday makers and businessmen. As Jill and her mother walk into the lobby, the concierge directs them to the conference room reserved by JASP airlines. The families of the other six cabin crew who lost their lives in the crash are already sitting down. Jill meets their accusatory eyes and finds herself lowering hers. Jill wishes she could leave now. She wants to straighten up and tell them all that it's not Carol's fault. But she knows she would choke on her own voice.

"You must be Carol's family." A sad but warm voice rises from the chill. "I am Liz Jones, Alan's wife."

They shake hands drawing strength from each-other. At least, they are not alone anymore. Liz is a small, red haired woman with freckles on her face and hands. She is softly spoken and Jill tries to reconcile in her imagination the woman she had so often heard Carol describe as the wife of henpecked Captain Alan Jones.

A top table has been erected for airline representatives and the insurers. A stocky man in his forties hovers and Liz introduces him to Jill and Felicity as Martin Stone. He is the head of the pilot union Flight Safety Department. From the way Liz looks at Martin Stone, Jill senses that they must all trust him. That he will make everything right. He offers his condolences as he shakes hands and smiles. He has clearly perfected his friendly style over a number of years. They all sit together towards the back of the room. There are about thirty family members and their friends, as well as the pilot and cabin crew union representatives.

Presiding over the top table is Sophie McDonald, Head of Human Resources in the airline. To her right is the chief pilot and head of cabin services. On her left is a representative from the insurers and a solicitor for the airline.

Sophie McDonald introduces the top table members and then swiftly gets to the purpose of the meeting.

"Thank you all for coming here today. We appreciate these have been difficult times for you, as they have been for the airline. You will have all received by now copies of the initial investigation findings but these are not yet final so please bear that in mind. Without wishing to seem lacking in compassion, the board needs to minimise the impact these events have had– not only on you and the other families of the passengers who have lost their lives in the accident, but also to move forward as swiftly as possible to protect the business as a whole. The AAIB and the investigation team have assured the Secretary of State for Transport that they will conclude their investigations as quickly as possible and have been given extra resources to achieve this. The Secretary of State for Transport, as you may know, has agreed with the Civil Aviation Authority that they will now complete a Coroner's investigation into the accident, including its root causes and this investigation is well on its way. They will report as soon as possible and their findings and recommendations will be made public. The investigation team will include people who are independent of the Civil Aviation Authority and will conclude with a public hearing at a date to be advised shortly here in Newcastle."

She pauses to have a sip from a glass of water. Her speech shows she is a business graduate pushed into human resources by a management keen like all airlines to reduce costs in the world of ever rising oil prices.

Sophie McDonald resumes her speech, "The board have decided that all crew members, regardless of length of service or rank will be treated equally. The board are prepared to offer, without any admission of liability, a payment to the next of kin of each employee the sum of £150,000, as well as three years pension contributions made by the employee and employer during their time of employment, whether they began the day the airline started or not. This is in addition to the payment made to you shortly after the accident. We feel this to be an extremely generous offer, especially as EU law clearly states that 'in all cases the carrier will only be liable for claims for which legal liability is established.' The board feels a lengthy legal case would be neither in your nor the airline's better interests. We have prepared the necessary paperwork for you to take away and review. Needless to say you should seek legal advice before agreeing to the offer. We are happy to answer any questions about the company offer or any aspect you wish to discuss but firstly we wish to invite the two union representatives from the pilot union and cabin crew to offer any views or comments on what has been said so far and which was presented to them yesterday for evaluation."

Martin Stone stands up and addresses the room, "The pilot union has reviewed the offer and we feel the airline is being very generous in these difficult times. We are working with the regulator to try and get the industry back on track as soon as possible. We recommend that the families of Captain Alan Jones and First Officer Carol Parker accept this settlement and have today written to them to that effect."

Nicola Matthews, the flight attendant representative, stands up, "We will discuss the matter with family members when the time is appropriate and when they have had the opportunity of proper legal representation. The memorial service was only yesterday and we feel these matters should not be rushed."

She sits down sharply. Nicola and her union focus on the welfare of the members and their families. Jill notices the very clear difference in approach.

An older family member of one of the deceased cabin crew stands up and asks the top table, "The initial report points towards pilot error, is that the view of the board?"

The chief pilot stands up to answer, "The report states this is the most likely possibility but the purpose of this meeting is not to apportion blame but to move forward."

Another family spokesperson stands up "Did the aircraft have any defects?"

The chief pilot responds, "The Civil Aviation Authority and the airline have investigated this and our view is the aircraft had no defects when it departed London and no defects were reported by the crew in flight. The Air Accidents Investigation Branch will give their view when they have completed their investigations in conjunction with the aircraft manufacturer and Rolls Royce the engine manufacturer."

The same family member fires another question, "The media said the aircraft should not have attempted to land in such poor weather conditions, other papers say commercial pressure forced the crew into this crash. What is your view?"

JASP's chief pilot replies, "Our crews are highly trained and professional individuals. If they thought conditions were not favourable for a safe approach and landing and had elected to divert, we would have supported their decision. 100% safety is the focus of our business. The reported weather conditions at the time of landing were just within the aircraft certificated limits."

Nonsense, thinks Jill. Carol had told her the story of a crew who went sick as they were too tired to do the last two sectors on a five sector day and felt it was not safe. They had been invited for "tea and biscuits" as they say in the industry and told very clearly to see a doctor or wind their necks in. She remembers Carol frequently talking about the cumulative fatigue of poorly constructed work rosters. The pressures of the industry on crews also came back to her when she recalled another incident her sister had recounted about the time she had been in

13

a rejected take off in Dublin. After abandoning the take off for a technical reason, the first thing that went through her head as they vacated the runway was had they screwed up – clearly signs of an industry in which crews fear the axe man.

Sophie McDonald brings the meeting to a close and as people start dispersing, Nicola Matthews introduces herself. Jill feels that, unlike Martin Stone, her kindness is not studied.

"I am here to represent the interests of the cabin crew and their families. I know these are hard days but if I can help, please let me know. My boyfriend is a pilot but with another airline."

Nicola gives Jill her business card. Martin Stone then breaks up their conversation, clearly a bit put out that Jill has warmed to Nicola. It is also obvious that Nicola wanted a longer chat. Liz Jones joins them. "Mrs Parker and Mrs Jones. If the union can be of any help please let me know. We are here to help." Martin Stone's voice has lost its previous tone of concern and is now hard in its formality.

Carol often commented on the union being too industry driven rather than member welfare driven. Martin Stone urges Mrs Parker and Mrs Jones to call if they have any questions. He checks the time on his wrist watch before striding out of the room. Left on their own, the three women exchange addresses and telephone numbers. Felicity invites Liz to pop in for a cup of tea and a chat anytime she likes. By all means, bring the little ones.

As Jill and Felicity leave the hotel, Jill puts on a cartoon voice, "OK, Mum let's go home and have a nice cup of tea."

Her mother smiles, Carol used to say that all the time when she visited her mother. A classic line from the Wallace and Gromit movies that she loved.

Chapter 4

Gary left school at sixteen, to join the Parachute Regiment. Everyone said it was one of the finest regiments in the world and he waited impatiently for his sixteenth birthday – the youngest age at which he could enroll. Gary is a Sergeant in 2 PARA. He has been in South Armagh, as well as in several hot spots around the world. 2 PARA became the Lead Element of the Airborne Task Force (ABTF) in September 2004 and has remained ready to deploy anywhere in the world at a moment's notice. Today he is on a NATO exercise entitled 'Operation Northern Drop', and is walking towards a Royal Air Force (RAF) Lockheed C-130 Hercules, the most numerous, transport aircraft in the West and which has been in production longer than any other aircraft in history. The prototype flew in August 1954 before he was born. 'Operation Northern Drop' is not one of the exercises he would rush to sign up for, but as he sees it, somebody somewhere dreamt this up so it must have a purpose in the bigger picture. He is going to fly across the Atlantic with in-flight refuelling before being parachuted to a training ground near Halifax in Nova Scotia. Spring is usually slow to get a grasp of this part of Canada and he knows it is going to be a cold jump even if it will be a low one to minimise the impact of the freezing temperatures. He smiles to himself as he remembers his previous trips there. Canadians know how to have fun. Halifax is Canada's largest naval and military base in number of personnel. Approximately two thirds of the navy's major ships are home ported in Halifax. 'Operation Northern Drop' is a small joint exercise with the United States 101st Airborne Division based at Fort Campbell in Kentucky.

As Gary walks across the Apron towards the awaiting Hercules on a chilly Wiltshire morning with forty other parachutists, one of his mates, Steve, catches up with him. "Hey Gary, how's it going, man? How was the funeral service?"

"Thanks for asking, mate, it was OK, didn't really know anyone but I am sure Dad would have liked it."

Steve gives Gary gives a tap on the shoulder to make the point that he cares.

Gary knows the Hercules well and has jumped out of them so many times it is all a non-event for him. The new kids will need keeping an eye on and that's his job as a sergeant. The Hercules he will fly on today comes from number 47 Squadron. 47 Squadron is one of the largest and most distinguished squadrons in the RAF. This isn't a Hercules like the early models but a C4 which the RAF replaced the older aircraft with in the late 1990s. As there are only forty of them on this exercise, there will be plenty of space to stretch out for the trip across the 'Pond'.

The doors shut and the six-bladed composite propellers on each of the four Rolls-Royce Allison turboprops spin into life. As the aircraft taxis for take off on runway 24, Gary takes the opportunity to start reading the initial crash report. Terry, the loadmaster, sees the cover. "You all right, mate?"

Gary smirks. "No worries, at least I can jump out if I don't like the ride or the stewardess."

The loadmaster smiles and gives him the finger.

As the aircraft leaves the runway and climbs away, Shaun an Irish lad pinches his nostrils with his fingers. "Pwah! Terry, put your socks back on. Your feet pong!"

Gary pays no attention, but notes the foul, dirty sock-like smell which he has already experienced on other Hercules flights. He is reading the transcript from the voice recorder from JASP flight 303. Although he has some knowledge of flying, most is lost on him. He turns over the page.

Co-pilot: 'The heading should be 090 not 050.'

Captain: 'Say again.'

Co-pilot: 'The heading should be 090 not 050.'

Approach Controller: 'JASP 303 turn left head three six zero and descend to 2500 feet.'

Co-pilot: 'Roger descend 2500 feet and turn left onto three six zero degrees.'

Something catches Gary's attention. He turns the page back.

Approach Controller: 'That's affirmative, these are radar vectors for an ILS to runway 25. Are you ready to copy latest weather?'

Co-pilot: 'Go ahead.'

Approach Controller: 'Roger, latest weather is wind one eight zero degrees at thirty-five gusting forty-five knots, overcast at three hundred feet, heavy rain, temperature plus 1, dew point minus 5, QNH 988 millibars. Braking action was last reported as medium 30 minutes ago by a Boeing 737.'

Co-pilot: 'Roger.'

Co-pilot: 'There's the socks again.'

Gary reads the last line again.

Co-pilot: 'There's the socks again.'

He turns towards Shaun who is now talking about some night in Armagh when he ended up the worse for wear on pints of Guinness Extra Cold.

Gary has to shout over the sound of the engines, "Shaun, what were you saying before?"

Shaun replies, "I was telling Alan about when some of us went out in Armagh and he carried me back to the car after some pints of the black stuff got the better of me."

Alan shouts out, "You're just a wimp paddy, Shaun."

"Fuck you!"

Gary cuts through the banter, "What did you say about your socks?"

"Not my socks, mate. I was taking the piss out of Terry because of the dirty sock smell earlier but it's gone now. Didn't you smell it? Like dirty socks, vomit or a wet dog type of smell."

Two of the men start barking in unison.

One of the soldiers kicks Shaun in the shin, "Only you would know what a wet dog smells like, you've had enough of them."

Before Shaun has the chance to fire back, Gary asks if anyone else noticed the smell, to which several say yes but most say they were not paying attention.

One of the corporals says, "I've smelt that before, why what's the score?"

The banter has eased off as some of them stare at Gary.

"Nothing, lads."

He sees that the soldiers don't buy that. He searches for something to break up the concern he has created. "Did you hear about the three Irishmen? One says to the other two, 'I noticed my son has a bottle of whiskey in his room, he hasn't told me about it, I think he is an under age drinker or a drunk.' The other one says, 'Jesus, I found some tampons in my daughters room, she must be having periods but didn't tell me or my Mrs.' The third says, 'That's nothing, I found condoms in my daughters room, I never knew she had a cock!'"

Later in the flight, Gary and some others are invited to the flight deck to see one of the in-flight refuelling procedures. The procedure goes to plan and the tanker aircraft soon clears away with fuel remnants briefly spraying the aircraft windscreen. When the cockpit work load returns to normal cruise levels Gary asks the crew what they make of the comment by the co-pilot of 'There's the socks again.' The Captain is in his late thirties, a career pilot in the air force. The co-pilot has been in the squadron less than a year. An engineer sitting in the jump seat is an old timer, not far from the easy life of retirement. He has the confidence and manner of someone who has seen it all before. The co-pilot asks to have a look at the report which he reads with the engineer looking over his shoulder. The Captain asks why he is interested in flight 303.

"My father lost his life in the crash, Sir. I have just been to the funeral."

The Captain's face softens, "I am sorry to hear that."

While the co-pilot and ground engineer read the report, Gary asks where they are. They have just passed 35 degrees West and talking with 'Gander Oceanic' radio control. The Captain points out their exact position on a chart.

The co-pilot turns towards Gary and speaks with a strong Aberdeen accent, "I think the co-pilot is talking about the fact that it's windy and that the 'wind sock' will be full because it's so windy."

"I think the co-pilot is talking about contaminated air," says the engineer.

Gary looks at one, then the other. "What do you mean, contaminated air – on the ground?"

"No," replies the engineer. "The air you are breathing right now, where do you think it comes from?"

"I don't know, I have never given it much thought. Air bottles, recirculated, outside?"

The engineer shakes his head. "No, if we had to carry the air we need for this flight we would need a massive tank. Yes, on commercial jets half the air is 'recirculated' as you say, but only after we have breathed it in. The only air we carry in tanks is emergency oxygen."

The engineer starts drawing as he talks. "What happens is, the air that enters the engine is mostly used in the propulsion process like in a car, it gets compressed, has fuel added, is burnt and expelled out the back. Some of the air that enters the engine is used to pressurise the aircraft and that air is also used for us to survive. This air is called 'bleed air' and the best way of thinking

19

about bleed air is like a diver's tank on his back. Bleed air is your complete life support system apart from the fact you don't have to carry it!"

Gary nods as he digests the information.

The engineer continues, "Sometimes the air supply – or the bleed air, as we call it – gets contaminated with engine oils. This can sometimes give the air a certain smell. Some people call it an oily smell and some call it a dirty sock smell. Sometimes the smell can be very subtle. If you were not looking for it you might not even notice it."

"On take off some of the crew were talking about smelling dirty socks today," says Gary. "Some said they had smelt it before but I've never given it much thought. For me the aircraft just has a different smell to, say, an office."

The engineer goes deeper into the lesson. "You see, what can happen is, under certain phases of flight when the engine is under greater load or in descent with less load, you can get some contamination because the engine seals are not working properly. I remember once in Iraq a flight engineer snagged an engine for this problem but then it was OK for a week and started again. Maybe on your father's flight they were having seal problems as well. It says in the report that the co-pilot says 'There's the socks again', so he is obviously concerned about it."

The aircraft hits some light turbulence. Gary smiles. "The co-pilot was a girl, actually, and you know what? I went to the same school as her older sister. Her name was Carol. Carol took me in a Piper Warrior a few times when she was building up her flying experience by hour building. Thanks very much for explaining all that stuff to me, it's very interesting. How often does it happen?"

The engineer replies as he hands Gary his sketches, "These new Hercules are pretty good, some of the older ones had some issues with oil fumes but I have no idea how often. I wouldn't worry about it. All is 'A OK' up here."

Gary changes the subject, "What's the latest on the weather for the drop site?"

The Captain replies, "We are waiting for an improvement which is forecast to occur but at present the weather has not cleared as quickly as was forecast and the low cloud is below jump limits. We will keep you posted."

Gary leaves the flight deck and goes back to inform the officer in charge about the drop site weather. Lieutenant Paul Morrison, a former special forces soldier on one of his last few trips before retiring is in charge. 'Mo', as he is known, is well respected by the lads and Gary has chewed a lot of the same dust as Mo in his time in 2 PARA. Mo asks Gary to tell the troops. Gary gives the lads an update. They are more relaxed now, some asleep, some reading books or newspapers, others eating. Unlike the luxuries of in-flight entertainment available on commercial airliners, military transport aircraft are a reminder of the early days of travel when books and magazines helped to pass the time.

Gary ponders over what he has learnt in the cockpit. The early start today and monotony of the flight get the better of him and he falls asleep.

He is woken up by Mo. "Gary the weather is fucking awful all around Halifax. Forecasters have screwed up again."

Gary yawns. "So we are diverting to Florida to sit on the beach for a week and drink beer and enjoy the views?"

Mo smiles, "I'll be doing that long before you, mate. No, we are switching to plan B. Plan B is to fly on to another drop site north of Winnipeg in Manitoba and bunk up afterwards at 17 Wing. The weather there is clear."

Gary knows that Winnipeg and 17 Wing is where the Canadian Royal Air Force 435 Squadron are based. They are the 'Chinthe' Transport and Rescue Squadron which specialises in air mobility, and search and rescue operations.

"I know the place. I did two months of search and rescue advanced training there once. Got dropped everywhere and had the arse bitten out of me by the flies one summer up north."

"The good news is that we will have a shorter exercise and therefore some time off, perhaps a long weekend."

One of the men overhears the informal briefing, "Perhaps some skiing as well, Sir?"

Mo quickly puts them back on track, "Let's see if you find the drop zone first, shall we?"

Gary and the lads are now back at the barracks at 17 Wing, having completed the exercise, are showering in the communal showers. They are clearly excited about the night ahead having completed a successful exercise and drop despite the extended flight time. It is Wednesday evening and they are off until Saturday morning.

As they walk out of the barracks in the direction of the bar, Gary shouts, "Hey lads, get me a beer, I'll be along shortly!" He finds the communications building, sits himself down in front of a computer and takes out the drawings the engineer did a few days ago. He types in 'Contaminated Air' into the Internet search engine. A long list of links comes up. He clicks on the first. It is an archive safety alert issued in New South Wales in Australia entitled, 'Contaminated Air – Warning To Divers'.

'A New South Wales diver was recovered unconscious from the water after breathing contaminated air from a surface-supplied breathing apparatus.' Gary clicks the back option and highlights the next link. At the fourth link his eyes widen. It is an archived UK parliamentary question from 20 January 2006 entitled 'Transport Aircraft (Contaminated Air)'.

'Paul Flynn: To ask the Secretary of State for Transport what steps he is taking in relation to contaminated air events on commercial aircraft.'

The reply from the Government reads, 'Ms Buck: The House of Lords Select Committee on Science and Technology report dated November 2000 (paragraph 4.41) found concerns about contaminated air events to be unsubstantiated.'

Gary clicks back, the next link is to questions in the UK Lords dated Tuesday, 25 October 2005. Three questions from a 'Countess of Mar.' The Countess of Mar asked Her Majesty's Government:

'With which government and non-government organisations responsibility lies for ensuring that the health of passengers and crew of United Kingdom airline companies is not adversely affected by exposure to contaminated air in cabins and flight decks after an aircraft has taken off.'

'What exposure standards currently apply to any synergistic effects of simultaneous exposure to numerous chemicals which may be experienced by aircraft passengers and crew during a contaminated air event in a reduced pressure environment.'

'Why filters are not fitted to commercial aircraft to prevent crews and passengers from being exposed to pyrolysis products from synthetic jet engine oils and hydraulic fluids during a contaminated air event.'

Gary immediately realises that contaminated air is an issue that has been discussed long time before he became interested in the issue. He focuses his research on the Lockheed Hercules remembering that the engineer said the early version of the aircraft had experienced problems. Gary types in 'Contaminated Air C-130 Hercules', he looks at a selection of unrelated pages then comes across a page which he realises is significant just from its title, 'Human Intoxification Following Inhalation Exposure to Synthetic Jet Lubricating Oil'. The 1977 paper records that, 'A recent case has dramatically demonstrated acute intoxication following inhalation of aerolised or vaporized synthetic lubricating oil. The patient, a 34-year-old Caucasian male in good health, was flying as navigator in a military C-130A aircraft when he noticed the gradual onset of headache, followed by slight dizziness, nausea, vomiting, incoordination, and diaphoresis.' The article states that such events are not uncommon and finishes with the sentence, 'The etiology of his symptoms was related to an inhalation exposure to aerosolized synthetic lubricating oil arising from a jet engine of his aircraft.'

Gary mutters, "Holy Shit" and goes back to the first page he read. The one that stated, 'The House of Lords Select Committee on Science and Technology report dated November 2000 (paragraph 4.41) found concerns about contaminated air events to be unsubstantiated.' He looks for the report on the net and finds a reference to it.

'After considering the available evidence on the issue, the House of Lords report (2000) concludes that the absence of confirmed cases of TOCP poisoning from cabin air and the very low levels of TOCP that would be found in even the highly unlikely worst case of contamination from oil leaking into the air supply lead us to conclude that the concerns about significant risk to the health of airline passengers and crew are not substantiated.'

It's getting very scientific, he thinks. 'TOCP poisoning', what is it? He finds that TOCP is in fact 'tri-ortho-cresyl phosphate', and that TOCP is an isomer of another compound called 'TCP' or 'Tricresyl phosphate', an organophosphate. The word organophosphate rings a lot of serious alarm bells in his head. Gary is still trying to remember why he knows the word when he types ORGANOPHOSPHATE into the search engine and there it is in front of him.

'Organophosphate (OP) compounds are a diverse group of chemicals used in both domestic and industrial settings. Examples of OPs include insecticides such as malathion, diazinon, chlorpyrifos, nerve gases such as soman, sarin... OP compounds were first synthesized in the early 1800s but it was

24

not until eighty years later that a chemist at Bayer AG, Germany, investigated the use of OPs as insecticides... The German military developed an arsenal of chemical warfare agents based on OPs. Massive OP intoxication have occurred such as the 'Jamaican Ginger Jake' palsy incident in the 1920s and 30s in the USA. Triorthocresylphosphate (TOCP) which causes demyelination and paralysis when ingested was used an adulterant in an alcoholic extract of Jamaican ginger. Thousands of people who drank 'Ginger Jake' during prohibition developed paresthesia of the feet and aching of the calves in about 12 days, followed two to three days later by ataxia, and paralysis. 20,000 Americans were paralyzed. This led to the discovery of some of the toxicological mechanisms of OPs. On 20 March 1995, the Aum Shinrikyo cult spread sarin nerve gas on the Tokyo subway system in which 12 people were killed and thousands affected.'

TOCP caused 20,000 people to be paralyzed and it is in the engine oils as well. Gary thinks there has to be a mistake but he looks again. No mistake. It is the link to sarin that rings the loudest alarm in Gary's head. He remembers the link between sarin and the Gulf War. Sarin is an organophosphate and sarin exposure is linked to Gulf War Syndrome. He has many friends who have suffered from Gulf War Syndrome.

Gary thinks about the Rosetta Stone found in 1799 which allowed the past to better understood. The Rosetta Stone is a stone with writings on it in two languages (Egyptian and Greek), using three scripts (hieroglyphic, demotic and Greek). Gary's Rosetta Stone is a published paper in English entitled, 'The Toxicity of Synthetic Jet Engine Oils' written by a professor Chris Winder at the University of New South Wales in Sydney. The 2002 paper explains in great depth what jet engines oil are but more importantly explains what the link to organophosphates is. The organophosphate TCP which he had been reading earlier about is in jet engine oils as an anti-wear additive at 3%.

Gary suddenly realises he has not printed any of this information out and it is getting late. Too amazed at what he was finding and trying to understand. He prints out the Winder jet oils toxicity paper and the quote from the 2000 House of Lords Investigation, as well as a selection of the other bits he has pulled together.

Gary sits back in the chair as the laser printer churns out the pages. Like at times in Iraq, Afghanistan and Northern Ireland, he knows he has walked into a real minefield. He puts his hands together behind his head, leans back and looks blankly at the wall in front of him, thinking. He looks at his watch. Should he ring Jill or do more research first? It is Wednesday evening in Canada, early afternoon in Newcastle. Gary then has an idea and types in 'University Winnipeg' and out comes the addresses he needs. That's where he will go tomorrow. He will get more information before ringing Jill. Just as he has been taught in the army. Get as much information as possible before acting.

Gary picks up the pages he has printed. He asks a member of staff which is the quickest way to the main bar and heads for the drink that he ordered two hours ago.

Information and good intelligence is everything in the military and Gary is an expert in gathering and collating such data.

Chapter 5

Gary gets out of the taxi at the Department of Chemistry at the University of Winnipeg and moves swiftly out of the cold morning air into the warm air-conditioned building. A thin Oriental man, walks past. He is wearing bleached jeans and has a green canvass bag slung over his shoulder. He must be a student. Gary asks him where he might find someone able to explain to him some aspects of chemistry and engine oils. The thin man removes small white earphones from his ears and tinny music drifts out of them. Gary has to repeat the question. The young man scratches his chin, then looks around the corridor, as though searching for someone to take over his burden. He finally points to the staircase, and gives directions in a soft Korean voice. Gary takes the stairs two at a time up to the second floor and walks down the neon lit corridor lined with notice boards. Timetables, seminar notices, textbooks for sale. He knocks on the frosted glass door marked 'Office'. A middle aged woman in a fluffy pink cardigan is staring at a computer screen. Strawberry earrings swing heavily from her earlobes as she speaks to him. She is clearly put out by having her work interrupted but softens as she eyes Gary from top to toe. "Try Dr Fedorova, in Room 203."

Gary finds the door to Room 203 ajar and walks in. There is what looks to him like high technology equipment, and he is comforted by the sight of a Periodic Table on the wall. The only thing in the room he can relate to. "Hello? What can I do for you?"

The girl does not look up from behind her laptop and appears too young to know the answers to Gary's questions.

"Excuse me, I am sorry to interrupt, I am looking for Dr Fedorova."

The girl stops typing and looks up with stern grey eyes. Still, her Russian accent softens her voice. "Why do you want to talk with Dr Fedorova?"

Gary finds himself speaking fast as he explains his query, as though he is on a quiz show. If he gives the correct answer, the girl will take him to Dr Fedorova. He is trying to understand what TCP and TOCP are and why they are in jet oils. "I am a soldier. It's all a bit too scientific for me. I was hoping someone at the University could explain it to me."

The large grey eyes mellow. "I am Dr Fedorova, Valentina Fedorova."

They glare again when she sees Gary's obvious surprise. She must get this a lot. A Doctor? She can't be more than twenty.

Dr Fedorova's eyes assess the large stack of papers on her desk. Gary feels disheartened. She is going to tell me that she is too busy to explain complex science to an uneducated soldier like me. Without looking at him, she brushes a strand of hair off her cheek and tidies it behind her ear.

Gary feels relief. Dr Fedorova looks up at the clock above the entrance door to the room then smiles. "I have a meeting at 11 but I would be happy to help you until then."

She invites him to take a seat and explain why he needs her help. He does so, conscious of the fact she is short on time.

"I am sorry about your father. My brother died in a car accident a few years ago so I understand in some ways how you feel. I too wanted to understand why."

Dr Fedorova starts to read the pages Gary printed out the night before at the base.

Gary looks around the room at the unfamiliar objects. Dr Fedorova is absorbed by her reading and does not notice her hair strand escape from behind her ear and flop forward. Fine, blonde hair. Gary first steals glances at her face then allows himself to watch her. Her skin is white and he imagines it must be very smooth. Her blonde hair is soft. She is biting the corner of her lower lip and frowns at what she is reading. She suddenly looks up at Gary and he feels himself blush and looks away, searching for something else in the room on which to focus his attention but he knows it is too late. She has noticed that he finds her attractive. He tries to distract himself and recalls his school chemistry classes. He remembers the joke he played on a friend which resulted in too much hydrogen sulphide, the rotten egg smell, being produced in a basic chemistry experiment and his teacher going ballistic with him. It puts a smile on his face.

Dr Fedorova is also smiling at him. "This is all very interesting, a lot more interesting than the work I am doing – analysis of metal ores'!"

Her tone turns business like. "How much do you know about chemistry?"

Gary is apologetic. "Not a lot. I left school at sixteen but I know water is H_2O and what the Periodic Table is. I also know there are plenty of chemicals that will kill you in a hurry and some which will leave you with life long injuries. I was in the Gulf and have met many people who suffer today with Gulf War Syndrome."

Dr Fedorova beckons Gary over to a whiteboard and starts writing, "If you were to select the following six types of atoms from the Periodic Table, notably Carbon (C), Hydrogen (H), Phosphorous (P), Nitrogen (N), Sulphur (S) and Oxygen (O) you could use these atoms as building blocks to make literally thousands of different compounds by using various combinations of these atoms. Like all compounds in life, it's the specific atoms and the way the specific atoms are arranged that makes each compound very different. At a basic level using just one type of atom, notably Carbon, just by the way Carbon atoms are arranged can either form the Carbon in your pencil which allows you to write or diamonds, the hardest substance known to man. Both are simply made of Carbon. The six atoms above can be arranged to make many molecules essential for life such as vitamin B2 which has the chemical formula $C^{17}H^{20}N^4O^6$ because it is made up of Carbon, Hydrogen, Nitrogen and Oxygen. The number beside the atom type in the formula is the number of those atoms needed to make that compound. So in the case of vitamin B2 you need six Oxygen atoms, four nitrogen atoms and so on. Do you follow this OK?"

"So far so good."

Dr Fedorova's eyes quiz Gary, as though trying to ascertain whether he is telling the truth. "You're a soldier so let's make it interesting for you. Another chemical formula we could look at using the same building blocks is $C^{11}H^{26}NO^2PS$. This is made up of Carbon, Hydrogen, Nitrogen, Oxygen, Phosphorous and Sulphur but this is not the formula of another vitamin but of the extremely toxic nerve agent known as VX, something you will know about."

Gary knows about VX. It is like sarin.

Dr Fedorova continues the lesson. "VX, when inhaled, is reported to be ten times as toxic as sarin, and the amount of VX that one can place on the head of a pin is reported to be sufficient to produce death in a human being. The important point is that every chemical structure is unique and you cannot always make direct comparisons with one chemical and another because it has the same types of atoms. The toxicity of each chemical compound needs to be evaluated individually, you cannot rely on similar compounds to say another chemical is safe. Also you cannot compare quantities of different chemicals equally as you have seen from the toxicity of VX, some compounds are lethal in minute quantities. Now turning to the engine oils, one of the ingredients that makes up 3% of the jet engine oil is reported to be 'Tricresyl Phosphate (TCP)'. TCP is an organophosphate or commonly referred to as an 'OP'. Why they use TCP in these synthetic jet engine oils I don't know but one of the papers you gave me said it was a good anti wear additive so I guess that's why it's in there. TCP is made up of Carbon (C), Hydrogen (H) Phosphorous (P) and Oxygen (O) atoms."

Gary is on a high from the intake of all this information. "What about the TOCP? The Government said 'the very low levels of TOCP that would be found in even the highly unlikely worst case of contamination from oil leaking into the air supply lead us to conclude that the concerns about significant risk to the health of airline passengers and crew are not substantiated.'"

Dr Fedorova is patient. "TOCP is an isomer of TCP. In chemistry, isomers are molecules with the same chemical formula and often with the same kinds of bonds between atoms, but in which the atoms are arranged differently. That is to say, they have different structural formulae."

Gary wants to know more. "How many isomers of TCP are there?"

Valentina picks up the paper from the University of New South Wales in Australia. "Let's have a look."

She reads through the paper for a few more minutes whilst Gary looks at the explanations written on the board.

She looks up again. "According to this paper, it states, 'Technically, there are ten possible tri-cresyl phosphate structures' so TOCP would be one of the ten but this part is important – 'The different isomers of TCP have different properties, and indeed, different toxicities.' I guess TOCP must be the isomer which is most toxic or present in the highest amount and that is why the Government focused on that one, but... Hang on... This page... Seems to. Let me just get my head around this for a second."

Gary can see that Dr Fedorova is struggling to understand it. He thinks to himself he had no chance if a doctor cannot figure it out.

Dr Fedorova, clears the black board and draws the formula of TCP and starts to explain. "Now TOCP is just one of the three 'Ortho' isomers, the other two 'Ortho' isomers are MOCP and DOCP. According to this paper from Sydney, TOCP is actually the least toxic, in the least concentration, of the ortho isomers. The paper states, 'In evidence to the Australian Senate Aviation Inquiry, it became apparent that TOCPs were present in TCP at a concentration of 0.006ppm, DOCPs were present in TCP at a concentration of 6 ppm, and MOCPs were present at a concentration of 3070 ppm. As these ingredients are present in higher concentrations than TOCP, and have a significantly higher toxicity than TOCP, it is suggested that a statement of low TOCP content is misleading as it underestimates the toxicity of the 'ortho' ingredients by a factor of 6.14 million.' Wow!"

Gary has lost the flow and cannot share Dr Fedorova's excitement.

"Sorry, Doctor, you lost me at the end."

Dr Fedorova spells it out, "To cut to the chase, as they say, the UK Government, in referring to 'TOCP', have down played the toxicity by 6.14 million times! It's very clever, they tell you about one isomer and it all seems very respectful science but in fact it's misinformation and the deceit is of the highest order, very clever. This is no mistake, this is deliberate!"

A middle aged man in a tweed jacket, with a bundle of papers under his arm walks in without knocking. He is a short black man in his early fifties, with gold rimmed glasses. He has a kind smile.

"Hi, Valentina. Sorry to interrupt, I thought I would collect you and walk to the meeting with you."

Dr Fedorova looks at the clock. It is 10.50. She introduces Gary to her colleague, "Charles, this is Gary, he is a soldier investigating a plane crash and we were discussing Tricresyl Phosphate toxicity in engine oils and breathing the stuff."

She turns to Gary, "Charles is a toxicologist and working with me on some inhalation problems we are investigating in relation to some mining activities in the North West Territories."

The two men shake hands. Charles is clearly trying to work Gary out.

"How would you be breathing engine oils?" asks Charles.

Gary replies, "It seems that the air you breathe in an aircraft comes off the engines and is known as 'bleed air'. Sometimes this 'bleed air' becomes contaminated with engine oils and you breathe the stuff in. It might have caused a plane crash."

Charles raises his eyebrows as he looks at Dr Fedorova in disbelief at the topic being discussed.

Dr Fedorova steps in. "These synthetic jet engine oils, Charles, are not your every day car engine oils but specialised oils which have the OP Tricresyl Phosphate and other chemicals added as anti wear additives and fire retardants. We were looking at the isomers of Tricresyl Phosphate."

Charles is a toxicologist. "I wouldn't just focus simply on the Tricresyl Phosphate or the isomers of interest, sure that will be of interest but it's the combined synergistic effect of exposure that will be important."

Gary cannot quite keep up but feels this is an important new piece of information.

The time approaches 11.00 and the meeting needs to come to a close. Dr Fedorova unplugs her laptop, closes the lid, and picks it up. Charles notices Gary's confused expression and explains, "You have to look at how all the chemicals you are simultaneously exposed to combine together and exert any toxicity. You could have two individual compounds which may be mildly toxic but combined together could be a thousand times more toxic. It's the combined synergistic effects of exposures to a selection of chemicals that always needs to be investigated, not the individual compounds alone. That's the main failure of current day exposure standards, they are for a pure compound on its own, how often does an exposure to a single compound occur? Usually, only in a factory where workers are handling say a specific chemical in some form of manufacturing process."

Dr Fedorova interrupts. "Gary, I am sorry, we have to go. It's a key meeting with the project grant holder. I hope we were helpful. I found it very interesting."

Gary expresses his gratitude to both of them.

Dr Fedorova opens the door and Charles walks out first. Then whilst half way out the door she turns to Gary. "I tell you what, write your email details on the board and if I get the chance I'll look at the issue a bit more and have a chat with some colleagues."

Gary finds himself grinning.

As Dr Fedorova and Charles walk down the corridor, she says, "That guy is a soldier in the British parachute regiment and his dad died in a plane crash earlier this year, hence his interest."

She pushes the button to call the elevator.

"Surely the air which comes off the engine is filtered before the crew and passengers breathe it?" says Charles, almost to himself.

The elevator doors slide open.

Dr Fedorova leans against the steel wall. "According to stuff he had printed out it's not!"

Charles frowns. "That can't be right. That would be completely stupid if there was the potential for passengers and crews to be exposed to neurotoxins, whatever the amount."

They watch the numbers rise on the level display, as the elevator goes up.

Gary walks out of the University building and waves down a taxi and tells the driver to take him back to the base. The driver switches on the meter. Gary looks out of the window. His head is throbbing. He looks at his watch. "Is there a main library in Winnipeg?"

The driver sounds irritated. "Sure, there is, Sir."

"Then take me there instead, please."

The librarian is a friendly elderly woman. Gary asks her where he can find newspaper articles.

The librarian leads him to a console. "All newspapers are indexed electronically, they are going back in time; at present you can search all major English language papers in the same way you use the net on this console. You can retrieve articles dating back to 1998 and also French language articles back to 2000. In five years' time they hope to have everything back to the last war in electronic format. What year were you looking for?"

Gary is not sure and the librarian courteously offers him any other help if he needs it, then walks away.

He starts to search through the archives. There is no shortage of articles on the contaminated air topic.

Dr Fedorova walks back into her office and reconnects her laptop. She looks up at the board. Gary has left his e-mail address and a thank you message, even if he has spelt her name incorrectly. 'Dear Dr Fedrova, thank you so much for all your help and patience. If you ever come to the UK please contact me for a free tour of London, Manchester, Newcastle... My e-mail address is 'Garybaseman@soldierconnect.co.uk'. Thanks a lot. Gary.'

Dr Fedorova smiles as she twirls a pen around her finger, then turns her attention to her laptop screen.

Gary is mastering the use of the search facilities on old newspapers and articles. This is clearly a global issue on the scale of the Gulf War Syndrome. The articles come from around the world but all have the same theme.

'USA: 26 flight attendants employed by Alaska Airlines sued that carrier, claiming that noxious fumes in aircraft cabins had made them sick. In settling the case in January 2001, the flight attendants signed a statement acknowledging that the company had not intentionally caused them harm.'

'Australia: Jet Fumes Drama Highlights Safety Fears.'

'USA: Unlocking an airborne mystery.'

'UK: Pilots seek truth on toxic cockpit air.'

'Canada: Christiaan van Netten, head of the Division of Occupational and Environmental Health at Canada's University of British Columbia, who is analyzing leakage incidence data, says leakage occurs in about 1 out of 1,000 flights and is usually traceable to equipment failure. He adds that incidence depends largely on the type of aircraft and the maintenance habits of the airline.'

'Norway: Thousands of airline employees are ill.'

'Australia: Australian Senate Investigation confirms crews sick from exposure to engine oil on the British built BAe 146 aircraft.'

'UK: Your pilot has been poisoned.'

'Australia: Smelly planes cause illness.'

'UK: Pilots poisoned by contaminated air. By Geoffrey Lean, Environment Editor. Airline pilots have been rendered incapable of flying their planes safely by polluted air pumped into their aircraft, a shocking report reveals. The report, compiled for an official investigation into the danger, says pilots suffer "alarming cognitive failures" - including being unable to remember vital instructions from air traffic control or if they had put down the wheels before landing - risking "substantial loss of life."'

Gary notes the date of the last article 'Published: 04 June 2006', 29 years after the paper he found last night on the navigator who was incapacitated on a C-130 Hercules he knows all too well. Gary logs on to the Internet to see if there is any more news on JASP flight 303 in the UK media but nothing. It is all news about oil prices and climate change.

Gary sits quietly for a while and takes out his wallet and a picture of his dad taken at a football game they went to a few months before the crash. He looks at the picture, just thinking about moments he can never have again. No more laughs, no more pints together, no more of anything. Just memories. If only they had spent more time together, he thinks, but it's too late. He puts his wallet away, stands up slowly and walks out. Gary thanks the librarian for her help and asks her where he can buy an international phone card. It is time to talk with Jill.

Chapter 6

Gary shuts himself in the phone booth in a local diner, then pauses to think about the significance of what he has learnt in the last few days. He considers the impact this may have on Jill and then gets out his mobile phone and brings up her number. Methodically, he punches in the digits onto the payphone pad. Jill's mobile phone starts ringing all the way across the Atlantic.

Her voice is deeper than usual.

"Jill, it's Gary ringing you from Canada."

"Gary from school?"

"No, Gary from the White House, you silly muppet."

He had not called her that since school.

"Hiya Gary, sorry I was fast asleep, I have been on night shifts."

Her voice perks up. "Where are you?"

Gary sits down on the floor of the phone booth and gets out his notes. "Jill, you need to really be awake for what I am about to tell you."

She raises her voice a little to confirm she is listening, "I am awake, let me guess – you won the Lottery and you're taking me on a two-week cruise and the taxi is waiting downstairs?"

Gary laughs. "No, sorry, love, it's a bit more serious than that."

"That *would* be serious if you took me on a cruise!"

"No listen, Jill, its about JASP flight 303."

Gary's tone has suddenly become sad.

Jill hesitates. "Hang on a second, Gary."

She sits up in bed and reaches out to part open the curtains. Another grey morning. She pulls the warm winters quilt up on herself and picks up her mobile again, this time ready. "OK Gary, I am awake, I am all ears, what's happening?"

"I don't want to stress you but have you read the initial Air Accident report?"

"Some of it."

"Was there anything there you didn't understand or was out of place?"

Jill sounds puzzled. "Not that I recall, some of it was a bit technical but no, why?"

"Can you get it now?"

Jill looks at her work bag and leans out of bed to reach it.

Gary asks her to go to the transcript from the voice recorder at the back of the report on page 23. He can hear the rustling as Jill turns the pages.

"OK, I got it, what am I looking at?"

"Look at the last line, where it reads, 'Co-pilot: There's the socks again'."

"Yes, here, what does it mean?"

"When I read it like you it meant nothing to me, but by chance I was taking off from Lyneham and the lads starting going on about a dirty sock smell. Anyway, to cut a long story short, dirty socks is one of several descriptions given to the smell of the air in an aircraft when the air supply is contaminated with engine oils from the engine. You see Jill, the air is taken from the engines on aircraft for passengers and crews to survive, that's where all the breathing air comes from. If the air becomes contaminated, as it seems to have been on Carol's flight, the crew and maybe the passengers will be exposed."

Jill is keeping up with the flow. "Gary, if they are exposed, what will it do to them?"

Gary shuffles to overcome the cramp of the small cubicle. "Now that's the really worrying bit. There was this navigator on a military flight in 1977 and he was incapacitated from breathing contaminated air. There's more... A lot more, hang on..."

39

Gary digs out the press articles. "Now listen to this, this is an extract from a newspaper article in June 2006, 'Airline pilots have been rendered incapable of flying their planes safely by polluted air pumped into their aircraft, a shocking report reveals. The report, compiled for an official investigation into the danger, says pilots suffer 'alarming cognitive failures' - including being unable to remember vital instructions from air traffic control or if they had put down the wheels before landing - risking 'substantial loss of life.' Isn't that absolutely incredible?"

Jill's voice goes very quiet as she starts articulating very slowly, "Are you saying what I think you're saying? Carol and Captain Jones might have been affected by contaminated air and this might have affected their thinking and their ability to fly the plane?"

Gary nods. "Jill, that's exactly what I am saying!"

Jill raises her voice a bit more and speaks faster, "Fucking hell Gary, if you're right then... This could... This could mean it was not their fault at all!"

He leans back against the glass wall. "That's it, Jill, you got the picture. I have been looking into this for a few days and wanted to check all the facts before ringing you. This morning I met with a Chemist and a Toxicologist at the local university and they were a massive help. They explained all about the toxicity aspects and..."

A sequence of fast bleeps tells Gary that the calling card is running out of credit.

"Shit!"

Gary scrambles out of the booth. His left leg has gone to sleep and he hobbles to the shop across the street. No one else is using the phone booth as he runs back. Thankfully, there is no queue. He redials the international number. "Sorry, Jill. Bloody card ran out."

"What you need to do is ring the Civil Aviation Authority (CAA), the airline and the pilot unions in the UK as soon as possible. I will ring the FAA, they are the American version of the UK CAA. Probably best not tell your mum, no need to worry her."

Jill agrees, "OK, I'll have a shower and get on it straight away."

"I'll ring you tomorrow, you take care."

Gary slowly picks up his papers from the floor of the phone booth. All the information overload and the jet lag start to catch up with him. He flags down his third taxi of the day and heads back to the base, drained. He feels like he is two weeks into a sortie, he is so exhausted.

Jill buttons up her blouse as she goes downstairs in her flat, her shoulder length hair is still wet after her shower. She pushes the start button on her computer and then fills the kettle to boil enough water for a cup of tea. She gets out a notepad and then tears off the front page which has notes she no longer needs, writes down 'CAA, airlines and unions' and picks up the phone.

A quick search on the net provides the required telephone numbers. A lady answers at the Civil Aviation Authority offices near Gatwick airport. After what seems like a huge hurdle, she gets a spokesperson on the line, "Hi, my name is Jill Parker, my sister was the co-pilot on the JASP flight 303 which –"

The spokesperson interrupts Jill in full flow, "I am familiar with the crash, my deepest condolences."

He clearly lacks any training in counselling. Jill knows she sounds irritable, "It's not your condolences I want, it's for you to listen to what I have to say."

The spokesperson gives way, "Please go ahead, how can I help?"

"I would like to know what the CAA makes of the comment on the bottom of page 23 of the Initial Accident Report, it's the section with the transcript from the voice recorder."

The spokesperson says he does not have a copy of the report to hand so Jill tells him what it says, "The last line of page 23 reads 'P2: There's the socks again'. What does that mean to you?"

"I am not sure, I am sure the Air Accident Investigation Branch and the section within the CAA dealing with that incident will expand on any aspects which it feels are appropriate to the investigations."

Jill probes a bit further but becomes cautious, "My research tells me that pilots use the term 'dirty socks' to refer to contaminated air. That is air in the cockpit or passenger cabin which becomes contaminated with engine oils."

The CAA spokesperson responds, "I appreciate, Miss Parker that these have been stressful times for you and your family but you must have faith in the CAA and the Government. We are in the final stages of completing a major report with the Air Accident Investigation Branch which is investigating these matters in full detail. If I recall, in 2004 the CAA published some research into fume events that concluded that symptoms reported in cabin air quality incidents could not be related to any particular compound or compounds. If we thought there was the very smallest chance of contaminated air causing any health or flight safety issue we would take action. All UK airlines take these matters extremely seriously. I know you are looking for reasons but I would suggest you have faith in the final report when that is released in the near future."

Jill knows she is being given the brush off but thanks the spokesperson politely for his time. She scribbles down a few notes. As a nurse she keeps records of everything.

Jill then looks through some paperwork, all on JASP airlines headed stationery. The correspondence her mum has received as next of kin from the airline since the accident.

She dials the number of Emma Hollingdon, the author of one of the letters.

"Hello, Emma Hollingdon."

"Hi, my name is Jill Parker, I am the sister of Carol Parker who was the co-pilot on flight 303."

"Hello, Ms Parker, how can I help you?"

Jill gets straight to the point, "On page 23 of the air accident investigation initial report, in the cockpit voice recorder part towards the end, my sister says, 'There's the socks again'. What does that mean?"

Emma Hollingdon is clearly lost for words, "I am sorry Ms Parker I am not a pilot but a manager within corporate affairs, I don't know what that means."

"Could you put me through to someone who might be able to help. I met the Chief Pilot the other day when he came to Newcastle to discuss the settlement, he might know. Can you put me through to him?"

Emma Hollingdon goes into corporate mode, "Ms Parker, the airline position which the board have instructed all of us to adopt is to wait till the final report or at least until a final statement from the AAIB before discussing the accident or its investigation. I am sure you will agree these things are best left to the experts."

Emma Hollingdon is certainly more friendly that the CAA spokesperson but it does not help Jill.

Next on her list of people to call is Martin Stone, the union rep. She takes out his business card from her handbag, still there from when they met at the Vermont Hotel with the other families. She rings the union head office number but she is told he is not in the office but on his mobile so she tries that number and it starts ringing.

Martin Stone clearly remembers who she is, "Hello, Ms Parker, how are you and your mother keeping?"

"We are both doing well. Thanks. I was wondering if I could ask you something?"

Martin Stone responds very quickly, "If it's about the settlement, I can tell you that Mrs Jones has agreed and sent me a copy of her signed agreement this morning."

"No, it's not about the settlement, I am letting my mum deal with that, I am ringing about a part of the transcript from the voice recorder."

"OK… Which part – do I need to get a copy? Because I am away from my desk at the moment."

"No, you will not need a copy. Basically, on page 23 of the air accident investigation initial report, in the cockpit voice recorder part, towards the end of the report, my sister says 'There's the socks again'. What does that mean?"

"I think it might be a reference to some smell in the cockpit."

Jill feels surprise and relief. At least he knows. "That's great. A friend of mine and I have been researching this and there are vast amounts of data on the Internet saying that contaminated air is often described with the expression dirty socks or wet dog type of smell. If the air was contaminated then this might be a reason for the accident. I rang the CAA but they told me to wait for the final report to come out, but if my sister and Captain Jones are being blamed for pilot error and it was not their fault, that's not right."

Martin Stone adopts a lecturing tone, "Ms Parker, I know these are difficult times for you but what the CAA told you was good advice. It's best to wait till the final report comes out before jumping to conclusions, especially from research on the Internet."

Jill fights her temper. "Hang on a minute, the initial report has pilot error written all over it, so waiting for a final report is a waste of time, it's my sister's name and abilities which are being questioned. She may just be another membership number to you but this is my dead sister we are talking about."

Martin Stone continues in a condescending manner, "Ms Parker, I am the Chairman of the Flight Safety Group. The view from the union is that contaminated air is not an issue to make a big fuss about. The CAA investigated these matters in the past and concluded there were no health or flight safety issues. Some have been outspoken about these matters, especially some Australian stewardesses but these were people who did not like the industry and had but one objective – to try and get a pay out from legal action."

Jill remembers what Gary told her about the air not being filtered, the C-130 navigator who was incapacitated in 1977 and the subsequent paper being published by the head doctor at the Air National Guard confirming it was due to contaminated air. She tells Martin Stone all of this and he continues to respond as if he was a teacher dealing with a disruptive student, "If there was any health or flight safety risk, the CAA would have mandated the fitting of filters. They haven't, so the CAA obviously think it's safe. The C-130 incident I am not familiar with but the military use different oils so that might be a reason or perhaps the doctors were wrong."

She eases out of the conversation, "Alright Mr Stone, I hear what you're saying. You're right, best to let the experts get on with their work and see what comes out. Thanks for your time anyway. Enjoy your weekend."

"You're very welcome Ms Parker, all of us at the union appreciate these are difficult times for you and your mother. Call again if you have any questions."

Jill slams the phone down in disgust and then closes her eyes to collect her thoughts, then looks at her fake Rolex watch, the benefit from a holiday to China a year before. It is time for her to get ready to go to work. She walks up the stairs and puts her uniform on, brushes her hair which is now virtually dry, and applies some pale lipstick.

Gary is finding it hard to join in the party atmosphere in the bar with the lads, his mind is on the other side of the Atlantic and focused on the data that is spinning round his head.

Terry, leans over to talk to Gary. He still has to shout over the loud music.

"What do you think about you and I doing a reconnoitre of the two targets bearing 090 at 25 meters."

Gary gives the thumbs up.

The targets are two very attractive girls in their early twenties sitting together and drinking cocktails. It is not yet spring in Canada but they are not dressed for outside, with low cut, short dresses. They are attracting the attention of all the males present.

Gary turns back to face Terry who now has his back to the girls and gives a view, "How long you been in 2 PARA, Terry?"

"Two years, mate, why?"

"Did they not teach you before you move in on a target you always assess the risk and defences first?"

Terry can sense something does not add up and turns round to look at the girls. They have just met up with two tall muscular mountain police officers whom they are obviously dating.

Terry turns back to Gary, "Bet they were no good anyway!"

Gary smiles, finishes his drink. "You could always go and ask."

Chapter 7

Gary walks back into the communications room and exchanges morning greetings with a young female soldier as he enters the building. He logs onto the Internet and finds the telephone number for the United States Federal Aviation Administration. He asks the receptionist if she has a phone he can use to dial a one eight hundred number in the USA. She points him towards a phone the other side of the room and he thanks her.

Like Jill the day before with the CAA, he finds it very frustrating trying to find someone to talk with on the issue. Everyone tells him this is someone else's responsibility or directs him to the FAA website. Finally, he gets somebody in statistical analysis. The man asks him what key words he is looking for.

Gary explains, "I am not sure but could you please try 'oil', 'smoke', 'contaminated air' and 'dirty socks'."

The FAA statistician is not finding the task very easy, "Oil is a very widely used word in the aviation industry, it could be used for 'engine oil levels' as well as 'oil part X, once a week'. I also need to know what aircraft type you are focusing on and if it's 'Part 121' operations or what."

"I am sorry I don't know what 'Part 121' is, I thought it was a bit easier."

"If you write in and outline exactly what statistics you want to know about then I am certain you will get a reply within twenty-eight days."

"OK, thanks for your help." Gary puts the receiver down impatiently.

As Gary walks out of the communications building he meets Lieutenant Morrison. He does not have to salute him as he is not in uniform. It is the rank of uniform you salute, not the person.

Lieutenant Morrison says, "Gary, can you meet me for a briefing on tomorrow's drop at 1800 outside your barracks?"

"Yes, Sir, will do. Just off for some breakfast, fancy joining me?"

"Another time, got a busy morning."

Gary looks at his watch, some hours away yet until they meet as time is always referred to Greenwich Mean Time (GMT) both in the military and in aviation.

Gary walks into the canteen, takes a stainless steel tray and helps himself to a good selection of Canadian army grub. As he turns away from the cutlery rack, some of the men on 2 PARA call him over to join him. Stories from the evening's night out are volunteered across the table, amongst hangover symptoms. Gary starts telling some of what he has been discovering. They are all fascinated despite the hangovers. The link to Gulf War Syndrome is very real to them.

Mike, a Cornish newcomer to 2 PARA says, "I grew up on a sheep farm and we used to dip sheep in all sorts of chemicals containing high levels of organophosphates. I think Diazonon was the name of one of them. The old timers used to talk about 'dippers flu' – a flu like symptom they would get after dipping the sheep. My uncle crashed his car one night and the locals all said he was drink driving. The thing is he was driving *to* the pub not *from* it. His doctor was convinced it was the neurological effects of inhaling all the chemicals and organophosphates from the sheep dipping he had been doing that day."

Gary and the others voice their amazement at the story, in-between mouthfuls of eggs and bacon.

"How come I've never heard of this stuff?" says Gary.

"Not too many sheep in Newcastle Gary, apart from some of those lasses down the Quayside on a Saturday night waiting in long lines to go clubbing, freezing with nothing on," says Tom, a city boy from Southampton.

Gary smiles, "At least our girls are tough and canny, not like your southern softies!"

He then turns to Mike. "What did they do about the sheep dippers?"

The banter stops as everyone's attention turns on Mike.

"Well," says the Cornishman, "the Government investigated it and interviewed lots of farmers and in the end it was all bollocks. The Government said you could not prove it was the organophosphates and maybe it was this or that. If you lived where I lived, every family who ran a farm knew someone who was sick. We all knew it was the sheep dip and the organophosphates but the Government said you could not prove it 100%. The question was asked if *interested parties* had sold the sheep dippers out to look after the interests of the farming business as a whole. It was the usual story, just like Gulf War Syndrome, confuse the issue so as to do nothing. They knew fine well people were sick. Some university did a study on it and they had no doubts but hey, they are just scientists, the bureaucrats always know best. My uncle died before his court action got to court. His lawyer who was a real wise old guy told my dad once, it's not 100% proof you need but greater probability than not, i.e. 51%. Well, we knew that but the Government white washed it all, probably to help with sheep exports or some bullshit statistics. The Government didn't care!"

Another soldier called Chris, who is from Chichester, joins in the debate, "Where I lived there was this girl called Georgina Downs, she was known as the Pesticide Nun. This woman was seriously ill from being regularly exposed to pesticides in her garden as a kid. The neighbouring farmer used to spray his fields and the pesticides were in the air where she

49

used to play. Anyway, she found out there were thousands of people sick from pesticide exposures so she started the UK Pesticides Campaign to try to get people the necessary protection. Her campaign led to Ministers requesting a study by the Royal Commission on Environmental Pollution (RCEP). The Ministers appeared to be hoping the RCEP would back the Government's position that pesticide spraying is not a serious health risk. However, the plan backfired and much to the Government's fury the RCEP ended up agreeing with Georgina's charge that the Government's policy is inadequate and that the chronic diseases reported in rural areas could be caused by pesticide exposure. But guess what? Just like Mike was saying about sheep dippers two of the Government's so-called *independent* scientific advisory groups the ACP and COT quickly brought out reports to say it was all bollocks and that the ill-health reported by rural residents was most likely to be psychosomatic! What a nerve, all they did was basically look after industry interests and to hell with those getting sick.

I know the nun was right, well she wasn't a nun as she was in fact an attractive woman of my age, but she was right because a cousin of mine got sick once from eating some fruit which had been sprayed with pesticides but nobody told him. You have to wonder what the country is coming to? Why do they always put commercial and industry interests ahead of people and the environment? The last I heard Georgina had got permission to take the Government to the High Court to challenge its whole policy and approach regarding the protection afforded to people from pesticides."

Gary sits back and takes it all in. He starts writing on a piece of paper. Organophosphates. Then he continues the list. Gulf War Syndrome, Sheep Dippers, Pesticide Exposures, Chemical Weapons... Engine Oils, Crew?

He then says, "If the same thing that happened in the Gulf, to Mike's uncle and to Georgina the nun, was also

50

happening in aviation then people would be sick, I mean crews would be sick. Do you agree?"

His theory makes sense to everyone at the table.

"What I should do is look and see if this is the case. Find the sick crews. I'll do that when we get back. Thanks, lads and thanks Mike and Chris... I am glad you guys signed up!"

Jill is in bed. She is staring up at the ceiling in the dark. Her mobile phone starts ringing.

She turns and looks at the display screen. The word 'international' is flashing.

"Hiya, Jill, it's Gary, I hope I didn't wake you again."

"No, Gary, I was awake and thinking about things. Can't really sleep. It's all a bit too much to take in."

"I know Jill, I'm finding the same, it's like being in a dream where you're in some sort of crazy surreal situation. Anyway, I haven't got long as I have to get the lads briefed for the drop tomorrow morning. It's a very early start but it's only a four-day exercise and then a few days later hopefully we will know when we will be on our way back. I rang the FAA in Washington but it was a waste of time. I have to write in to find anything out. How did you get on, did you ring anyone?"

"Yeah, I rang the CAA, the airline and the pilot union. I might as well have rung just one of them as they all said the same thing. 'Wait for the final report.' It's very frustrating. I wish I knew some people who actually fly. I am going to have to look and see if I can trace any of Carol's friends down and ring them."

"That's a great idea,"

Gary goes on, "Can you keep researching this when you can while I am on the exercise and when I get back we can sit down and look through everything?"

"OK, I will but this might all be for nothing as Martin Stone told me that the oils used in the military are different from commercial aircraft. Gary? are you still there?"

"Yeah, I was thinking about what you said but even if that was the case why was there an article in 2006 about pilots being poisoned in flight?"

"Maybe every aircraft uses different oils. Maybe the military plane, the C-310 –"

"C-130."

"Sorry the C-130 – maybe that and all other aircraft all use different types of oil."

"I see what you mean. I need to find out. If the C-130 uses the same oil as the Boeing 757 then who cares about the rest, because if that navigator can be incapacitated then so could your sister."

"That's a point, unless the oils back in 1977, I think you said it was then, are very different to the oils today, then it would be a different issue."

"You're right, what we need to do is find out if the oil used in the C-130 is the same as in the Boeing 757, and is that oil the same as back in 1977. OK, I'll find that out tomorrow if I can when I go to the airport on the way to the drop. As soon as I know when I'm back I'll let you know and we can catch up. OK, let's keep in touch and see what else you can find. I'll do the oils."

It's pitch black outside when the wake up call comes into the barracks. The plan is to jump at first day break. Terry and Mike look at their watches. They love the job but this is the worst part. Early starts with big time zone changes. The detachment from 2 PARA quickly get up and enter the truck for the ride to the aircraft.

Mike asks Terry, who is a corporal, what it's like, jumping from the aircraft they are approaching. Today, the are dropping from a Boeing C-17 Globemaster III, a four engined United States Air Force transport aircraft, not something the relatively new members to 2 PARA have done many times before.

Terry fills him in, "Well that's an easy one, you jump and one thing is guaranteed 100%, you fall – it's gravity my son!"

Terry sees that Mike would like a bit more help than that, "It's OK, the Yanks like an easy life so they make it real easy for them. It's just like the ones we have and I think it's easier than the Hercules."

Mike smiles.

The truck arrives near the side of the aircraft on the floodlight and cold apron where the aircraft is parked.

Gary asks Terry to count the lads onto the aircraft as he walks towards an airmen standing near the ground power unit (GPU) plugged into the side of the aircraft. The GPU is supplying the aircraft with electrical power whilst it is on the ground.

Gary asks the airmen, "Excuse me, are you an engineer?"

The airman pulls the scarf down from across his face to reply. It is a cold morning and the wind is adding to the chill. "I certainly am, power plant licensed engineer, why – do you need one?"

"I was wondering, what type of oil would the engines on this aircraft use and how would it compare with the oil in, say, the engines of the C-130 Hercules?"

The engineer's look shows he thinks it is a wind up, "What are you, some sort of trainee pilot or something?"

"No, I am just interested out of curiosity. The lads and I were having a chat as one does and just wondered."

The engineer pauses a few seconds and gives him the benefit of the doubt. "The oils we use all have to be approved against U.S. Military Specification MIL-PRF-23699. I'll show you."

The engineer takes him on a short walk to van. He opens the back of the van and in a cardboard box sits a dozen or so cans of jet engine oil. The airmen picks one up and shows it to Gary, pointing to the bottom side of the can. "You see it's written here. Approved against U.S. Military Specification MIL-PRF-23699. Different oil manufacturers make these specialised synthetic jet engine oils such as BP or Shell or this fellow here made by ExxonMobil."

He rotates the can. "This is Jet Oil II, this is the most widely used jet engine oil in the world. We use it in nearly all aircraft such as on the Boeing C-17 Globemaster or the C-130."

Gary is impressed with his knowledge and wants to know what commercial aircraft use for oil, thinking about Martin Stone telling Jill that military aircraft used different oils.

"I get it. Most military aircraft use the same oils such as this oil ExxonMobil Jet Oil II, but what about civil aircraft such as the Boeing 747 or Boeing 757?"

"They use the same buddy, it's all the same. We even fly those aircraft in the military so it would make no sense having different oils, would it? The Boeing 757 is a military C-32A."

Gary wants to be sure. "Are you 100% certain that the oils you put in the engines of this aircraft, a C-130 or a civilian Boeing 757 engine are the same?"

"Absolutely, they may have different manufacturers but they're all the same, it's like putting gas in your car, lots of different companies selling the same stuff, but I guess a bit different in that there are only a few companies making these specialised jet engine oils. ExxonMobil Jet Oil II has been around for decades, it's the most popular but I wouldn't put it in my coffee if you know what I mean."

Gary is running out of time as he hears Terry shouting his name. "What about a can of Jet Oil II in the 70s or 80s – is that the same as a can of Jet Oil II today?"

The engineer replies, "When I went through training back in 1982 they told us it took over ten years to develop the specification for these oils and to change them would take at least another ten years. It worked in the 60s so why change it? I would say it's essentially the same shit today, why wouldn't it be?"

Gary hands him back the can and smiles. "Thanks a lot for the lesson, buddy, how about I teach you to jump out of the sucker?"

The engineer replies in a loud voice as he closes the back of the van, "I fix the suckers so I don't have to jump out when I go fly! Have a good one, brother."

Gary takes his seat in the aircraft. They had space on the C-130 but the space they have today is a big step up. It appears the USAF are doing pilot training and the use of the aircraft fits into the exercise. Gary has another piece of the contaminated air jigsaw but knows there are many pieces missing. He knows that the oils used on the C-130 where the navigator was incapacitated is the same as on JASP flight 303 and therefore perhaps inhaling the oil fumes had an effect on Carol and the Captain.

His mind is a mess with so many "what ifs." He has more questions than answers. After the aircraft gets airborne he suddenly looks up and Lieutenant Morrison is right in front of him, talking to him.

Gary has heard nothing, "Sorry, Sir, did I miss something?"

He notices a few of the men looking at him quietly and immediately realises something is amiss. The lieutenant tells everyone to go and check their kit, a polite way of telling them to leave him and Gary alone. Mo and Gary have seen a lot of hot spots together and there is mutual respect.

"Gary, I was talking to you for half a minute and you were somewhere else... I have overheard the lads talking about some of your research and your father's plane crash. Look I know these are hard times for you and clearly your mind is elsewhere. You're a good soldier, a very good soldier. If you are putting time into something to the point you can't hear me that means two things."

Lieutenant Morrison carries on, "It means it must be *very* important and you should be somewhere else, not about to do a jump out of an aircraft on this exercise."

Gary smiles in acknowledgement that he agrees.

"Gary, that shoulder of yours needs looking at, it's obviously causing you a lot of discomfort. I am sending you back to the UK, report back for duties when you're combat fit again. The crew on this aircraft will take you back to base after the drop."

Mo winks. Gary remembers the time he injured his shoulder in Afghanistan with the lieutenant, on a night reconnaissance mission. He also knows they both know it healed a long time ago.

Gary is very grateful and plays the part, "Thank you very much, Sir, that's probably best. My shoulder has been keeping me awake a lot recently. I'll see you all soon back at base, have a good jump."

The aircraft comes to a halt on the apron and the engines are shut down. After the loadmaster has opened the forward port door he points towards to a van which has been arranged to pick Gary up and gives him the thumbs up. Gary shakes the loadmaster's hand and walks towards the awaiting van.

After a short drive, he gets out of the van and walks to the communications centre near his barracks with all his kit, much to the surprise of the soldier manning the desk in the communications centre. Within fifteen minutes, he has a booking to London.

Jill is fast asleep in the lounge. It is very late and it takes some time for the ringing to register in her brain. She realises she did not make it to her bed.

She rummages in her bag and finds her mobile.

"Jill, it's Gary. Sorry to wake you again but I am coming back."

"What do you mean you're coming back?"

"Listen, I found out this morning that the oils on that flight where the navigator was incapacitated are the same as on Carol's Boeing 757! What the union told you was bullshit! It's a long story but I have a flight from Winnipeg with Air Canada at 17.05 local time, a connection in Toronto and arrive in London with Air Canada tomorrow morning at 11.05. When I get to London I will either get a train to Newcastle or get a flight. I will sort that bit out tomorrow. Jill, we need to get to the bottom of this. Something tells me something does not add up. Whilst I am flying back, can you see if anyone has investigated air quality on aircraft and dig, dig everywhere on the net?"

Jill shares his excitement. "I know what you're saying, I agree a lot of this does not add up. How could Martin Stone tell me the military used different oil?"

"An engineer told me this morning, it's all designed to a specific military specification so they will all be the same and that the military fly commercial aircraft as well!"

"OK, I will seriously start digging and getting more information. Ring me when you know when you're arriving in Newcastle and I'll meet you at the station or airport and... Take care, Gary."

"Don't worry, see you when I am back home."

Jill drops the phone back into her bag. She finds herself wishing Gary would stop waking her up. The sleep starvation is getting the better of her.

Chapter 8

Lying in bed, unable to sleep, Jill is uncomfortable at the idea that Gary has been doing the bulk of the work. She turns over to see the radio alarm clock. 06.00. She does not even reach out for the curtain to check the outside world. She knows it is still pitch dark. It is all very overpowering, the authorities are investigating these matters yet nobody seems to be investigating any possible link between the comment Carol made on that fatal morning and what the relevance of the comment was.

She throws off the duvet with a mixture of resolution and resignation, and swings her legs off the bed. On the way to the lounge, she makes a brief detour to the kitchen and pushes the 'on' switch on the kettle almost spitefully.

Jill boots up her computer and rubs the sleep out of her eyes to focus on the screen. On her notepad, she writes 'investigations into aircraft'. She starts her Internet research by typing in 'commercial jet aircraft types' which quickly lists all current jet aircraft, and starts at the top of the list. She comes across a webpage with a quote from a UK MP, Paul Flynn in 2006.

'In many cases the contaminated fumes are a result of burning engine oil leaking into the ventilation system. The two aircraft types most affected are the BAE 146 and Boeing 757, which are flown by a number of regional and international airlines.'

The Boeing 757 is reported by Mr Flynn as being one of the two most affected aircraft. There is so much evidence on the net of contaminated air from jet engine oils, she can't really take it all in but she finds that the AAIB certainly know about this happening before.

There are countless incidents telling the same story on the Internet. Incidents in Australia, USA, Canada, Norway and numerous other countries around the world.

England, 5th November 2000. Aircraft type was a British Aerospace BAe 146 with CAA reference number of 200008340 and aircraft registration of G-JEAK. The incident report records, 'Co-pilot incapacitated and Captain performance seriously impaired whilst on the approach to Birmingham. Commander also felt light headed and had difficulty in judging height during the ensuing approach and landing.'

England, 7th November 2000. Aircraft type was a Boeing 757 with CAA reference number 200008363 and aircraft registration G-CPEL. The incident report records, 'Oily metallic smell had also been evident during previous sector. On this occasion, numerous ATC calls were missed, prompting ATC to ask aircraft if everything was all right. Captain then forgot to slow aircraft during approach until reminded to do so at 3.7d. Crew unaware that they were becoming partially incapacitated.'

Northern Ireland, 8th December 2004. Aircraft type was a British Aerospace BAe 146 with CAA reference number 200408975. The incident report records, 'Flight crew incapacitation due to possible air quality problem. Co-pilot felt unwell (faint and breathless with shaking hands). Captain had headache with 'flu symptoms' and was in a state of euphoria although successfully landed the aircraft while operating as single crew. Co-pilot sent to hospital and Captain suffered headache and flu symptoms for 24hrs.'

England, 10th February 2006. Aircraft type was again a British Aerospace BAe 146 with CAA reference number of 200601036 and aircraft registration of G-JEBB. The incident report records, 'Fumes on flight deck and in forward cabin. The Captain and two cabin attendants were aware of fumes during the cruise. The Captain reported being unable to concentrate and one of the cabin attendants reported slightly blurred vision.'

Australia, 31st March 2000. Ansett Australia Airlines. Aircraft type was again a British Aerospace BAe 146. ATSB incident report 200001175 and aircraft registration of VH-JJZ. Report from Captain reads, 'When switching air supplies from the APU to the engine air supplies, we got this odour in the cabin I call it the dirty sock smell. I have smelled it numerous times in the past... About a minute later, I felt just a slight light-headedness coming about, so what I did was I took the oxygen mask. I did not actually properly don it; I just took it and held it up to my face at that point the autopilot was already on and just took a few whiffs to sort of clean my system out. It is pretty much standard procedure and it is there at the ready in case you need it. What happened, as I pretty much expected it would, was that the symptoms of this sort of light-headedness went away pretty much straightaway... The light-headedness thing sort of came back again and a very, very dull headache transpired, so I started breathing the oxygen again. Lo and behold, it started to go away and, as the flight progressed and once again I was not breathing oxygen the whole time it went away and then it started coming back again. And then later I just had very dry scratchy eyes, a sore throat, that sort of thing, a taste in my mouth, and the only way I could describe it is it tastes like it smells. So at this point I am already saying, 'There is obviously some sort of a problem here we are going to have to sort out but, once again, what engine is it coming from, what pack is it coming from?' There was really no way of telling because there was no way to isolate it. So the flight continued and, on descent at the lower altitudes going into Melbourne, I then became aware that with the points of light, when you get down low at night it was a very clear, brilliant night, there was some blurring in my long-distance vision... It was not until that point, in walking across the ramp at Melbourne, that I realised that I had a slight disorientation. I do not really know how to describe it, not staggering falling over drunk, but it was very obvious that there was something wrong, that there was a minor incapacitation.'

Australia, Brisbane incident 1997. BAe 146 incident report which reads, 'a pilot in command of a BAe 146 reporting that the smell of oil coming through the air supply was far worse than usual with the passengers and flight attendants complaining bitterly of the smell. The First Officer also complaining of the smell experienced worsening red / weeping eyes. On final approach to land the Captain slowly became aware of feeling "as drunk as a skunk" as if having consumed about 6 Scotches. The captain reported having trouble judging the distance to land with everything seeming "wonky" including the runway. The Captain reported that the symptoms similar to intoxication removed all consideration of handing over control to the First Officer. The pilot grounded the aircraft and stated that further flight would not even be considered until fresh air was obtained to 'sober up'.'

USA, 30th April 1998. US Employee Accident Report. Aircraft type is an MD80. Report reads, 'After landing smell of burning odour in cabin. Experienced burning sensation in eyes, throat, face & skin flushed with a lot of difficulty breathing. Felt 'out of it'.'

Canada, 27th July 2001. Internal Company Incident Report. Aircraft type is a Boeing 767. The report reads, 'Immediately after take off there was a very hot oil smell throughout cabin which lasted for 20 minutes but was very strong for 10 minutes.'

If her sister died because of the effects of these fumes, all the incidents she is reading about could easily have been the writing on the wall. Perhaps flight 303 was when crews' luck finally ran out. How many incidents are there? How much writing was on the wall? Yet more questions for her notepad. She knows she really needs to speak with someone who really knows. Someone somewhere must know these things – who?

The incidents she has found often have the UK CAA or UK AAIB as the investigating authority and frequently end with a CAA statement of, 'CAA Closure: The hazard is adequately controlled by existing requirements, procedures and documentation.' Jill wants to know what the, 'existing requirements, procedures and documentation' actually are. It is clear by the frequency of events she is finding that they appear to not be working. It is not long before she finds exactly the sort of investigation she has been looking for, an investigation specifically looking at contaminated air on either the Boeing 757 of BAe 146. The investigation report is entitled, 'The Australian Rural and Regional Affairs and Transport, Air Safety - BAe 146 Cabin Air Quality. November 1999 to August 2000.' She starts to read through the extensive investigation report.

Gary is at the check-in desk for Air Canada in Winnipeg. The check-in agent runs through the routine security questions, then asks him where he would like to sit.

"Window in first class would be nice."

The agent has heard it all before, smiles and hands him his boarding card. "Perhaps on your next trip, Sir, here you go, flight departs at 17.05 from gate C32."

Jill makes notes from the Senate investigation and after some hours gets to the recommendations made by the investigation.

'The Committee notes from the evidence it has received the considerable concern amongst a number of aircrew and medical specialists that some aircrew might experience health effects, both short term and possibly long term, from exposure to cabin and cockpit air in the BAe 146 aircraft.'

'The Committee considers that, in view of continuing concern about aircraft cabin air quality, CASA (*Australian aviation regulator*) should, after assessment and consideration, give consideration to requiring fitting of such filters to all commercial passenger jet aircraft flying in Australia.'

'As the Committee notes in Chapter 3, the issue of the chemical conduct of Mobil Jet Oil II and its probable effect on health is a matter of contention between Mobil, the operators of the BAe 146 and aircrew and pilots.'

As Jill sits back for a few seconds and digests all the data, Gary's flight to Toronto takes off from Winnipeg. She wonders if such a thorough investigation as the Australian Senate Inquiry called for filters to be fitted on commercial aircraft in 2000, what happened. She scribbles 'Air Filters?'

Jill gets back to the research and soon discovers that bleed air filters are not fitted to aircraft – only the recirculated air is filtered which does not help this issue. She then finds a question asked in the UK House of Lords by the Countess of Mar from October 2005. The questions asked Her Majesty's Government, 'Why filters are not fitted to commercial aircraft to prevent crews and passengers from being exposed to pyrolysis products from synthetic jet engine oils and hydraulic fluids during a contaminated air event.'

The Government reply given by Lord Davies of Oldham includes the statement that, 'Filters are not required on commercial aircraft because European airworthiness regulations already require aircraft ventilation systems to be designed to supply air to an acceptable standard, free from harmful or hazardous concentrations of gases or vapours.'

If the air supply that pilots and passengers are breathing is contaminated with engine oils which contain neurotoxins then the aircraft ventilation systems are not doing what the government say they should be doing.

What a fob off, she thinks. She goes back to the Australian Senate investigation and looks to see who chaired it. She finds it was chaired by Senator John Woodley. The Internet reveals that he was a former Democrat Senator who stepped aside because of ill-health in 2001. Senator Woodley is a retired Uniting Church Minister with links to the Caboolture Uniting Church.

Directory Enquiries provide the telephone number of the Caboolture Uniting Church in Queensland Australia. Jill rings the church and obtains Reverend Woodley's number. She hesitates. What will she discover? Will he speak to a nurse from Newcastle, ringing about a crash he may or may not know about? She takes a deep breath. In for a penny, in for a pound. She dials.

"Hello, I am very sorry to trouble you, Sir, my name is Jill Parker. I am ringing from Newcastle in Northern England. I am ringing about the Senate investigation you chaired in 1999-2000 on the BAe 146."

Senator Woodley replies in a strong and caring voice, an ability gained from his years working in the church and in the Australian Senate. "I remember it well, the recommendations and findings certainly rattled a few cages. What is your interest in the inquiry, are you a crew member or a journalist?"

"No, Senator Woodley, I am neither. I do not know if you know about the plane crash we sadly had here in Newcastle in January. Well, my sister was the co-pilot on a Boeing 757 flying for JASP and lost her life.

Senator Woodley knows about the accident. "I certainly do remember reading about it, something to do with bad weather? I am very sorry to hear of your loss, it must be very hard on you."

Senator Woodley pauses for a while, then continues. "What is the connection between the accident and the BAe 146 inquiry we did?"

"Well, it's a bit of a long story and it may sound a bit crazy at times but I wanted to speak with someone... Well it might have something to do with what you investigated."

Jill does not have a chance to continue her sentence.

"Contaminated air ?"

A shiver goes down her spine. "How did you guess?"

"It was not a guess, but before I say any more, please tell me what you know." Reverend Woodley's tone is methodical.

Senator Woodley has listened very carefully. "I applaud you for the knowledge you have gained on these issues so quickly. These are issues I am very interested in. These are very technical issues and many play on the technical and scientific complexities to confuse crews and the public. Yet it is so very simple. As you know the oil contaminates the air supply and passengers and crews breathe in the contaminated air which is harmful – it's that simple. What still amazes me today is how passengers do not realise that the air they breathe is not filtered. They confuse the recirculated air with the bleed air.

It does not surprise me that the aviation industry has managed to pull the wool over the public's eyes for so long. During our inquiry we were advised by BAe that they believed their aircraft had a very good safety record as it had never suffered a fatal accident due to an aircraft technical failure. When BAe was asked by Senator Forshaw to clarify what they determined constituted a good safety record BAe advised this was based on fatalities due to technical failures. The Committee did not feel that assessing an aircraft as being safe based on fatalities alone was appropriate, as to do so ignored many other factors, especially the in-flight problems and health effects which had prompted the inquiry in the first place.

A matter which continues to concern me is how the public is not informed when they have been exposed to contaminated air and what the potential consequences of that exposure could be. I have tried to remain informed about the issues involved but I'm sure there will be some developments of which I am not aware. Our Report was tabled in the Senate in

October 2000 and I retired in July 2001. In 2005 I attended and spoke at a conference which was organised by one of the UK pilot unions and sponsored by some filter manufacturers and the aircrew group AOPIS, set up in Australia just after the Senate Inquiry finished. You did not mention their name but you should contact them if you have not already done so."

Jill writes the name 'AOPIS' on the notepad and continues to listen carefully.

Senator Woodley continues, "The 2005 conference in London was an amazing yet wasted conference in that every interested party was offered a slot in the program. Some twenty-five leading authorities spoke from all around the world yet the union – probably too frightened of what they discovered and its potential impact on jobs – failed to even issue a press release. I remember very clearly that the Boeing 757, as well as some other aircraft in addition to the BAe 146, were reported to be suffering continued problems with contaminated air. I remember presenting my speech in London which, if I recall was entitled 'The Politics of Aircraft Health and Safety.' I chose that title because the whole issue is in reality more about politics, power and money than it is about medical evidence, medical treatment or medical science. You have told me about what you know and focused on the technical issues of the debate but you need to be aware of the very sinister side of these matters."

Jill has already started to realise there are several hidden agendas at play.

Senator Woodley continues. "After we concluded crews were getting sick, losing their careers due to ill health, filters should be fitted, oils reviewed for their toxicology effects, the UK House of Lords quickly looked at the wider spectrum of air travel and as you mentioned, sharply concluded that contaminated air was not an issue based on a the red herring of TOCP. Some alleged that the UK Government just acted to protect British Aerospace whose aircraft had been the center of our year long investigation. I met in London with the Chair of the House of Lords Committee, Baroness Wilcox and also with the public servant who was the Secretary to her Committee, a most charming gentleman, who never left her side apart from a few minutes during lunch when he went to the toilet. While he was away she confided in me that she felt she was being conned by the bureaucrats and, having read the House of Lords Report, I believe she was!

It is rumoured that in Australia, BAe paid Ansett Airlines and East West Airlines a million plus dollars in an agreement dated September 1993 in relation to contaminated air problems. This fact was not disclosed by BAe when questioned at the inquiry but was the subject of a question in the UK House of Lords in July 2006. Lord Tyler who had investigated these matters asked Her Majesty's Government whether they were aware of any payments made by British Aerospace Regional Aircraft Limited to Ansett Transport Industries Operations Limited and East West Airline Operations Limited, under an agreement dated September 1993, in connection with design flaws in the BAe 146 aircraft allowing contamination of cabin air by oil and other fumes.

The senate investigation was basically called for by a lovely stewardess called Judy Cullinane and a talented pilot called Susan Michaelis who had won the Sir Donald Anderson Award. Both had been seriously affected by exposure to contaminated air. Judy – who was finally compensated in a significant out of court settlement for her injuries – once revealed the sinister side. For some considerable time whilst she was a plaintiff against her employer, a car used to park outside her house and follow her, take pictures of her and all the usual intimidation tactics industry goes to silence the brave. In the end, as I mentioned, she was compensated but probably not what she deserved. They were both smashing girls. I met so many affected crews, there was no doubt in my mind they had been affected by the fumes."

Jill, who has been making lots of written notes, replies, "Senator Woodley, it's absolutely amazing, especially when you think that all this was known in 2000."

"Not 2000, this has been known since the 1950s. I remember that in 1983 – which was before the BAe 146 first flew – that a Dr Johnson and Dr McNaughton if I recall the names correctly, published a paper which concluded that smoke / fumes in the cockpit was not a rare event and a clear threat to flying safety because of the acute and long term effect toxic effects oil and hydraulic fluid substances had when heated. You should realise, Ms Parker, that like the tobacco industry the airline industry cares little for the impact contaminated air has on crews and passengers when they can get away with it. The tobacco industry led the way. For fifty years, cigarette manufacturers employed a stable of scientists willing to assert (sometimes under oath) that there was no conclusive evidence that cigarettes cause lung cancer, or that nicotine is addictive. An official at Brown & Williamson, a cigarette maker, once noted in a memo: 'Doubt is our product since it is the best means of competing with the body of fact that exists in the mind of the general public.' The industry relies on misinformation. I remember, during the hearing, that an industry doctor tried to blame ill effects from contaminated air exposures on the contraceptive pill. It still makes me chuckle when I remember the union spokesperson pointing out that male pilots were not on the contraceptive pill but still reporting contaminated air exposure symptoms after exposures.

Jill smiles and Senator Woodley carries on, "Another matter you might want to remember, is that we were not the first to conclude crews would be adversely affected by working on the BAe 146. In 1992, the Industrial Relations Commission of New South Wales ruled that cabin attendants who had supporting medical evidence that they were being affected by working on the BAe 146, would be exempt from working on the aircraft. What you should realise is that the industry attempted to convince us that this was not an aviation safety threat, merely a health issue. However, our committee found that the aviation regulations required pilots to be in a suitable state of health for flying an aircraft and therefore acknowledged the regulator link between crew health and air safety. Some other interesting facts worth knowing, are that Ansett Airlines had set up a committee specifically to deal with contaminated air and was called the 'BAe 146 Cabin Odour Inquiry Committee'. A panel selected by that committee actually concluded that short term symptoms associated with odours that had been reported on the BAe146 and other types were substantiated. You see there is so much evidence for those like you who take the time to look. Anyway, if you hang on a few minutes I think I have the contact details of the fella who hosted the London conference – can you hang on?"

Jill can see that the issue is, from a cover up view, on the scale of asbestos or smoking but has been kept out of the public's radar more successfully.

Senator Woodley returns, "OK, here it is, his name is Charles Cosgrove, he was a Captain who lost his medical certificate and was no longer able to fly due to the years spent on the BAe 146. He lives in a small village called West Ridelton. He will know how to contact a chap called Gordon Cooper who was a Boeing 757 pilot who used to know everything there was to know on these matters. Gordon lost his health to these matters as well. Find Charles and he will point you to Gordon."

Jill is overwhelmed. "Senator Woodley you have been very kind to give up your evening and I appreciate all the information you have told me about, it's all very enlightening but also very sad. "Please let me know what comes of your investigations. God bless."

Jill puts the phone down. She knows now this is big industry she is up against. An industry like many that will do anything to protect itself and to ensure they continue to achieve their primary objective. Increasing the share price.

Chapter 9

The next obvious step is to find Charles Cosgrove. This time, Directory Enquiries are not as helpful. The number is ex-directory. Jill looks across the room to the clock. 10.15. She walks over to the window and pulls open the curtains. Daylight has come again without her noticing. She digs out a UK road map from the top of the bookcase, and blows off the dust. The pages are frayed. She looks at the index and looks up West Ridelton.

It occurs to her that her mother might worry if she does not answer the phone for a few days. She dials her number but the answering machine clicks in. Jill remembers that her mother must be out shopping. "Hi Mum, it's Jill, I just wanted you to know if you were thinking of popping around, I am going to go down south for a few days. I'll be on my mobile, take care. Love you."

There is no point trying just yet to explain all this to her mum. The union, airlines offices, as well as the CAA are all in London and that's where Gary and she need to be.

Jill walks out into the cold wet morning. She opens the boot of her car and throws in a small overnight bag and a thick coat. The car starts and she puts in a Madonna CD, one of many she will have time to listen to during the journey.

After a four and half hours she drives into the small village of West Ridelton. It is like any other English village, with a church steeple, a pub called *The Green Man* and a tea shop with white lace curtains on the windows. With a bit of help from local residents, she finds the house of Charles Cosgrove. Before she can even start to think if he will be home she is relieved to see an older man in his large double garage to the side of the house, inspecting the engine of a vintage car. She parks her car in his driveway, and starts walking towards him. The man takes his attention away from the engine and turns to look at the visitor. With veteran skill, he looks her up and down and smiles approvingly. Everything about his demeanour illustrates him as a lover and connoisseur of pretty women.

Charles Cosgrove is well-spoken. The benefit of an expensive education, years in the RAF and a subsequent life as a radio presenter. "A very good afternoon to you even if the weather has failed to be kind to us. Can I help?"

Jill smiles. "Good afternoon, I am looking for Captain Charles Cosgrove, would that be your good self?"

Charles is full of life, "It certainly is, I didn't remember it was my birthday today, it's not every day I get such charming visitors. Have you been a car enthusiast for long?"

Before she can even reply Charles assumes she is and has no problem discussing one of his passions in life and highlighting the features of the car he was investigating when Jill arrived, and which is evidently for sale.

Charles goes into sales mode. "Well this is the E-Type for sale, it's a beautiful S1 Coupe. May 1963. 3.8 litre in gunmetal grey with a quality blue/grey leather interior. It's only got 18,000 miles from new. This car was last owned by a fanatical E-Type enthusiast for twenty years, having covered just a hundred exercise miles during this period. Needless to say, it has a full service history and of particular benefit is that by being a mid 1963 example, it features both footwells and modified rear bulkhead, together with the rare cross style aluminium dash and centre console. Most of the paintwork is original and the interior and carpets are, naturally, immaculate."

He pauses, sensing the visitor's lack of enthusiasm. "Is it not quite to your taste?"

"It looks fantastic but I am very sorry I have come to see you not about the car for sale but about contaminated air," replies Jill, rather sorry to disappoint him.

Charles's smile fades. "I see, I was half expecting a lady who had indicated she might pop by to have a look at the car. I do apologise for the sales pitch. Contaminated air, now there's an issue I have not spoken about for a few years. Why don't we go into the house, it's a bit chilly out here. What is your name?"

"Jill Parker."

Charles closes the garage door by remote control and leads her to the house. He hangs up Jill's coat and invites her to sit down in the living room. In the past couple of minutes, Charles's flirtatious manner has turned sad. "Contaminated air, what's your interest in contaminated air?"

"My sister was killed on JASP flight 303 last January. She was the co-pilot. On the voice recorder transcript she mentions dirty socks", Jill explains how Reverend Woodley had told her that he had chaired a conference on these matters and might know how to contact Gordon Cooper, the former Boeing 757 pilot who Reverend Woodley had said 'knew all there was to know about these issues.' Charles listens intensely to what Jill is telling him.

Charles stands up. She is not sure whether he looks tired or angry. He gives her a forced smile. "Wait a moment, please."

He leaves the room. She looks around the living room wondering if perhaps she said too much and whether Charles thinks she is mad. She looks around the living room. It is an old house with black beams propping up the ceiling. There are several pieces of memorabilia from his flying days, including a picture of a fighter jet and several trophies in a cabinet.

Charles walks back into the room, a letter in his hand. "I suppose you're wondering, if there was contaminated air in the cockpit; could it have played a part in the accident and does contaminated air have any long term health effects?"

Jill searches his face. "Yes."

"Well, I can tell you as a former test pilot and Captain on the BAe 146, that it is certainly very possible that contaminated air affected their judgment and that contaminated air has long term health effects."

He hands her two letters dated from 1998 signed by the Civil Aviation Chief Medical Doctor. They state that Charles was considered a risk to flight safety, long term unfit and that his consulting neurophysiologist believed he may be suffering from some sort of chemical exposure in the BAe146, and long term exposure to organophosphate chemicals.

"Having read those letters you might understand why I was really amazed and annoyed back in February 2004. You see, the Government with its usual spin and misinformation had the cheek to reply to a question in parliament on contaminated air and say, 'The Civil Aviation Authority is not aware of any adverse long term health effects in flight crew that can be traced back to the cabin environment.' It really is a disgrace what they try and get away with!"

Jill rereads the letters and looks up at Charles, "I am sorry you lost your career to contaminated air. Why were you considered a risk to flight safety?"

Charles sits down. His hand is shaking as he pats the armrest of his chair. "I was considered a risk to flight safety because I was making errors whilst flying due to the neuropsychological effects these chemicals have on your brain. During one particular flight I could not remember if I had raised or lowered the undercarriage and that's very worrying for an airline captain. These chemicals can seriously affect your ability to fly.

It's the same story all the time. I have no doubt that your sister and the Captain could easily have been affected by contaminated air. If she mentions dirty socks you know the air is contaminated. When you told me what you know, you did not mention emergency crew oxygen."

"What do you mean?"

Charles sits back in the chair and slowly rubs his palms together. His fingers are still shaking. "Well, this is the biggest irony of all these events. If the cockpit has smoke in it, crews are meant to go onto oxygen and in fairness I suspect most would, however they are also meant to go onto oxygen if they *suspect* the air is contaminated but with no visible signs of contamination, this is what the aircraft manufacturers say you should do and if I recall the CAA even sent out a memo called a FODCOM on these matters in 2000, I think. But it's a joke, crews have accepted these smells as normal for so many years they usually don't bother, on top of that your ability to smell anything very rapidly goes. You mentioned Gordon Cooper – now he knows all this stuff but I remember him telling me one fact which stuck in my mind even if I am getting older. According to the American Conference of Industrial Hygienists – the ACGIH – they said that your ability to smell the concentration of something within two minutes is already only 25% of what the concentration actually is. What this means is when these events occur many crews think they are transient which they might be or they actually might be continuous. Either way the fume effects very slowly take over your cognitive faculties without you realising. It's very much the same as hypoxia."

Jill cuts in. "I know quite a lot about hypoxia. I am a nurse. I have seen the videos where they have pilots in altitude chambers being taught to identify symptoms of hypoxia."

"The training you talk about is only given to military pilots, sadly, but the point is hypoxia and contaminated air exposures are similar in that you frequently feel fine and have no idea your brain is slowing down. Another point is that after a flight where you have been exposed to contaminated air or hypoxia usually your short term symptoms clear making you think you are OK again. There was a colleague of mine who was a training captain in Chicago for a US airline. He told me a story once where he was training these two pilots once and went out of the cockpit for a while, basically to chat up one of the girls on a Boeing 757 and when he came back as the aircraft started to descend, he could smell that the air was contaminated. He sat down and watched the two pilots flying the aircraft and they were mentally really slow and missing radio calls from air traffic control but when he asked them how they felt they both said they felt fine. Needless to say he instructed them to put on oxygen masks but it just shows the complete lack of education on these matters that exists. Gordon Cooper with some others was banging the table for years to get contaminated air detection systems fitted but the airline industry did nothing, probably too scared of how often the darn things would be going off. Isn't it amazing that when you think that an aircraft, like a space craft or a submarine, is pretty much a sealed environment entirely dependent on an air supply to sustain life and yet space craft or submarines both have extensive contaminated air detectors, yet commercial aircraft worth millions have nothing. They rely entirely upon a crew's sense of smell, with some airlines even saying that the most sophisticated form of monitoring is the human nose. Amazing, really, especially as there is no requirement for pilots to have a sense of smell to be a pilot in the first place. Additionally, many contaminants have no smell like carbon monoxide for example. It's all completely mad, it's like the madhouse is running the industry. You mentioned the pressure group AOPIS that part sponsored the conference in 2005, they made a documentary, I think in 2003, entitled 'Aircraft Air Contamination – An Ongoing Health and Safety Issue,' you should get a copy because there is a pilot called Nevan Pavlinovich who makes a comment I never forget – he said 'If there is an accident it won't be an accident as everybody knows

76

about it' and he was completely right. In 2007, another documentary came out entitled 'Welcome Aboard Toxic Airlines.' I wonder when this issue will ever be resolved?"

Jill has made some notes but the more she hears the more surreal the whole things starts to sound. "Charles, this may be a stupid question but if this air supply, this bleed air, can sometimes get contaminated with engine oils, why do they take air from the engines in the first place?"

Charles smiles. "That's a very good question and which old timers like myself know a lot about. You see, it has not always been like it is today."

Jill looks at Charles with deep concentration not to miss any key part of what he is saying.

He explains. "You see, the early jet aircraft like the Douglas DC-8 or the Boeing 707 used to take bleed air from the engine but would not allow it to feed directly into the cabin as they subsequently did. They used the bleed air to turn a thing called a 'blower' which itself would take in outside air which could not be contaminated with oil. Then with supposedly more efficient engines and the ever increasing need to make engines and aircraft more economical in the late 60s and 70s, they introduced direct and unfiltered bleed air like most aircraft have today. Ironically, the new Boeing 787 took us back to the 50s as it does not use engine bleed air, some suggest it is industry's way of fixing a problem they know about without admitting anything."

Charles can see that Jill is worn out with the day. He notices dark rings under her pretty brown eyes. "Let me get you a cup of tea and perhaps a sandwich before you set off."

Jill accepts his kind offer and they discuss other issues over some sandwiches which Charles prepares to accompany a pot of Ceylon tea, her favourite. Charles is the quintessential English gentleman. He tells her about his time playing county cricket and rugby for the Saricans. Jill looks out the window and can see that the daylight is fading rapidly and she still has to get to Heathrow and find a hotel before picking Gary up in the morning.

She gets her papers together, then asks, "Charles, where can I find Gordon Cooper?"

"Gordon dropped off the scene in disgust with industry and his union who took, in his view, a pro industry view at the expense of its members' health. The truth is he was right as well. Last I heard he was living in Sussex, in Storrington, but I don't have a number. He always reminded me of the engineer who tried to stop them launching the Space Shuttle Challenger in January 1986, the engineer predicted a disaster was coming and it looks like he was right. I wonder if he knows."

Charles helps Jill put on her coat and she turns to him and gives him a kiss on the cheek. "Thank you for inviting me into your home and for taking the time to share your obvious knowledge and expertise on these matters. Good luck with selling the E-type."

As Jill drives off, Charles returns to his house, walks into his study and sits in front of an open box on the bureau. It is the box where he kept the letter from the CAA. He puts the box in his lap and looks at the memories he has from the years where he helped to campaign these issues. Then Charles puts the box back on the table and puts his head into his hands. "What a waste!" he shouts. But he is alone in the house.

Jill checks in to the Wiley Tyrell hotel near Heathrow Airport, a typical airport four star hotel for those on very short stays waiting for a flight home or to some exotic part of the world. Apart from the sandwiches Charles gave her she has eaten very little, she is very tired and has driven 350 miles. She picks up the room service menu and orders some dinner. She reviews her notes from her meeting with Charles whilst she awaits her order. When the tray is delivered to her room she sits up on her bed and decides to watch some television whilst eating her meal. She gathers the pillows behind her and puts the tray on top of her legs.

The news comes on. "This is the eight o'clock news with Diane O'Sullivan and Simon McDonald. This evening's main stories. Carbon Dioxide levels reach a new record high. Scientists say carbon dioxide levels are higher than even computer models forecast. We will have a full report shortly. Other news: the opposition party have strongly questioned the government on its handling of the recent reformed education bill; fresh evidence from the JASP airlines crash in January links suspected crew error to alcohol and Manchester United sign the American football star John Speed. First, to our special climate change story with our environment correspondent Susan Cook..."

Jill slides the tray down from her lap on the bed. She is a keen environmentalist but she is not taking any of the news in, she just wants to hear about JASP flight 303. Fifteen extremely slow minutes later the news comes to flight 303, 'In a development to the investigations of the crash of flight JASP 303 in Newcastle last January, investigators issued a statement late this afternoon which may impact on the findings of the investigations. The short statement linked the two pilots to a Lebanese restaurant in London where it has emerged the crew ate the night before the accident. According to the restaurant owner the two pilots drank a total of two bottles of red wine at a time when they should have been alcohol free. The final public hearing day and findings are due shortly and this statement seems to endorse previous findings which suggested the crew's judgement was not what it should have been. Now to sport...'

Jill cannot breathe. Not again. Not a second time. Carol can't have done this again. She panics at the thought that her mother may have heard this. She dials her number.

"Mum, it's Jill."

Felicity's voice is relaxed. "Hello, pet, are you having a nice time?"

"Mum, have you seen the news?"

"No, I haven't – why what's happened?"

"Mum, the news says the investigators have issued a statement claiming that Carol and the Captain were drinking when they shouldn't have been."

"Oh my God, Jill – is it true?"

"I don't know but the investigators made the statement. I will try and find out more tomorrow morning."

Felicity stammers. "You don't think she…"

"I don't know, let's wait and get all the facts, you know what the media are like. Don't stress Mum, I'll call you tomorrow when I know something."

Jill turns the television off and starts taking slow deep breaths. She can cope with this. She has to cope with this. She counts between breaths but they become uneven, shaken with sobs. Tears stream down her face and she wipes them impatiently with the back of her hand. Breathe. Calm down. You can do it. No! I won't do it anymore. I want to be eight again and come back home from school and tell Carol all about my day. She asks why she can't come with me. Mum tells her she is too young to go to school. I want my sister. I want my sister back. Bastards. It's as though they are trying to kill my sister again. I want my sister back.

Chapter 10

As Gary walks out of arrivals he hardly glances at the crowd of people waiting to meet friends and relatives, he is thinking about how to get to Newcastle as soon as possible. He walks past Jill, oblivious to her presence until she gives him a punch in the arm. "Hiya, Gary."

"Jill, what the hell are you doing here?"

"I decided yesterday to come and meet you but a lot has happened in the last twenty-four hours. Have you heard anything?"

Gary is still getting over the surprise and obviously does not know what she is talking about. "No, I've heard nothing about anything in particular, what exactly are you talking about?"

Jill points towards a Café Nero nearby and suggests they go there.

She takes a sip from her tea, "Gary, you need to know something. I know you lost your dad and I am very sorry, very very sorry. There is not an easy way to tell you this but yesterday afternoon, the accident investigators released a statement saying that Carol and the Captain were drinking when they should have been alcohol free. In a nutshell, they believe that this is why they made the errors of judgement they did. I am very sorry, I know you will have a lot of anger for me, I am shocked myself, I never thought she would, well do that type of thing again."

Gary raises his voice. "What do you mean *again?* Has she been busted for flying pissed before?"

Jill notices that they have attracted the attention of people nearby. "Gary, sorry, I wasn't clear. No nothing to do with flying

Gary. She was nineteen. She got stopped driving back from a club and was over the limit. She got done for that."

"How much over the limit?"

"Well, not by much at all really."

Gary is glaring. His blue eyes are piercing. "How do they know all this and why has it just come out now? Where is the statement? What are the actual facts?"

Jill wishes he would stop attacking her. She is fighting back the tears. "It was on the news last night. They mentioned that Jill and the Captain had drunk two bottles of wine at some Lebanese restaurant."

"So she was drunk!"

"Gary, please."

Jill's voice is failing her. She wants to grab hold of his hand but he jerks it away. She wants to shout and beg him to stay but all she can do is sit nailed to her plastic chair. Gary knocks down the carton coffee cup as he gets up from the table. Jill thinks he is going to shout but he grabs his bag and walks away.

Jill knows people are watching her and she looks down so no one sees that she is crying. A wave of hot black coffee runs down the table at her and starts dripping onto her skirt.

Gary's hair and face are wet from the teeming rain. He wants to punch something. Jill? No. His father is dead. He wants it to be Jill's fault. Or Carol's fault. He wants to be angry with somebody. The pain in Jill's face is in front of him but he tries to see something else. Why should he care? Her sister killed his father. He hears a car horn and someone swear at him. He has crossed the road without seeing the traffic. He knows he is in the wrong but sticks two fingers up at the driver and keeps walking. It's all so bloody unfair. His mother and now his father. He remembers Felicity's face at the funeral. It was raining just as heavily. He wonders how Jill is. He finds himself hoping she is

82

not going to drive whilst so upset. She had dark rings under her eyes as she was telling him about the new findings. New findings that Carol and Captain Jones were drunk.

Something in his mind does not add up. How come it has taken so long to come out? Nobody has mentioned it in the preliminary accident report. Also, did they not blood test the pilots? Surely, if they had and they had been positive, they would have released the information by now.

Gary realises that he is walking aimlessly and walks back into the airport terminal, to catch the Tube. A man in a pin stripe suit is standing just inside, reading a copy of the Financial Times. Gary's eye wanders to the bottom of the front page. 'FJFT Insurers shares down 12% due liabilities on JASP flight 303'.

Jill. He must find Jill. He reaches out for his mobile in his pocket. There is a missed call. He did not hear it ring. It is from Jill. He feels a sudden surge of relief. There is no message. He keys in her number. His fingers are shaking. He hears the ring tone. Please pick up, Jill. I am sorry. I'm an arsehole. Please pick up.

Jill's voice is very faint. "Hello?"

"Jill? Where are you?"

There is no answer. Is she going to tell him to get lost? That she never wants to see him again? "Jill, tell me where you are."

She hesitates. "On level 2 of the short term car park."

"Please wait for me. I'll be right there."

Gary sprints across the Terminal, following the sign posts to the short term car park. He stops off at a newsagent and picks up one of each daily broadsheet. The dazed sales assistant watches him like a freak, and offers him a bag but he dashes out, the papers rolled up the best he can under his arm.

Jill is sitting behind the wheel of her red Golf, her face in her hands. Gary taps on the passenger window and startles her. For a moment, she stares at him, as though unable to decide whether or not to allow him in. Finally, she opens the door from the inside. He swings his bag and the stack of newspapers on the back seat and climbs in next to Jill. Her face is ravaged by tears. "Jill, I am so sorry. I didn't mean it. I just wish there was someone I could blame."

She nods quickly, and her face scrunches up as she sobs uncontrollably. Gary puts his arm around her as she buries her face in his shoulder. She is shaking and he kisses her forehead, his hand smoothing her hair. He wishes he could see her smiling at him. He holds her. "Don't cry, Jill. We'll be all right. We'll get the bastards. I promise."

In a coffee shop in Fulham, Jill's face has regained some colour. Her eyes are still sad but there is renewed trust in them as she looks at Gary. They are reading through the day's newspapers.

"Look, Gary, it says here they went to a Lebanese restaurant near Shepherd's Market the night before, called Al Bustan. It also gives the owner's name as the witness who has come forward, her name is Danielle Bechara. It doesn't mention anything about blood tests. What do you make of it?"

Gary looks up from the paper he is examining. "I think we should take a trip to the restaurant and hear it for ourselves before we accept what we are being told. Maybe they got the wrong people or got the dates confused."

"I know what the papers are saying but I knew my sister and she was extremely professional. Yes, she got busted when nineteen but it was a one-off. OK, she might have drunk the night before it but I find it very hard to believe that. She loved her job and she was always on time for work. It was her day off the next day so why do it? Why would the Captain do it? I know it was the anniversary of her first solo that day but still you're not going to risk your career."

"Maybe they were an item?"

"Gary, that's crazy, no way!"

"OK, Jill, I just thought I should ask. Let's go the restaurant and see what's what."

They walk back to the red Golf.

"Jill, don't forget I knew Carol too, I trusted my life with her when she took me flying, I always thought she was extremely level headed and sensible. I find this whole alcohol story just before the coroner's hearing all a bit of a coincidence, all a bit too cosy."

Still, as they approach Mayfair, they agree that if the evidence from the Lebanese restaurant is conclusive they will drive home later that day and accept it. If there is any doubt they will stay with a friend of Jill's who works south of London and will try and find Gordon Cooper.

They look for somewhere to park. Before they get out of the car Gary has an idea. "I've used this technique in reconnaissance missions before. I'll go in and just act like a normal tourist. Wait twenty or so minutes and then come in and ask to speak to Danielle Bechara, the boss and I will get a flavour of how she deals with you."

Gary gets out the car and heads to the Al Bustan restaurant. It is a fairly new restaurant with seating for about sixty people. There are about twenty customers having lunch. A waiter asks him if it's a table for one and Gary is offered to sit where he would like as they are not busy. He opts for a table near the till and desk area. After a few minutes a young waitress of Eastern European looks and with a Slavic accent approaches. "Good afternoon, can I get you something to drink, Sir?"

"Can I have an Almaza beer and a mixed meze please?"

"Not a problem, I'll bring it to you very soon, Sir."

The beer and the meze arrive fairly quickly. Gary is already eating the food when Jill walks in. The same waiter who greeted Gary asks again if it's a table for one. Jill very politely declines and asks if Ms Danielle Bechara is in.

"Yes, she is, Madam, can I say who it is?" replies the waiter.

"Yes, my name is Jill Parker."

"Very good, Madam, if you can wait a few minutes I will see if she is available. Please take a seat."

Jill and Gary do not even share a glance. Danielle Bechara comes out from the back. She is an older lady wearing a lot of gold jewellery, of average height and build.

"How can I help you? I am Danielle Bechara."

Jill stands up as she introduces herself, "I have come from Newcastle to see you. My sister was one of the pilots on the flight that had the accident in January and according to the media ..."

Danielle Bechara indicates the chair. "Please sit down."

When they have both sat down at the table Jill continues. "If I understand things correctly, according to the media you said my sister and the Captain came to this restaurant the night before the accident and drank two bottles of wine. Are you sure?"

Danielle Bechara does not flinch. "Of course I am sure, that is why I told the authorities. They sat over there and drank two bottles of Château Musat. I know because we don't sell much of that wine. It's very expensive."

Jill's heart sinks. "Why did it take you so long to come forward?"

"I saw an article in the paper and recognised their pictures so then I rang the authorities. They took their time to contact me."

Jill tries not to sound upset. "How do you know it was the night before, how do you know for certain it was them? My sister was very professional. I cannot believe she would do something like that, it does not make sense."

The Eastern European waitress comes to Gary's table but is clearly taking an interest in what Danielle Bechara is telling Jill. "Is there anything else I can get you, Sir, some coffee perhaps?"

"Yes, that would great, thanks."

Danielle Bechara is relentless. "I do not doubt your sister was a fine person but all I can tell you is what I know."

Jill thinks of another angle. "If they were here do you have a copy of the credit card bill? That would show the time they were here and *if* they actually were here."

Danielle Bechara does not like the implication that she is lying. Her bird of prey eyes harden. "They paid cash, a lot of people who drink pay cash. Perhaps they paid cash because they knew they were doing wrong. Perhaps they were in denial of a drinking problem or perhaps they just threw caution to the wind. I can only tell you what I know and that's what I told the authorities. People are accountable to themselves, I just run a restaurant. I am sorry for you and your family. I am sorry."

Danielle Bechara gets up. Jill's head is spinning. Without looking at Gary, she gets up and leaves the restaurant. Her emotional state is clearly noticed by the Eastern European waitress who opens the restaurant door for her as she leaves. The girl clearly feels sorry for her by the way her hand brushes Jill's shoulder as she closes the door behind her.

Gary gets her attention. "Excuse me, I overheard the conversation those two ladies were having. Very interesting. Where are you from?"

The young waitress looks suspicious. "I am from Poland, but why are you interested? Are you with the media?"

"No I am not with the media, I am a soldier. I have worked with many Polish soldiers, they are first class soldiers."

The waitress lowers her guard. "My brother is a soldier in the army. If you're not with the media why were you interested in the conversation?"

Gary treads carefully. "As a soldier I have been trained in counter intelligence and interview techniques. If I was a betting man I would say the Lebanese lady was not telling the truth."

The Polish girl looks uneasy but he knows he has caught her interest. "What makes you think that?"

He has her exactly where he wants her. "Years of training and experience… What's your name?"

"Katarzyna."

"Beautiful name. That's 'Katherine', isn't it?"

She blushes.

Gary orders the bill and settles in cash.

He also slips a generous tip into Katarzyns's hand, and a piece of paper he has quickly scribbled on. He gets up and walks out before she has the time to look at the contents of her hand 'I need to talk to you about this. It is bigger than you imagine. Please call me on this number and say nothing. PLEASE.'

Back in the car, Jill is remembering the last time she saw her sister. They had gone out to the Gateshead shopping centre with their mother, shopped and had lunch. Felicity had bought a brown skirt and Carol was insisting that it was 'too old' for their mother.

Gary opens the car door. She looks at him with defiance. "I bet you hate us all now. To think of all the lives lost because she was drinking. I never thought she was that stupid."

Gary takes her hand. She tries to pull away but he holds on to it. "Jill, listen to me, that woman might have fooled you but I would bet a year's wages that she is lying, she was not convincing. My years in the army taught me to recognise the body language of those who are a threat or telling the truth. I don't buy it. If she convinced you she probably would convince most people."

Jill frowns. "Gary, I know you're a good lad and a good friend but you don't have to say these things."

"Jill, trust me – she is lying."

"Why would she lie!"

Gary looks out through the windscreen. "That's the bit I haven't figured out yet. She has either been bought or she's mistaken. I am fairly certain the waitress in there knows something. I left her my number. Let's see what comes of it. For now I am going to carry on digging on the contaminated air issue. What are you going to do?"

Jill is still frowning. "You're a great lad, Gary, you're right, I knew my sister and no ugly lying bitch is going to change that!"

They both burst out laughing at her comment.

Jill turns the ignition key. "OK, what next Gary?"

"Why don't we go and see your friend, ring your mum, make a few phone calls and decide what to do next. What do you think?"

They arrive at the terraced house where Jill's friend Sarah lives. Jill tells Sarah the basics. She knows she can be trusted but asks her to tell no one.

Sarah lives in a rented town house in West Kensington with another girl who is away on holiday, and is fascinated by Jill's story. "Let me know what I can do to help. I have two spare rooms as my house mate is away and she won't mind you using her bed. The kitchen is over there; Internet there and telephone near the sofa. Please make yourselves at home."

Gary sniggers. The girls turn to look at him. "It makes me think that we are terrorists on the run in a safe house. It's like being at work again but we're on the good guy's side."

Jill picks up on the joke. "Are you not always on the good guy's side?"

Gary gives a look expressing the realities of military operations. "Usually. We try to be!"

Gary logs onto the Internet and Jill gets on the phone to her mother. Sarah, proud to be involved in their mission, puts the kettle on.

"Jill, your tea still black?"

"Yes!"

"Gary, how do you like your tea?"

"NATO standard please Sarah, milk two sugars, thanks."

Gary checks his e-mails and a smile appears on his face. He has an e-mail from Dr Valentina Fedorova. It seems like months ago he was learning about synergistic effects of exposure. She has been doing some research. As he reads the e-mail he recalls the date he suggested if she ever came to the UK. Valentina has attached several papers to her e-mail, some he already has. One is entitled, 'The toxicity of Jet Oils' by a Chris Winder from University of New South Wales and JC Balouet from Paris. After reviewing the paper again, he thinks that Paris is not too far away and perhaps worth a trip. The other papers all support the view that exposure to pyrolised / heated engine oils will not be good for you. He sends Valentina a reply to thank her and reminds her of the offer to be a tour guide one day. He is not aware of the grin on his face, nor does he see Jill watching him. She decides not to ask but there is an imperceptible discomfort in the pit of her stomach.

When Gary has finished on the Internet he turns towards Jill who has been on the phone to her mother and tells her what Valentina sent through.

Jill raises her eyebrows and probes Gary, "Oh! Yes! Nice Dr Fedorova, you sure you're telling me everything?"

Gary's tone rises an octave. "Of course, you know me. I am just a quiet boy. What about your mum?"

"Mum is very upset and gone to stay with friends as not only are the media hassling her but she has had calls from people saying Carol killed their loved ones and being very aggressive on the phone. The other thing is, she has signed the pay out contract with the airline as they said the option might expire in view of the new information. What she did say, was how come they never did a blood test on Carol and the Captain after the accident."

"It's a good question, something we need to look into", says Gary, glad to take the focus off Valentina.

The next morning, over breakfast cooked with a scout's dedication by Sarah, Gary suggests going down to Sussex to find Gordon Cooper. Jill does not need a lot of convincing. Charles said he knows all there is to know on the matter.

After finding their way through the busy and slow roads of South London and Croydon, Jill and Gary head south on the M23 motorway. Whilst on the M23 they pass under the approach path for flights arriving on the westerly runway at Gatwick Airport. As they both look at an aircraft flying overhead, Jill reminds herself and Gary of how Charles could not remember if he had put the under carriage up or not when he was flying.

Jill turns in her seat to look at Gary, "At the meeting with the airline the other day, I met the main Health and Safety rep for the cabin crew. Her name was Nicola Matthews. Do you think it's worth my calling her as she would surely know if the cabin crew were blood tested. She seemed like a really nice girl and not like the pilot union guy Martin Stone."

Gary agrees. She takes out Nicola Matthews's business card and calls her mobile.

Gary looks at Jill when she hangs up, "So, what did she say?"

"Apparently, it's all a bit vague. She thinks that they might have tested but it has not been mentioned before. She suggested, as I am a nurse, I go up there and find out. That's a great idea, when we get back I'll go and ask a few questions. There is bound to be someone I know there."

"Good. As soon as we get home let's do it. If she was blood tested then we need to know who found out what."

A few minutes later Jill's phone rings. It's Nicola Matthews again. "Hi Jill, I thought you should know that there is a lot of misinformation being put out by the airlines and the industry and you need to be aware of this. Let me give you a good example of misinformation within the aviation industry. A leading company doctor once wrote in a 'Cabin Crew News' article in October 2003 that tricresyl phosphate in the oils was not harmful if absorbed through the skin or breathed in. What he forgot to tell the crews was that the NTP Chemical Repository for tricresyl phosphate actually stated that, 'This compound is toxic by inhalation, ingestion or by absorption through the skin.' Cabin crew trust their employers to look after them, like passengers they never think their health will be put at risk, yet it frequently is. Anyway I just wanted to tell you if you had not realised that you need to be ready to filter the misinformation from the truth. If you have any doubts about it, here is another example. In 2006, whilst the UK regulator were continuing to say contaminated air events were rare and most events were being reported, the US FAA director of Flight Standards Service was saying that the FAA had growing concern over numerous reports of smoke / fumes in cockpit / cabin and that their data analysis indicated numerous events were *not* being reported."

Jill is no longer shocked, "Thanks a lot, Nicola, I have already come to that conclusion but appreciate the heads up. Guess the difference is that the UK CAA is entirely funded by the airlines they regulate! Slight conflict of interest would could say. Take care."

After stopping for a coffee and petrol they finally arrive at the town of Storrington and set about finding Gordon Cooper. Storrington is a lovely small village just north of the South Downs in the picturesque West Sussex countryside. Besides the three spellings in the Domesday Book, Storrington has had considerable name changes through the centuries. It was not until 1735 that the name changed to Storrington. They drive past the church of St Mary the Virgin which was built in the 11th Century.

Chapter 11

Compared to London it is a sparsely inhabited part of the country and, after asking the local pub landlord and the owner of the convenience store, Jill and Gary eventually find out where Gordon Cooper lives. They drive out to a house near the foot of the South Downs. Jill's phone rings. It's Nicola Matthews again.

"Hi Nicola…. That's OK… Please do… Right… That's very interesting, I think I got the drift of that. You rang at the right time because we are about to knock on the door of Gordon Cooper's house so I will ask him all about that. Nicola, thanks a lot, that could be a real break, thanks a million."

Gary has been trying in vain to follow the conversation. "What's going on? What's the great news?"

Jill slowly turns towards Gary, "That was Nicola from the cabin crew union. Get this. Some years ago her union part-funded a blood test to not only prove exposure to tricresyl phosphate but time of exposure!"

"Bloody hell Jill, if Carol was blood tested and we can get some of her blood then we can see if she was exposed on the flight. Is that possible?"

"Nicola said Gordon Cooper knows all about the test as it was done during his time in the union."

"Why did Martin Stone never mention it?"

"That's a very good question but the more I learn about the union the less I see it as a union. Let's hope Gordon Cooper is in and sheds some light on all of this."

They arrive at a two story house built around 1940 with a large front garden. It is surrounded by fields and woods, and the nearest neighbours are at least a mile away. Only the sound of chirping birds disrupts the quiet frosty morning.

The door is answered by a broad, tall, balding man. "Can I help you?"

"Are you Gordon Cooper?" asks Jill.

Gordon looks at each of them in turn. "Who wants to know?"

"My name is Jill Parker and this is Gary Bamford, we're from Newcastle. We've come to see you today because my sister was the co-pilot on JASP flight 303 and Gary's father was also on the flight. Both lost their lives. We think…"

Gordon interrupts her, "Contaminated air?"

Jill and Gary exchange glances. "How did you know?"

"I knew that one day somebody would knock on my door to talk about contaminated air. I am sorry about your sister and your father. If it's due to contaminated air it was totally avoidable. Would you like to come in?"

As they walk into the house, the words reverberate in Gary's head. It was totally avoidable.

The library is a well-lit room with a fireplace. Small flames crackle and add warmth to the room. The shelves are lined with hundreds of books about climate change, industry cover ups and various other environmental topics, such as Chernobyl, Bhopal, Exxon Valdez, and many others.

Jill seems to have read Gary's mind. "Why did you just say it was totally avoidable ?"

Gordon looks ponders over his answer. "The industry have known of this problem for over fifty years, yet have failed to fit filters, failed to introduce contaminated air detection systems and allowed a scenario to exist where most crews globally accepted contaminated air exposures to be a normal occupational hazard. The industry should have addressed these matters years ago but they knew this one was one of their worst nightmares. Besides, what makes you think contaminated air is linked to the accident on JASP flight 303, the media reported strong winds, no technical faults and crew error. What makes you think differently?"

Gary leans forward and hands Gordon the initial accident report, "Read the text at the bottom of this page."

The elderly man takes a pair of reading glasses from his breast pocket and reads aloud. "'Co-pilot: There's the socks again.' I see what you mean. It looks like the media forgot that part or failed to pick up on that clue. His face clouds over. How did you find me?"

"Charles Cosgrove told me about you." says Jill, "and Senator Woodley told me about Charles."

Gordon chuckles. "Well, you have been digging up some good folk, how are they both? Is Charles still selling antique cars?"

He leads them into a storage room and points to over a hundred lever arch files on the issue of contaminated air. "Where shall we begin? The industry cover up, what they could have done, the lies, the misinformation? Let's start with my showing you examples of flights where crews experienced contaminated air on the Boeing 757, British Aerospace BAe 146, Airbus..?"

He shows them printouts of pages and pages illustrating over 1200 events he was aware of during his time in the union. Five hundred contaminated air events are from UK Boeing 757 crews.

He reads out some of the finer details, "Have a look at these: 'First Officer partially incapacitated due to fumes; toxic fumes in the flight deck; crew removed from duty feeling unwell; passengers with paper up their noses due fumes; all crew had headaches and effects' and so forth. You can see for yourself, nobody can say they didn't know. Both the union and the CAA databases were missing most events but they both had enough to see the problem was real. It was estimated that we had less than 4% of all events as crews simply didn't bother reporting most events and nothing has changed from what I am told. Many crews never reported events at all. I remember one fellow telling me he had smelt fumes every day he had flown the 146 yet never reported it once in his life! Is that completely crazy or what? You have to be in the industry to understand why this is. Basically, ignorance and fear.

We told the CAA that under reporting was going on and they had the nerve to tell us that pilots were professional, they would report all defects and many fume events were not in fact safety related. Those guys were in fantasy land or denial of what was really happening. How can any form of contaminated air, present in the cockpit, not be a safety issue? You see for them to accept what we were telling them, would have meant they had to act. Acting was the last thing they wanted to do with regard to getting crews to report contaminated air events. I believe their motive was to protect the industry that funded them. Can you imagine if they had really told the crews to write up every event? Aircraft would have been grounded everywhere and that would have been a financial disaster for airlines. It was easier to put their heads back in the sand. Also, don't forget the events listed on the database are just UK events, if this is what we have from the UK what is the global scale of these events? I used to smell contaminated air on the Boeing 757 in varying degrees on over 75% of the flights I did."

He continues. "I remember I had an event once and both the co-pilot and myself *thought* the contaminated air had cleared but I started to feel spacey so we invited in one of the cabin crew to the cockpit and before we could say anything she was waving her hand in front of her face and telling us it stank! If your sister had been experiencing fumes it might have been all flight. When she refers to dirty socks this could have simply been an increase in concentration for a few seconds which triggered her awareness. This would have been a higher exposure above the continual background exposure they might have been experiencing. If this was the case it is very plausible that the crew would make mistakes. I remember one incident where a pilot said after an exposure they felt they were landing the aircraft having drunk six Scotches with the runway moving around the place. You have to look upon exposure to contaminated air as equivalent to flying under the influence of alcohol but not being aware you've drunk anything or suffering from hypoxia. The point being, you often think you are OK but don't realise you're not 100%. You must also realise you become very quickly desensitised to these smells. Within a few minutes you will perceive that the smell has gone but it might not have. When you walk into, say, a chemist or a bakery there is a certain smell but within minutes your perception of the smell changes. That's why as a passenger or crew member it's vital you get a good smell of the air when you first walk onto an aircraft. If it smells of dirty socks, oily or like a gym, I would get off as soon as possible."

He continues. "There have been several accidents where crew have died and it has been put down to crew error. Not all these accidents will have a contaminated air element but some of those accidents might have had an element of contaminated air as a contributory reason. No one can say it's not possible, as aircraft do not have any contaminated air detection systems so if the crews were partially impaired due to contaminated air they would not know, the crew would make a mistake and game over. Take the Boeing 757 Cali accident in South America in 1995, same aircraft as your sister flew. Put down to pilot error and loss of situational awareness but how do you know their minds were running at 100%? A Boeing 757 managed to forget to slow down or lower the flaps and under carriage going into London Heathrow once so it is very possible that in Cali with the same aircraft type contaminated air *might* have been a contributory factor. We have reports of contaminated air events on the Boeing 757 from way before 1995.

Another example could be Kegworth. Kegworth was an accident that occurred in England on 8th January 1989. The aircraft was a Boeing 737-400. The accident occurred on the third sector of a four sector day. The crew shut down the wrong engine when carrying out the fire checklist under a bit of pressure. Again how do you know for the last two sectors the engine that went bang was not giving off fumes and affecting their cognitive ability in some way? The Helios crash of 2005 is another possibility for contaminated air being a contributory factor. The crew became incapacitated in the climb due to hypoxia and the plane crashed some hours later when it ran out of fuel. Why did they not use oxygen and make mistakes? Contaminated air would *easily* have done that. The accident report even acknowledges that the air conditioning system had oil in it weeks before the crash and it could be an intermittent fault

I am not saying contaminated air was part of those events but it *might* have been. Granted, you will never prove either one way or another but the worrying thing is nobody wants to look at it! Pilot error will always be the easy option! A contaminated air detection system would have provided the answer in all these cases.

Crews just see contaminated air events as part of the job – it's normal so why would they think it's affecting their ability to do the job unless someone tells them what it can do to you, or you make the link? In my day, we tried to educate crews but it's like telling people not to smoke, they don't listen until they have effects and they wake up to the realities of smoking. Certainly in my mind the regulator never did what it should have and own the problem. Why? Because to do so would have been too bad for the industry. Can you imagine the regulators telling airlines to tell passengers they have been exposed to neurotoxins as they walk off an aircraft? It's all a question of vested interests. I resigned from the union because they would not protect crew health above commercial interests, in my view. Some said the union had become an extension of the regulator. I could go into the politics of the union in great detail but two examples sum it up. I remember an influential person in the union saying 'Do we really want to know? It's like Pandora's box, you might not like what you see' – an excuse to put industry interests ahead of crew and passenger welfare in case the industry would suffer. Another guy in the union once said, 'if a few people die from ill health due to contaminated air you have to look at the industry as a whole, it's a risk assessment'. I was aware of members who lived their lives every day with serious neurological problems. There was a chap who had flown for 25,000 hours and thousands of hours on the BAe 146. Every day he lived with a burning sensation in his tongue, tingling in his extremities and other serious neuro cognitive problems. He and his doctors had no doubt contaminated air was to blame. The union did nothing for these people. These pro industry views were not in the members better interests in my view and for that and other reasons I resigned, I did not want to be part of it anymore."

Gary wants to know more about the cover up, "You mentioned a cover up when we entered the room. I know many say the Government covered up the Gulf War Syndrome and have done the same on countless other issues but tell us more about the cover up of this issue, I can see myself it does not add up but what else do you know?"

Gordon smiles. "Do you have all day to listen? There has been so much misinformation and lies over the years I worked on these matters it would take all day to tell you everything but let me give you a few examples. In Australia, an airline called Ansett was plagued with contaminated air problems on the BAe 146. The engine manufacturer did some air sampling and finally wrote a report which said no tricresyl phosphate or TCP was found. Those who read the draft report say it was reported as found and minutes from a meeting also report TCP as being found. It's amazing what the lawyers remove from reports which will impact financial interests!"

"On the issue of TCP, let me give you another example of misinformation. In 2005 there was a conference in London on contaminated air at which Professor van Netten from British Columbia presented evidence that TCP was being found on pilots clothing, in dust filters, HEPA filters and on the walls of the cockpit. As well as his reporting finding TCP in aircraft, numerous doctors and scientists stated how they were seeing medical effects in crews exposed to contaminated air both short and long term health effects. Despite the conference reporting finding TCP and the medical effects being clearly shown the Government wrote a letter stating that 'Representatives of DfT and DH attended the recent international conference on contaminated cabin air, but no new evidence on the presence or the effect of low levels of organophosphates in aircraft cabins was presented.' Misinformation on a grand scale but the union did nothing. Statements like that just support my view of most Governments. They put the need to protect and serve industry ahead of the needs of the people and the environment which should in my view come first. Industry should never be put ahead of the environment or peoples welfare in my view.

Talking of the union doing nothing, there was a pilot called Palmer Warden who had recorded carbon monoxide on over 80% of flights he did in 2004. This guy contacted the union Chairman and told him about his findings and as far as I know he is still waiting for a reply! Another way of saying we are not interested. I told the CAA about it and they were not interested either.

Another gem of misinformation they come out with, is to carry out air monitoring with poor techniques and then say that everything is below the appropriate exposure standards. What exposure standards? Exposure standards for synthetic jet engine oils do not exist so how can it be below an exposure limit? The Australians led the way on these matters, some say because there was no conflict of interest. Let me find an article here."

Gordon sifts through all the articles he has and finds the one he is looking for. "Here it is, it was in a Royal Australian Air Force (RAAF) magazine published in 2004 called Aviation Safety Spotlight. The article was written by one of the RAAF head doctors Dr Bhupi Singh and entitled 'In-Flight Smoke and Fumes'. Let me read this part – 'The aircraft cockpit and cabin are unique workplaces that cannot be compared with industrial and other workplaces on the ground. Aircrew members are required to perform complex tasks requiring high level cognitive skills, which may be much more sensitive to insult by hazardous contaminants in the smoke/fumes, such as Tri-Cresyl Phosphate (TCP). Therefore, the maximum permissible limits for safe exposure recommended by the Occupational Safety and Health Administration (OSHA) of USA, and American Council of Governmental Industrial Hygienists (ACGIH) for industrial workers cannot be applied to aviation.' Pretty clear message. It's like the paper you mentioned before from 1977 which confirmed back then that crews were becoming incapacitated but nobody acted."

Jill acknowledges the true scale of the misinformation and Gordon delves further. "In the UK, contaminated air and a crew's ability to be listened to, was a real mess. British Aerospace, who had contributed to the Labour Party in the UK who were in power, were very closely linked to the Government. For instance, the once Chief Operating Officer of BAe Systems, was given the job of head of the new Office of Government Commerce (OGC) in February 2000 on a reported salary of £180,000 (plus 3% bonus), making him then the highest-paid civil servant in the country. The Chairman of the CAA used to be Chief Executive and latterly Chairman of Shorts Brothers plc, the

Belfast-based aerospace company and also used to be President of the Society of British Aerospace Companies. The CAA was 100% funded by the airlines it regulated and the head of the confidential crew reporting programme known as CHIRP joined British Aerospace Commercial Aircraft in 1980 as Senior Development Test Pilot and was involved with the development of the BAe146. You see what I mean? No wonder many crews felt all bases were covered by safe hands."

Jill suddenly remembers the blood test Nicola had mentioned. "Gordon, sorry to interrupt you but I was told about a blood test that was being designed to prove exposure to tricresyl phosphate – what happened?"

Gordon explains, "The Biomarker of exposure test. That was one of my initiatives, how to prove not only exposure but also time of exposure. I found an absolutely top scientist called Professor Ashington, a complete genius and really nice guy all in one. I approached him and his University to develop a way of proving exposure to tricresyl phosphate. It was a lot of money but the best money we ever spent. I remember the day I signed the contract to underwrite the cost, we all drank champagne to celebrate and then I went to unions around the world to raise the money. It wasn't difficult as many unions could see the sense, apart from my union who probably were too scared of the impact the blood test would bring to the industry. Anyway, Professor Ashington did the work and developed a blood test. The approach he took relied on analyzing a number of proteins which were permanently modified when an individual had been exposed to the tricresyl phosphate in the oils. I can't remember all the science but, in a nutshell, different proteins which were decorated had different half lives. Depending on what showed up you could then say when the exposure took place. They got the accuracy down to hours, if I recall correctly."

Jill asks, "Why was the test not used?"

"Last I heard was the oil companies tried to block it on all sorts of publication technical legal grounds and loopholes. I don't know whether the legal issues ever got resolved, best thing would be to contact the Professor. I think he retired to some small place in British Columbia, I might have a phone number somewhere, I would have to dig it out. If I recall, he retired in a town called Smithers where another doctor lived who by coincidence had also been involved in the contaminated air debate. This other doctor whose name escapes me flew on an internal Canadian flight and his beautiful young black Labrador dog died from carbon monoxide poisoning after travelling in the cargo hold. The doctor set up a website after the name of his dog Sila called silaflysafe.com to see how many other dogs were dying in aircraft and he had a growing list when I last heard but I digress. I assume you're thinking of using the blood test to show if your sister or the Captain were exposed in flight to tricresyl phosphate?"

Jill replies, "We don't know if blood was taken but I am a nurse and it would have been routine to take a blood sample especially as she was in A&E. What is confusing is, if they took blood then surely they would have tested for alcohol poisoning. The media and the AAIB are linking Carol, my sister, and the Captain to a Lebanese restaurant in London and drinking too much wine."

"That's the media story," Gary interjects, "but I talked with a waitress who works there and my gut feeling is this is a stitch up."

Gordon puts down the papers he is holding and takes an even greater interest into what Gary is saying, "What makes you think that?"

"I am in the parachute regiment and was specially trained in these areas and my gut feeling is she knows the story the boss of the restaurant is putting out is wrong. I left her my

104

number yesterday and I am waiting for her to call me. If she does."

"When did the alcohol part come into the investigation?"

"That's the point, only a few days ago and yet the accident was in January."

Gordon drags his index finger and thumb down his chin. "I see, that's interesting. Have you contacted the airline, unions, media or regulator?"

Jill says, "Yes, I did some days ago…"

The expression on Gordon's face stops her in her tracks. He is nodding and half smiling.

Gary, catches on to what he is thinking. "I know what you're thinking. No mention of alcohol until Jill starts to make some phone calls. Obviously hits a nerve and suddenly the story breaks. Now that would be very evil."

Gordon glances at Jill before replying. "Is it any more evil than not telling the pregnant passengers who have flown and been exposed to contaminated air that they have been exposed, especially those who might then have miscarriages as a result? Is it any more evil than not telling crews and the passengers who end up with respiratory or neurological problems that those problems may well be linked to chemical exposures on aircraft?"

He looks at Gary, "Is it any more evil than the way they treated the Gulf War Veterans? As I said, commercial interests have a lot of muscle in Governmental circles. Maybe it's a coincidence."

Jill remembers another coincidence. "My mum recently signed a contract as a full and final settlement from the accident as the media were knocking on her door and the airline said the offer might not stand for much longer in view of the recent news. It's all very good timing for the airline."

Gordon looks at the clock, "I have to meet someone so leave me your contact details and I'll see if I can find a number for Professor Ashington. You need to see if there is any blood to test but be careful, if they are making the story fit a hidden agenda they will remove or amend all the evidence they need to. If you prove contaminated air caused this crash then the airline industry will be on its knees. It's a multi billion dollar industry and they will make sure nobody changes the status quo."

Gary writes his number down and hands it to Gordon.

Gordon also gives them his number. "Here is my number, if you ring, be careful. Assume the worst."

"I know exactly what you mean we do that all the time, assume everyone is foe."

Gordon pauses in thought for a few seconds and then looks at Jill and Gary, "I have just had an idea." Gordon goes to an old address book and writes down an address and telephone number. "This is the name of a guy in Paris. He was a big campaigner in these matters but last I heard taking a break to focus on other issues, a true Frenchman. He is what you call an 'environmental forensics' person. He knows a lot of people and would be of great help. He also used to be an air traffic controller when he did his national service. I would go and see him. He might have some contacts that can dig out all sorts of things. His name is Jean-Christophe. Let me ring him and see if he still lives at this address."

As Gordon dials the number he carries on talking, "I would go and see him as soon as possible. Hello Jean-Christophe it's Gordon Cooper... I agree it's been a long time... Listen *mon brave*, I have a couple here looking into a contaminated air crash and I think they should come and talk with you, is that possible?"

Gary looks at Jill and raises his eyebrows and Jill smiles back.

"Hang on, Jean-Christophe, I will ask them." Gordon replies into the phone to a question from Jean-Christophe.

Gordon lowers the phone from his mouth and looks at Jill and Gary with a grin, "He can see you tomorrow, is that soon enough?"

Gary smiles, "Let's do it. Tell him I will be there by lunchtime tomorrow – somehow!"

"OK, Jean-Christophe, it's on. They will be there tomorrow lunchtime. Let's talk again soon as they are just heading off... *Salut mon brave.*" Gordon hangs up. "I think it will be worth the trip."

Jill and Gary thank Gordon for arranging the meeting. He replies, "One last thing before you go. Jean-Christophe just informed me of a new book recently published on the issue called the Aviation Contaminated Air Reference Manual. He said you need a copy of the book. I think I will get one as well and get up to date."

As they walk to the front door Jill turns to Gordon, "When you did all the campaigning, did you get a lot of help?"

Gordon smiles. "When a union wants a problem to go away and basically tells you to trust the regulator rather than listen to its members' actual health effects you get very little help. There were a few good folk who helped, however, most left the industry. They saw the evil side of the industry and the union, I suppose as I did. Anyway, ring if you have any questions and please let me know what's going on. I'll make a few calls and see if some old contacts have some information."

As they head out of Sussex, Gary makes a suggestion. "Why don't you go home tomorrow morning with the car and I will go and see Jean-Christophe in Paris and then fly from Paris to Newcastle. Gordon seems to think he will be able to help. What do you think?"

"It will cost a lot of money but I agree it has to be done. We should be able to book your flights online tonight at Sarah's house. When I go to the hospital do you think they will be looking out for me?"

"I doubt it. They don't know about the blood test so they will not cover that avenue."

Gary's phone receives a text message. He seems very excited by it. "Listen to this - 'If u want to know about story we talk about yesterday then come tomorrow night exactly at 6 p.m. DO NOT reply to this text. Katarzyna'. She must know something, this is fantastic news. Jill, I think we are winning!"

"That's great news, but what about Paris?"

"Why don't I get the train first thing in the morning to Paris and get back in time to be at the Restaurant at 18.00 instead of flying? It takes less than three hours by train to Paris and is a lot less hassle than flying."

"That sounds like a great idea, you could be there for breakfast! Don't forget to have a chocolate croissant for me. When I get to the hospital tomorrow I think I will go straight away, as the hospital will be busy and although I don't work in that hospital, I will not look out of place. If I go on the night shift, which I was thinking, I might look more out of place in the blood bank or in the Pathology Department or wherever they have the blood stored."

"The busier the place is the more you will blend in. We do that on reconnaissance trips in the military, as well."

Chapter 12

Gary is looking out the window into the dark and wet morning rushing by on the first train for Paris. Last week seems like a year ago and his active duty with the parachute regiment like a dream from another lifetime. A stewardess walks past.

Her attention is caught by the passenger beside him, a young skinny business man in a cheap suit who obviously got out on the wrong side of bed, "Excuse me, the lights in the bathroom are not working again, don't you guys ever fix anything? It was like this last week, too."

The stewardess – in her mid-thirties – has obviously encountered the type before. She replies with a wide smile, revealing a row of pearly teeth. She could not be friendlier, had the passenger just paid her a compliment. "I am very sorry, Sir, I'll get the pilot – sorry, the driver – to call the fault in. There are toilets in every carriage so I am sure you will be able to find one with working lights which will help you find what your looking for."

Gary catches the joke straight away and guffaws. The young business man gives Gary an aggressive look, then decides to back out of the situation, intimidated by Gary's obvious physical strength. The two passengers sitting opposite do not speak English and obviously have not taken any interest in the proceedings. The young man replies in a weaker tone, "OK, thanks."

The Stewardess walks away, her smile still fixed on her lips. Gary's eyes follow her, his brain quizzical. He leaves his seat. "Excuse me, Miss, I don't want to complain about anything but I liked your joke. Why did you say the *pilot* and then the *driver*?"

The stewardess looks pleased at having her joke appreciated. "It's early morning syndrome. I used to fly as a stewardess before I got married and had kids and sometimes forget I am on a train."

"You seem to imply that the pilot calls in defects, what did you mean?"

"In the airlines every defect is written up and the pilots usually call the defects in at base or at the destination to get them fixed during the turnaround if they are important otherwise they get fixed when suits. Why are you interested?"

Gary says enough to keep her talking. "No, nothing, really, I was reading a book about an aircraft accident and there was an issue with a possible defect so your comment got my attention as I didn't understand how it was done."

"I see. Well, let's say the aircraft was taxiing out for take off and the IFE packed up."

Gary interrupts her, "IFE ?"

She explains, "Sorry, the In-Flight Entertainment system. Let's say that packed up and you were about to do a twelve-hour flight. You would tell the pilots who would try and fix it and they might call it in or talk with engineering to try and fix it. Sometimes, you might even go back onto the stand if it was a quick fix as a twelve-hour flight with nothing to keep the passengers happy would be a nightmare."

Gary is delighted with the new piece of information. "OK, I get it, anyway thanks for explaining that."

He walks back to his seat and – eager to share the joke – winks at the passenger beside him who does not respond.

Jill is driving along listening to music when her phone starts ringing. She mutes her stereo. "Hello."

"Jill - it's Gary, how's the traffic?"

"It's fine no bother, looks like everyone has slept in today. Train OK?"

"Yes, it left spot on time, felt like I was in Switzerland, it was so punctual. Look I have just been speaking with the stewardess…"

Jill can't resist the opportunity, "Oh yeah! Seems to be a pastime of yours chatting up…"

Gary interrupts her but can't help snorting with laughter. "No, not like that, listen. To cut a long story short she used to fly and told me when there is a defect on the aircraft if it's important, crews will contact their operations folk and tell them, or if the defect occurs before they leave, the crew might take the aircraft back to the gate to get the problem fixed. In the initial accident report there is no mention of this so perhaps they didn't ever contact the company but if there was contaminated air to the level to cause the accident perhaps they called it in. Can you contact one of Carol's colleagues and find out about these things or ring Gordon or Charles and find out. Actually, best somebody who worked with Carol, so we know what they do today and in her airline. I think it's worth digging a bit, what do you think?"

"Yeah, nothing ventured nothing gained and all that. OK, I'll do it later when normal people are awake."

"I know what you mean, I could really do with a good sleep. OK, I will call you when I get back to the UK. Good luck and don't take any chances."

"I won't, good luck in Paris, see ya."

Jill reselects the music and heads further North towards home as daylight starts creeping up.

The train arrives in Paris at the Gare Du Nord. As Gary walks out of the station into a tranquil and dry morning, he admires the architectural marvels of the German born architect Jacques Hittorff who was responsible for a lot of the work at the station in the 19th Century. It occurs to Gary that many architecturally stunning buildings in Paris were saved during the Second World War thanks to the early surrender of the French.

The Gare Du Nord is in the heart of Paris, not far from Montmartre and the Sacré-Coeur. It is just after 9 a.m., so he decides to have the chocolate croissant Jill told him to have along with a cup of café au lait, in true French tradition, at a nice café whilst he briefly watches the morning pass by in what is in his view one of the most beautiful cities of the world.

Jill picks up her phone and dials the number of a girl Carol lodged with once, when she started at JASP. "Hi, is that Stephanie… It's Jill Parker, Carol's sister. I am sorry to trouble you – I wanted to ask you a few questions about Jill and the job."

"Jill, you have to understand what Carol and the Captain did was stupid, unprofessional and brings bad publicity onto the airline. I am sorry, I don't think it's appropriate for us to have this conversation. Good bye." She hangs up.

Jill is in shock. Perhaps Gary and she are wrong. Perhaps contaminated air is real but not a factor on flight 303. Her head is swimming. She talks to herself to rework the logic. She knows if the Polish girl in the restaurant denies the story they were drunk she is home and dry. She tells herself she is on an emotional rollercoaster. Gary. Where would she be if Gary was not helping her? She turns the music back on. Bob Dylan is singing 'Hurricane'. The lyrics of the song reminds her of the whole story she is in – a boxer framed as it was the easy option. She takes a deep breath and smiles to herself, feeling stronger. I will survive this, she repeats to herself. I will get out a winner out of this dreadful chess game.

Gary waves down a taxi and asks to go to the address where Jean-Christophe lives. As he sits in the back of the taxi enjoying the trip down the back streets of Paris, he thinks about the international scale of the problem and how people, crews and scientists around the world have reported crews and passengers suffering effects from exposure. This is truly a global issue. Despite the language differences and the cultural differences the medical problems being seen by doctors are the same. The common link is the lubricants, wherever in the world these events occur, the aircraft are all using the same specialist synthetic jet engine oils.

Gary arrives outside the building located on the Quai de Jemmape, in the 10th Arrondissement. He gets out of the taxi, surveys the area with a glance, and pays the driver. He walks into the early 20th Century building and heads for the top floor. He knocks on the door and a dog starts barking inside. After a while the locks to the apartment door click and the door is opened by an older man, unshaven with fluffy hair as if he has just got out of bed.

The man looks at Gary through his glasses. "Vous cherchez quelqu'un?"

"I am sorry, I don't speak French. I am looking for Jean-Christophe."

"You have found him – not at his best this morning, as I have been working most of the night, but you have found him all the same. What can I do for you? Are you military?"

"Yes, how did you know?"

"The combat boots and the haircut are a giveaway. I was in the army, military service, many years ago. How can I help you?"

"My name is Gary Bamford. Gordon Cooper rang you yesterday. I am investigating an accident which might be linked to contaminated air. He said you had contacts and might be able to help me?"

"Of course, I was expecting an older man. I don't know why. I just imagined you would be older. Have you come from England especially?" enquires Jean-Christophe.

"Yes, I just arrived this morning and I need to be back in London by 18.00."

"You're definitely a man on a mission. If Gordon sent you it must be important. Gordon is a fantastic *brave*, a true good guy. Come in. If I can help, I will. Please come in and take a seat. Don't mind the dog. She barks on the retreat!"

Gary enters the apartment. The dog, an old black Briard, rushes to sniff his boots, then wags her tail as a sign of apology for the earlier barking. It is obvious from the paperwork everywhere that Jean-Christophe lives alone and does a lot of research.

Gary explains, "My father died in an accident in January in Newcastle when a Boeing 757 crashed on landing. The unanimous view, is that it was a pilot error and recently it's become pilot error due to alcohol effects. On the transcript of the voice recorder the co-pilot who also died, and whose sister is helping me, said, 'there's the socks again'. Gordon is fairly convinced she must have been talking about contaminated air. My investigations all started..."

Gary goes through all he knows, what Gordon and others have told him and Jean-Christophe listens much like Gordon did the day before. Over an hour flashes by as if it was a second.

"So what do you think?" asks Gary when he has finished.

Jean-Christophe sits back in his chair whilst stroking the top of the black Briard's head on his knee. "I took a break from this war a year or so before Gordon finally gave up and realised the union bosses were as bad as the industry bosses. From what you're telling me I think they got too complacent and grim reaper has finally played his cards. What is more, the fact the alcohol story is new, I am convinced your meeting tonight will be very enlightening, you need to make sure she goes to the police or to a lawyer and gives a full statement if she tells you what we think she is going to tell you. Do you have the initial report with you?"

"Yes, it's in my bag."

Jean-Christophe looks at the report, "Let me have a look at the report and make a few calls. In the meantime, you should watch one of the DVDs the group AOPIS made back in 2003 for an Australian pilot union, I have it somewhere in my organised mess!"

"Thanks a lot, I appreciate your help."

Jean-Christophe finds the DVD and puts it in the player, "I will show you the 52 minute longer version as it will be of great interest to you."

"OK, thanks."

Jean-Christophe sits back and starts to read the report and then makes some calls in French whilst Gary watches the DVD.

When the DVD finishes he turns to Jean-Christophe, "What a great DVD. That pilot Nevan Pavlinovich said very clearly 'If there is an accident it will not be accident as everyone knows about it!' With all that evidence why did no one do anything?"

Jean-Christophe explains, "That DVD was the first documentary on the issue, the second was called 'Welcome Aboard Toxic Airlines', that was even better but I don't have a copy of that one. You can get it on the net. Something you must do. That guy – Nevan Pavlinovich – do you know what happened to him?"

Gary shakes his head.

"That guy fought the system like many have and in 2003 was fired by his employer on the basis – and this is the really crazy part – on the basis that they could not provide him with a safe working environment as they could not guarantee that the air would be free from oil contamination! You see what they get away with – it is because it's all about money and profit, Gary. Let me tell you about how I got into environmental issues and fighting for justice in many corners of the world. Although I had been involved since a kid, I stepped into these issues full time on 16 March 1978. Do you know what happened on that day?"

Gary shakes his head again, "Sorry, I have no idea."

"On 16 March 1978 the oil tanker Amoco Cadiz bound for Rotterdam ran aground off the coast of Brittany in Northern France following a sudden engine breakdown. Over a period of two weeks, the entire cargo was released into heavy seas. By the end of April, oil and emulsion had contaminated 320km of the Brittany coastline and at the time the incident resulted in the largest loss of marine life ever recorded after an oil spill. Like your father's accident this was also a totally avoidable disaster. You see as soon as the Amoco Cadiz radioed her problems, a tug began to proceed towards the scene. When the rescue tug arrived, the captain of the Amoco refused to accept assistance from the tug. The reason for this was his uncertainty about the costs involved. Money! The Captain of the Amoco Cadiz did not want to agree on a towage according the Lloyd's Open Form. Instead, the captain argued that he was not actually in serious distress and required a contract on a regular towage rate which is of course far cheaper. The tug captain disagreed and insisted on the Lloyd's Open Form, as the Amoco Cadiz was doubtlessly in distress. Meanwhile, the tanker continued to drift rapidly towards the coast. The negotiations never got resolved and the Amoco Cadiz crashed against the rocks off the coast of Brittany and cracked suddenly in two. At the subsequent hearing with the ocean court, the tanker's captain was found guilty. One of the questions put to the captain of the Amoco Cadiz was, why he did not lower the anchors to help stop the tanker drifting. The captain gave the almost unbelievable answer that he did not want to risk loosing his anchors. Well, he saved his anchors but he lost his entire ship!

I digress – but the point of the story is the same the world over. Money and profit versus health risk or environmental damage. On flight 303 they could have fitted filters, used non toxic or less toxic oils, done better maintenance, fixed design flaws or even fitted contaminated air detection systems years ago. Even if it did not crash because of contaminated air which seems very unlikely, on how many flights around the world have passengers been exposed to contaminated air and told nothing by the airlines? It's human rights to be told you have been exposed to a known neurotoxins and hazardous chemicals. The reason they do not have contaminated air detection systems, is because they know they would be going off too frequently, the aircraft would be grounded and the cost to the industry would be too high. These are the so called cost risk assessments. How much will they pay out on this crash, whatever it is it will probably be less than the cost of fitting filters and detection systems to all aircraft.

Anyway, let me tell you what I have found out, things you might like to know and dig further into. Firstly, the voice recorder transcript is extremely interesting. For two reasons. Look at the transcript carefully."

Gary looks at the page as Jean-Christophe points the key parts out. You see here the approach controller gives the command, 'JASP 303 reduce speed 210 knots and turn right heading 090.' The Co-pilot replies with the wrong heading, 'Roger turn right heading 050 JASP 303' and the approach controller has to correct her.

Sure, people make mistakes but she is making a lot of mistakes. Later on the approach controller tells them, 'JASP turn left heading two six five degrees, cleared ILS runway 25.' The Co-pilot replies with, 'Roger turn left heading two sixty degrees, cleared ILS 25.' This time the approach controller doesn't pick up the mistake. When the aircraft has to be transferred from the approach controller to the tower radio frequency, something that happens on every approach, the approach controller has to ask them three times before they respond.

The transcript also shows the co-pilot highlighting that they are too fast and amazingly, the landing checklist never gets done although they seem to have done the relevant actions.

It is clear all was not well long before the accident. The GPWS, that is the Ground Proximity Warning System even went off, albeit very briefly, because they were late in putting the landing gear down. This is one of those approaches they should have thrown away and started again but it's hard to do that especially if you're becoming incapacitated and your judgment is being seriously affected. They might well have got away with it apart from this day the weather was right on the aircraft limits and they needed to be sharp. The last wind given by the tower controller was when he cleared them to land, he says, 'JASP 303 clear to land two five, wind now three four zero forty gusting fifty.'

The saddest part of the whole thing is the comment by the co-pilot split seconds before the crash. She says to herself and not to the Captain because it was not recorded on the intercom but recorded on the roof mike. She says, 'This is no good, we need to go around.' She wants to abort the landing. Her brain knew it was wrong but she didn't have the ability to do anything. Had she been alert she would have taken control or told the Captain to go around."

"I don't think I would have the heart to highlight that part to Jill, her sister."

Jean-Christophe carries on, "The other reason the transcript is very interesting, my friend, is because it's lacking time in seconds, it only shows minutes. Look here, the crew and ATC are talking here and here, and the time is in minutes. Now look at this one from the Concorde crash in Paris in 2000. The times are in seconds."

Gary has lost track, "What do you mean, what's the significance?"

"I think it would be very significant because if they were flying under a toxic effect as we suspect it might show up. For instance when someone is drunk there is more of a delay to their response. It might show up in the timings not to the extent a drunk person would but it might show the delay in cognitive response. A delay would indicate some form of cognitive impairment. For instance, when they are told by air traffic control to turn left or right, they should answer straight away if they are completely alert. Sure, sometimes you might be distracted and there might be a temporary delay but not all the time. If all their replies are delayed this would show a slow mind rather than occasional distractions. It's only in minutes so we can't tell if the reply is immediate or 5, 10, 15 or even 30 seconds later. Worth checking out but it's clear to me this crew were not working effectively, they were making a lot of mistakes before the crash. But then again *if* they had been drinking then..."

"How do you know all this stuff?"

"That's a story for another day as you are short on time but I used to be an air traffic controller during my military service. Next thing is the defect thing. I rang a buddy who is an engineer and he confirms if they pushed back and had fumes then or in the climb they might have called it in. Definitely worth checking out. I also found out that all airlines have different insurance policies. Some have a cheaper policy based on various exclusion clauses like if they will not be flying to certain trouble spots. There are also penalty clauses they can sign up to in an attempt to reduce insurance costs like you have with car insurance with higher excesses. For instance, if the airline's own maintenance screws up then they accept to forfeit x % of the insured value. Now JASP was a relatively new airline, maybe to save costs they too had a high penalty on insurance and it helps to have crew error as they will get a full pay out no doubt. Worth looking into..."

Jean-Christophe looks at his notes and continues, "Yes, another thing worth making a few phone calls about, is the previous crew who flew the plane, now the report says that the previous crew were interviewed and said the aircraft did not have any defects. That's fine but they may know a lot more than the report tells you."

Gary takes notes and then remembers something. "A buddy of mine from college is in the Army doing communications and all sorts of surveillance stuff for the military and government. I will give him a call, he might have a take on all this."

The dog which has remained calm for Gary's entire stay suddenly jumps up and starts barking, seconds before there is a loud knock on the door. Jean-Christophe can see Gary is startled and reassures him as he walks to the door, "It's OK, that will be Michelle, I suspect. Michelle was a stewardess whose career was ruined by exposure to contaminated air and who works nearby. I asked her to come round. I thought it would be an interesting experience for you to actually meet a victim of these issues.

Jean-Christophe opens the door whilst holding the dog by her collar.

He greets the visitor in French. Gary stands up to be polite. The visitor is nothing like Gary imagined. Michelle is a tall and extremely beautiful brunette in her mid thirties. Jean-Christophe takes her coat under which Michelle is wearing a very smart short skirted suit. She speaks excellent English with soft French vowels.

Michelle smiles at Gary, "Jean-Christophe tells me you are investigating a contaminated air crash and you have never met anyone affected by contaminated air exposures. Am I as you imagined I would be?"

"Well, I didn't really have time to imagine as Jean-Christophe only just told me you were arriving. But I guess I didn't expect someone to look like you. You are, well, shall we say stunning. I guess I imagined you would look sick."

Jean-Christophe laughs and Michelle smiles. Gary does not get the joke. Jean-Christophe beckons them all to sit down.

"We laugh because your reply is exactly what everyone says, who does not understand the issue. When people have cancer they often look well in the early days. The injury we have, Aerotoxic Syndrome as it is known is often more of a neurological illness. Many of us look OK but our injuries are not immediately apparent to the person in the street. Our neuropsychological injuries are all roughly the same in that it affects our memory processing and not our actual memory. What I mean to say is that we can remember long term things like you can, but it's the processing of short term things part that is not right. I struggle with processing too many tasks simultaneously. If I am rushed or given too much to think about my mind fails me. For instance, if I am cooking a big meal for friends I often over cook something or burn my cooking as I often forget something. If I pace myself I get by. For me, I also suffer from massive nausea and brain fog, like being permanently jet lagged if I do too much cognitive work or if I am exposed to certain chemicals. I have friends who have bad respiratory problems but I am OK. We are all affected differently. You have a saying in English, 'don't judge a book by its cover' – well the same goes for crews and passengers like me who suffer daily from Aerotoxic Syndrome.

"I am sorry, I did not mean to belittle your injuries. I appreciate very much your coming to meet me, it was a good idea of Jean-Christophe's. It helps me understand these problems more. I don't know if Jean-Christophe told you but my father died in a Boeing 757 crash earlier this year, which I believe is linked to contaminated air."

"Yes, he did."

"Can you tell me about your exposure?"

"I was a stewardess and then a purser and I had often smelt contaminated air on the aircraft but, like everyone else, just assumed it was harmless. Looking back, it was clear I was having effects but I just put the effects down to something else. How was I to know any better, the airline never told me what the risks were! In 2005 I was coming back from an East Coast trip and"

"East Coast?" asks Gary inquisitively.

"Sorry, the East Coast of the United States. Airline jargon. So, anyway, I was coming back from an East Coast trip and as we pushed back from the gate an extremely strong smell of sweaty socks invaded the cabin (more towards the back) and to a lesser extent the cockpit. Run up to take off was exceptionally short – about 4 to 5 minutes. Crew from the back rushed to tell me that the smell was unbearable at the back and that the crew and passengers had stinging eyes, headaches and nose and throat irritation. I immediately informed the flight deck but got little attention as we were lining up for take off. We took off, anyway. After take off the back purser informed me that there was a mist in cabin. I informed the flight deck of events in the cabin. I insisted that all crew put on oxygen masks or used bottles and masks. Our flight deck crew had no knowledge as to the toxic nature of jet engine oils. The smell in the cockpit was not as strong as in cabin. The co-pilot reassured the Captain, saying that he had often smelt this funny odour on the Airbus A320 and thought it was due to a slight oil leak - but no problem. I asked the Captain to go back but he wasn't interested – old school – and did not want any trouble. Soon afterwards, the mist cleared and we could no longer smell anything. I am sure we had become desensitised and wrongly thought the air was clean. On descent towards Paris, a slight smell of sweaty socks was reported again to me from the rear cabin. We could also smell it in the front.

Upon arrival – and a hard landing that was – four cabin crew and myself reported to the company medical centre and we were told that the incident was not serious (however, we were congratulated on donning masks and oxygen briefly) and that no test was available in France to measure levels of organophosphate intoxication."

Michelle then loses concentration and stops for a few seconds, a symptom of her injury. Gary observes but remains quiet. Michelle then carries on.

"The company doctor told us that he personally follows the oil leak dossier and seemed quite informed on the subject - however, he was very proud to inform us that only four incidents were reported the previous year. After we had argued with him, he ended up agreeing that if crew do not have information about oil leaks and contaminated air, they do not report on what they reckon to be very minor and non health affecting incidents. Aircraft continue to fly with known leaks because of this industry's 'we don't care' attitude. Little help is available on the medical side as reliable tests are not available to measure subject intoxication.

The next day, I woke up at about 4 a.m. with seriously bad nausea and have never felt OK since. I lost my job about four months later. That's my story and I could fill this room with people who have similar stories. Perhaps we were genetically more susceptible but we have equal rights to be protected don't we? If your father died because the crew ignored the potential consequences it would not surprise me at all. It was only a few months ago I met a girl from Canada who told me that their flight attendant manuals now have information about the risks of exposure to contaminated air and what the health effects can be but they still don't tell the passengers! It's not on any safety card you find in the seat pocket in front of you! It would be nice if all flight attendants had manuals like that.

Crew do what they are trained to do and contaminated air isn't on the airline training program for obvious reasons."

Gary notices that her speech has slowed down and her voice become a little more faint. Although still looking at him, her blue eyes seem vacant now. "I am sorry to hear about what you have been through, I can see it's hard on you. I could see when you spoke you struggled at times. Now I can see what you mean. I never realised that someone could be affected by just one flight so badly."

Jean-Christophe joins in the conversation, "People can get sick from one exposure or repeated exposures, each exposure is different and everyone is different. You see, Gary, apart from the impact contaminated air has on a pilot's ability to fly the aircraft or the impact it will have on the ability of the flight attendants to evacuate the aircraft in an emergency, how much do you know about the health risks?"

Jean-Christophe can tell from Gary's look and response that he has not really delved into these areas, "Not a lot – can you explain it to me?"

"This is a major scandal. You see, passengers and crews will can experience short term or long term – what is named Aerotoxic Syndrome effects, but as nobody tells them they have been exposed, they don't realise it was from contaminated air. They ignorantly assume it's due to bad food, jet lag, long day at work, the journey, etc. You will find the full list of symptoms in this Aviation Contaminated Air Reference Manual."

Jean-Christophe opens a large reference manual specifically looking at the whole contaminated air issue.

"The short term symptoms of Aerotoxic Syndrome effects will include things like neurotoxic symptoms, such as blurred or tunnel vision, disorientation, shaking and tremors, loss of balance and vertigo; neuropsychological symptoms such as memory impairment, headache, light-headedness, dizziness, confusion and feeling intoxicated; gastro-intestinal symptoms, such as nausea, vomiting; respiratory symptoms, such as cough, breathing difficulties i.e. shortness of breath, tightness in the chest; cardiovascular symptoms, such as increased heart rate and palpitations and also irritation of eyes, nose and upper airways, and so forth. That's the short term side of the issue and let's not forget the increased chance of miscarriage if you're pregnant, or the impact on young children. I know many stewardesses who have had miscarriages – why do they appear to be so much higher than the national average? Why has a proper epidemiological survey not been done?"

Gary agrees, "I see your point. What are they hiding? What are they scared of finding? The truth?"

Michelle nods in agreement.

Jean-Christophe continues, "Now let's look at the long term symptoms of Aerotoxic Syndrome. These will include things like neurotoxic symptoms, such as numbness in fingers, lips, limbs; neuropsychological symptoms such as memory impairment, forgetfulness, lack of co-ordination, headaches, dizziness, depression, sleep disorders; gastro-intestinal symptoms, such as, nausea, vomiting, diarrhoea; respiratory symptoms, such as breathing difficulties, tightness in chest, susceptibility to upper respiratory tract infections; cardiovascular symptoms, such as chest pain, heart palpitations; skin symptoms, such as skin itching and rashes, skin blisters, hair loss; irritation of eyes, nose and upper airways and sensitivity, such as signs of immunosupression, chemical sensitivity leading to acquired or multiple chemical sensitivity and general symptoms such as weakness and fatigue leading to chronic fatigue type symptoms, exhaustion, hot flashes, joint pain, muscle weakness and pain and so the list goes on. You see, Gary, the problem we have with Aerotoxic Syndrome from a passenger or crew perspective is that you don't walk off the aircraft with a blue head or yellow eyes. The impact of being exposed to a mixture of chemicals targets numerous organs and systems in the body and hence the wide spectrum of symptoms you may have. Obviously, you will not get them all, you will get some of them. This is because we are different genetically. The really sad part is, these symptoms have been pretty much known of since the 1950s! All I did with another top guy called Professor Chris Winder in Sydney, was to write them up, summarise them and give them a name. Chris was one of the guys who really did a lot on this issue, a really nice guy. That was way back in 2001. As you mentioned, the Australians led the way on these issues and the article we did was published in the Journal of Occupational Health & Safety, Australia & New Zealand."

"Where did the term Aerotoxic Syndrome come from?" asks Gary.

Jean-Christophe replies, "People had been networking and discussing these matters from around the world for some years before it was given a formal name. The term 'Aerotox' was first named by a guy called Harry Hoffman, a former flight surgeon in the US Navy, with highest credentials. In 1998 the head of the Aerospace Medical Association told me that If you want the scientific and medical community to work on the issue, you have to describe the symptoms, the supposed causation or links that could be established, and name such a syndrome, so that people can know what this is about and refer to same language. In a nutshell this is how we decided on the name. Several alternative names were discussed but I believe the name is correct, although the aviation industry does not like the 'toxic' part."

"I never knew that," states Michelle as she turns towards Gary who acknowledges that the history of where the name came from is very interesting.

Jean-Christophe picks up some other notes, "Another important part of this is how the industry has misinformed the public for years on the health issues. If the industry and the airlines allow passengers, some of whom will be pregnant or crews to breathe in contaminated air then obviously the public will assume it's safe. Do you agree with that point?"

"That makes sense," says Gary.

Michelle adds to the conversation, "In all the years I flew, never once did I ever hear the pilots telling passengers that they had been exposed to contaminated air or what the health consequences might me."

Jean-Christophe continues, "Well, look at the misinformation they put out. In 2004, the UK Civil Aviation Authority, those nice people who are 100% funded by the airlines, put out a paper, not published in a peer reviewed journal as no doubt it would never have been accepted, but released all the same, a paper entitled Cabin Air Quality. In section 4.1 they state 'A general assessment of the toxic potential of the components and thermal degradation products of aviation lubricating fluid has been carried out and no single component or set of components can be identified which at conceivable concentrations would definitely cause the symptoms reported in cabin air quality incidents.' Anyone who reads that paper – like the public – will incorrectly assume all is well and nothing to worry about. Would you agree with that thought process?"

"Of course," nods Gary.

"First of all, research was done apparently partly under contract for British Aerospace. The work remained the commercial property of British Aerospace and was never made available for public review – something many would say is hardly independent research. The next point is, the CAA never talked with any doctors treating crews for contaminated air exposure effects and never talked or communicated with the crews either. It was all bullshit. To put the icing on the cake the CAA paper even added the get out clause statement which should have been in bold writing on page one 'Although some references are made concerning long term health effects, the scope of this research did not include an attempt to determine the extent of any such risk.' Despite that, a CAA doctor subsequently stated that research undertaken 'did not suggest that there is a health risk for passengers including infants or crew.' Do you see what they do? It is all a well-orchestrated misinformation campaign. Just like the UK House of Lords saying there were no adverse health effects from contaminated air exposures in 2000, even though they said no records were being kept and this was based on poisoning from a chemical called TOCP which was one of the chemicals present in the engine oil anti wear additive called tricresyl phosphate. They knew when they made the comment that TOCP was the least toxic of the ortho isomers of tricresyl phosphate in the lowest amounts. It's amazing how they forgot to mention that part! They never expected anyone to check!"

Jean-Christophe looks at his watch, "Oh Merde! ...Sorry, look at the time – you need to rush to get your train back."

Gary, Michelle and Jean-Christophe keep the pleasantries to a minimum by simply exchanging telephone numbers and Gary rushes out of the flat in search of a taxi to get to the station. At the Gare Du Nord, he has not even the time to get a sandwich before boarding his return journey to London and his 6 p.m. meeting with Katarzyna.

Chapter 13

Jill approaches the Newcastle General Hospital from Westgate Road, on foot. Dressed in her nurse's uniform she does not feel out of place. She is also wearing some uncorrected vision glasses and a black wavy wig – both previously obtained for a fancy dress party. The disguise will reduce the chances of her being recognised by those she knows in the profession, as well as anybody who might subsequently want to look at any CCTV footage. She is familiar with the hospital layout, even though she has not worked there, except for a section of her training. Jill knows that hospitals do not keep blood very long. However, in view of the fact this was an accident with an ongoing inquiry, all evidence would have been kept until notification was given to dispose of it.

Jill is aware that it is vital that any blood she can obtain today was taken whilst Carol was still alive. Biochemical investigations carried out on post-mortem blood are generally of limited value. The measurement of electrolytes such as sodium and potassium has no value after death. Also, blood glucose concentrations generally fall rapidly after death and are an unreliable guide to glucose concentrations prior to death.

She walks through the front entrance and looks at the list of doctors within the hospital. From there she walks into the records department. There is a young nurse working on a computer. She glances up at Jill who oozes confidence.

"Doctor Roberts is wondering why he has not had an answer to his email from yesterday about the blood test records for a John Parson who was deceased earlier this year."

The young nurse looks flushed, "Sorry I am only temping here to cover maternity leave. I don't know about this request but if you wait a while the full time staff will be back very soon. I do know all this year's data is still in the filing cabinets as we are about three months behind scanning in the data due to the recent system upgrade, if that helps at all."

"If you're a temp then you don't know Doctor Roberts. He doesn't wait for anything and that's why I am here. I'll have a look myself to cover whoever has been incompetent. Tell the full time staff when they get back I'll be down later to talk to them about this. They owe me one." Jill turns and walks to the cabinet with 'P' as a surname, pleased she gave the temp false information to cover her tracks.

The temp lacks experience and maturity to deal with the situation other than to see that Jill is a nurse and goes back to staring at her computer screen and entering data. Another staff member is on the phone and looking out the window.

Jill looks through the records till she finds 'Carol Parker,' checks the date of birth and confirms this is her sister's data. For a split second she pauses at the words 'deceased' and 'Do not discard – Aircraft accident'. The records have her sister's arrival time and time of death. The records have various pages attached, which Jill looks over. She glances quickly at the temp, the staff member still on the phone and then at the door to review the risk as she takes in all the information. Her heart rate is elevated, the adrenaline is pumping, she can feel the stress and fear setting in despite being on the side of justice. The hospital will not take kindly to what she is doing and if she is caught she will probably lose her job. She hurries through the file. All the reports are here, such as Hematology, Biochemistry, Immunology and Serology. Jill then finds the attached 'Biochemistry Results' and starts to read: Sodium; Potassium; Calcium; Phosphate; AST; ALT; and so forth.

Finally, in what seems like an eternity, she finds the report on increased levels of toxic compounds including hydrogen cyanide, hydrogen chloride, nitrogen dioxide, formaldehyde, ammonia, and toluene confirming inhalation of toxic fumes most likely resulting from the fire that was reported following the accident. Then, 'Alcohol Analysis Report'. It is a report from the laboratory. This is exactly what she was looking for but first she scans the room and the door again to make sure all is safe. Then she starts to read from the top. 'Enzymic methods for alcohol analysis commonly used by clinical laboratories may give falsely elevated results in critically ill patients or post-mortem specimens. Analysis for alcohol was carried out by gas chromatography as this is more specific than enzymic methods of alcohol analysis and is also able to detect the presence of other alcohols such as methanol and isopropanol, or the products of keto-acidosis such as acetone…' Jill skips past the science and the preamble to get to the conclusions. 'Results of the analysis are attached.' She looks through all the biochemistry results again, nothing. She pauses a short while, puts the file back, looks around the room and realises that nobody has been paying much attention.

As she walks to the door four female nurses walk in, and two glance in her direction but before they even start to wonder who Jill is or what she wants, the staff member who was on the phone starts talking to them. "That must have been the longest tea break ever."

One of the four is quick to argue back, "Are you kidding? have you seen the queues in the canteen?"

The temp turns to one of the female nurses after they have debated the canteen queues and says "That nurse was sent down by Doctor Roberts to…"

The door shuts closed with Jill having left the room grinning not because she was not caught but because she knows how they play the game. She knows if her sister had been tested positive for alcohol, the report would still be there. There is no report, not because it is being used elsewhere but because she believes someone else went through the file as easily as she did and deliberately removed it.

She makes her way to the blood bank. At the bottom of the biochemistry report it stated in a way only a doctor or nurse would understand, FFP placed in BB with a date and a signature. FFP means Fresh Frozen Plasma and BB is short for Blood Bank. For hematology, biochemistry, blood bank, immunology or other laboratory tests, plasma is obtained from whole blood. To prevent clotting, an anticoagulant such as citrate or heparin is added to the blood specimen immediately after it is obtained. Usually, the anticoagulant is already in the evacuated blood collection test tube when the patient is bled. The specimen is then centrifuged to separate plasma from blood cells. Plasma can be frozen below -20°C nearly indefinitely for subsequent analysis or use and that is what has been done. Her sister's Plasma is being stored in the freezer in the Blood Bank and she knows that, unless the person who has already been through her sister's files was a doctor, they might have made their first mistake.

Jill is mentally well prepared for the challenge as she walks into the Blood Bank section. She opens the door and sitting facing the door at a desk is a young male nurse filling out some paper work.

"Hi honey, Doctor Roberts wants some FFP urgently for a Carol Parker. He said you got about 10ml on ice to rerun some tests. Somebody screwed up the result data on some tests and it looks like we are going to be working late. What a nightmare, today of all days."

The young male nurse is a bit taken back, not used to such bubbly and cheerful nurses just walking in like that in such an authoritative manner. Normally, it's a telephone call for some blood to be rushed to A&E in a hurry. "OK, let me see what we got stored."

He starts to type data into a computer and asks, "What was the name again?"

"Carol Parker, deceased in January."

132

"Deceased... OK, here it is – Carol Parker, yeah I remember – she is one of those we are holding pending release authority. We only have 4 ml. I am not familiar with the release rules on these."

Jill holds her nerve, and raises her tone. "How did you get this job? Section 26 rules for internal release of FFP for internal biochemistry work do not come under coroner release laws. Besides, all we need is 3 ml. Now if you want to ring Dr Roberts and tell him your pissing him around because you don't know your internal hospital 'regs' then be my guest but judging by the mood he's in you would be a brave man."

She claps her hands, a little too hard, to stop them from shaking. "So come on let's get going, I got a hen night party tonight down the Quayside to go to."

The young nurse gets up in a flash. "Sure, no problem, I remember that rule now, I'll put it in an ice pack to transfer it to the lab."

He goes into the back room. The minutes tick by and Jill starts to consider making a dash for it. Is he on the phone looking for Dr Roberts? She keeps asking herself should she go or stay? The young male nurse returns with a small polystyrene container, "OK, I put it on dry ice. Can you just give me the doctor's details again for the release."

Jill replies, "Dr Roberts in Biochemistry. Thanks a lot, see you soon. You're cute."

Jill walks into the corridor and through hospital maze of busy corridors towards the hospital entrance. She puts her coat over the container. She cannot wait to be out of the hospital but makes sure she does not walk too quickly to attract attention. As she reaches the front doors a voice calls out, "Excuse me!"

She freezes, as her ears start buzzing. She knows she has been caught, she is in serious trouble. She considers making a run for it but her legs feel heavy. She turns around slowly. A man is looking not at her but past her and calls out to a nurse again. She realises it is an old man talking to a sister walking past her. She breathes again, turns sharply and heads straight out the hospital doors quickly, but not so quickly as to be noticed, to her car. She unlocks the door, and then freezes.

Behind her comes a male voice. "Excuse me, nurse."

Jill turns slowly towards the voice. Two tall and physically fit young men in their twenties are standing looking at her.

Jill quickly thinks about getting in her car and driving off.

Who are these men? But before she has decided what to do, one of them speaks.

"Sorry nurse, you look very pale, I did not mean to startle you. Can you tell us where we are best to park for the X-Ray section?"

One of the men seems to be looking at her car number plate. She feels very vulnerable but there are a couple of people walking nearby. After a pause Jill replies, "Anywhere around here, there isn't a specific car park for the X-Ray section."

"Thanks a lot," replies the man who turns and walks off with his companion.

Jill gets in her car, her heart is racing and her breathing very heavy, her hands are trembling. She puts her coat on the passenger seat and the container on the floor and then quickly opens the car door and is sick on the street. Sick with nerves. She glances around to check that nobody has seen her being sick. She closes the door, wipes her mouth and breathes out heavily, relieved she has got away with it.

She has pulled it off. She starts the car and drives off.

Jill drives home quickly so she can put the plasma in her freezer. In her state of euphoria she is home in no time, parks the car and walks with the container in the cold wind to her house. At least, it will be warm indoors.

When she opens the front door the cold of the house strikes her straight away. She closes the front door, takes off her coat and then shivers slightly. The house is surprisingly cold. She looks at the thermometer on the wall, 13 Celsius. It should be about 21 as it was warm when she left. She pauses for a few seconds, and then opens the door to the downstairs cloakroom and puts the container on the floor inside and closes the door again. She walks slowly through the living room and then sees that the back door is wide open. She freezes. She has been broken into. She looks around the living room and listens for any sound that the intruder is still in the house. Nothing. She goes towards the door and finds it undamaged, no sign of a break in. She knows she left the door closed. She wonders if she locked it but knows she has not been out of that door for several days. She surveys the downstairs slowly and looks out the windows to see if anyone is parked outside observing her every move but nothing. Everything seems in place, maybe she left it unlocked and the wind blew it open. She thinks that unlikely but if it was a break in why is nothing missing? She opens a kitchen drawer, takes out a chopping knife and slowly goes upstairs. Room by room she looks around her small house. Everything seems in place, nothing is missing.

She goes downstairs and returns to the back door. She opens and closes it a few times to check its functionality, tries the lock a few times, all seems normal. She closes the door one final time and locks it.

As she opens the drawer to replace the knife, she suddenly registers. Something is missing. Her computer. The monitor is still there but not the computer. She knows this is linked to her research, and the certainty chills her. Then she thinks that perhaps she disturbed a break in but if that was the case the room would not have become so cold so quickly. They probably waited for her to go out and did it then. The thought that she is being watched frightens her.

Jill goes back to the cloakroom, retrieves the plasma and takes it to the kitchen. She opens the freezer and pulls out a large bag of frozen peas. She opens the bag and goes to slot the plasma inside when the grim reality of what she is doing overcomes her. This is her dead sister's plasma. She looks at it, the container is cold in her fingers so she quickly buries it in the bag of frozen peas, puts it all back in the freezer and slowly closes the door.

Chapter 14

Gary's train is speeding back through Kent. The train is a lot emptier on this journey and, in the distance, motorists are turning on their headlights. He picks up his mobile. After a couple of rings, he answers, it's Gordon Cooper.

"Hi Gordon, I have some information for you. I wanted to ask you about company radio frequencies and if you think the crew on flight 303 might have called in a defect if they had one."

"Well, on that note, I can tell you that the initial accident report forgets to mention the aircraft was on the ground for 52 minutes after it left the departure gate before it got airborne. Why – I don't know. It might have been air traffic control delays as airports get even busier first thing or maybe they had a defect. The problem is, that even if they did call something in, where would the evidence be, it's not on the cockpit voice recorder recordings although they only start after the aircraft is well on its way to Newcastle. Air traffic control will not have kept the data that long, that's a great shame."

Gary remembers again about his friend in communications, "There might be a little bit of hope, I have a friend who works in the military in communications and surveillance stuff. I will ask him. That's really interesting about the delay getting airborne. If they were being exposed that would have given more time for the contaminated air to take effect on their faculties. Jean-Christophe has highlighted that the cockpit voice recorder timings on the transcript are in minutes only and should be in seconds as well, so we can see if there is any continuous delay in crew response so I was thinking of looking into that. Jean-Christophe also took me through the insurance aspects. He said you had a brother in that sector and he might be able to see if they had any increased premiums for faulty internal maintenance."

"That went through my mind last night, Gary, especially when the alcohol story was taken off the shelf to make this stick in a hurry and the insurers are seriously taking a hit on this one. Anyway, my brother did some digging, and guess what? They were short on cash obviously when they set up JASP. JASP had serious penalties on the hull value, i.e. the value of aircraft itself and they had responsibility for that towards the lessor of the aircraft. Public liability was fine but, in a nutshell, if it was proved to be maintenance errors which were foreseeable and which caused the accident then they are basically out of pocket the hull value of the aircraft and some other costs. This would be a really serious hit for the company which is seriously strapped for cash coming out of a poor winter season. As for the timings, even if you show there is a delay, they will argue it is due to alcohol, they are very clever. I would focus your efforts elsewhere."

"This gets better by the day," adds Gary, who has ceased to be surprised.

Gordon carries on with what he has unravelled, "It turns out that that the crew who last flew the plane before the crew of 303 took over, was a Management pilot called Dave Callaghan and no bonus points for knowing he is one of their senior managers, so I would not take what he has reported as reliable, I don't know who the co-pilot was. I have feelers out looking for the data. Now what else do I have for you? Oh, yes. Got a telephone number for Professor Ashington which I will text you shortly, don't forget they are eight hours behind. I haven't rung him yet. Any word on the blood?"

"No, nothing yet, Jill is on the case. Gordon, that's really helpful, I'll get on the phone to Jill and if she comes up trumps I'll get her onto Professor Ashington."

Gordon interrupts, "That reminds me of the most important point. Did you know the final hearing date is next Monday? That means if you can't produce evidence by then it will become virtually impossible to ever get justice. The papers seem to think it's a done deal and are really hitting the crew hard and are calling for mandatory blood testing of crews before flying. I think the odds are seriously stacked against you but you haven't yet been dealt the dead man's hand. Keep me posted and I will keep digging around."

"I am glad I came back from Canada early. Thanks a lot Gordon, I'll keep you in the loop. All the best."

He hangs up and wonders whether to ring Jill first or his friend in communications. The latter seems more imperative. He has to dig his number out of his diary as it is not in his phone. Alan Godbold, Cardiff.

"Alan, it's Gary"

"Hey, Gary, how's it hanging man, let me just turn the television down… What you up to?"

"It's a fairly long story and a mind spinner as well but I need your help, can you help me?"

"What's the problem?"

"Well, keep this between you and I, and I'll fill you in when we next meet but in a nutshell – do you remember the flight my dad died on? Well, it was a JASP Boeing 757 with a flight number JASP 303. What I want, is to know if you could get the transcripts of all communications the aircraft made with its company on VHF or through ACARS. Is that possible?"

"Did the flight leave from London?"

"Yes it did."

"I know some guys who might have some communication data for the London area as they monitor a shit lot of frequencies for counter intelligence purposes. I know they even scan the corporate jets data relays as they feel terrorists might use that as a way in. I'll see what I can do."

"Another request mate. Do you still have mates who could get into JASP airlines database and files and get me all they can on the JASP flight 303 that crashed recently?"

"Bloody hell mate, you don't want much do you?"

"Alan, this is probably the most important request I have ever made, mate. Whatever deal can be done, I'll cover my end."

"This must be important, I'll do my best. You know that."

Gary has known Alan since primary school. He knows he is trustworthy, "That's great. Just one thing – it's really urgent."

"Well, if you get off the phone I'll get on with it, buddy."

Gary clears the line with Alan. His phone starts ringing. Jill's name flashes on the display.

"Where are you – can you talk?"

"Yeah, I am back in England on the train heading for London, will be there soon. I've had a really productive day, absolutely brilliant, so much to tell you. Just been on the phone with Gordon, the final hearing is on Monday. Look tell me what your news is and I'll call you later with mine as I will have to go to the restaurant as soon as I get to London."

"Listen, I came home today and someone had broken into my house."

"Jesus!"

"Get this – the back door was open and the only thing I can find missing is my computer! I know the back door was locked when I left. What do you make of it? I haven't told anybody yet."

"That's fucking clever of them."

"What do you mean ?"

"It's a clear message to you, a warning. We can get to you anytime. They left the door open so you can't prove it's a break in because the police would wonder why the only thing they took was a computer worth next to nothing. The police would assume you left the door open as there is no sign of a break in.

We play these games on special ops. Put the laser gun sight on someone to tell them had we wanted to, they would be dead!"

"Hang on Gary, I am only a nurse. How do you know for certain it was not some kids or just a normal break in?"

"If it was a normal break-in they would have taken other stuff, Jill. Besides, you're not a nurse. You are a nurse meddling into a multi million pound cover up. You'll be OK for a while as they have made the point. I know it will shake you up, that's the whole idea but if they wanted to harm you they would have. So trust me, you'll be OK."

"I am scared. But it shows me we are right and that just fuels me more. Besides, they can have the computer. I've got some great news. I got some lovely wine for you today. I'll put it out for you to admire when you get home."

For a few seconds Gary is wondering what the hell Jill is talking about and then he catches on that Jill has started to assume she is being watched, "That's really nice of you, what type?"

If Gary is following this the wine will be red meaning she has her sister's blood.

"Red, of course, full bodied, they tell me."

"That's excellent. You're a top lass you know, you'll make someone a lovely wife one day."

"Is that a proposal, Gary, you've got class – I'll hand it to you. No getting down on one knee for Gary, a telephone will do the job."

Gary knows that she is hiding her fear under the banter. "Jill, I'll call you later and we can talk about it when I am home and cracking open that bottle of wine. Take care, call you later."

"Good luck Gary and Gary, one last thing… Thanks for all you're doing. You know I really appreciate it."

"I know Jill, let's talk later."

The train arrives at London Waterloo station at 17.20 and Gary makes his way to the Lebanese restaurant by taxi. He gets out a few streets away as he instinctively decides to survey the area around the restaurant for a while just to review the risk. Nothing seems untoward, so at five to six he enters the restaurant.

A waiter, in his thirties, of Arabic features asks him if he has a reservation. Gary tells the waiter he hasn't but asks for a table for one. The restaurant is virtually empty. Just one couple on their own near the window. A short time afterwards the waiter gives Gary a menu and asks if he would like something to drink.

"A Lebanese beer would be great, thanks."

Gary can feel the fatigue, not just the physical fatigue but the mental fatigue. He drinks his beer slowly and looks at the menu but his focus is on his watch. 18.00, 18.05, 18.10, 18.15.

The waiter who is obviously keen to take his order returns a second time, "Can I take your order, please?"

Gary picks the first thing that grabs his attention. "Yes, can I have the Mohammara Bil-Jawz, the Feta Cheese Salad and the Mujadara. Thanks."

A few minutes later, the door of the restaurant opens, Gary looks around quickly. It is just a party of four followed soon afterwards by a party of three. It is 18.20 and there is no sign of Katarzyna. Did she mean outside the restaurant? Has he misunderstood? Does he have the right day? He looks again at the text message, he is not mistaken. There is only one choice. He dials the number and puts the phone to his ear. 'You have dialled an incorrect number.' He redials, same message. He has the feeling he has experienced in combat, that gut feeling something is not right. His only saving thought as he looks around the room is at least here someone is not going to open up on him with an AK-47 or rocket launcher although the adrenaline is flowing as high, just the same.

The waiter returns with his meal, "There you are, Sir, one Mohammara Bil-Jawz, one Feta Cheese Salad and the Mujadara. Are you sure you would not like any water or wine this evening?"

"No thanks."

Gary has to engage the waiter; he does not want to do this but he is running out of options, "Excuse me, I haven't seen you working here before, where is Katarzyna?"

"I am new, this is my first day, Sir. If you mean the Polish girl, she had to go home due to family problems."

Gary relies on his instinct that the waiter knows nothing of the bigger picture, "That's terrible, mate, I have some money for her. I am a private driver and she was giving me some business on the side from the restaurant. You know how it works. They want drivers and she calls me. She gets commission. Actually I have £ 100 for her but I don't want the boss knowing."

The waiter is clearly new to the business but likes the sound of the extra earning potential he was not aware of when he signed up for the work. He is clearly keen to help and perhaps equally benefit from the scam.

"I think I know where her address is kept, they might be able to tell you her address in Poland or when she will be back. If I can help, can I send you some work as well?"

"If Katarzyna is going to be away, I am happy to give you my number and perhaps we can have the same arrangement as I had with her? Don't mention this to anyone or your boss. If your boss finds out she will want some as well. She makes enough money already!" replies Gary with a slight laugh.

The waiter turns and walks away. Gary can tell he knows nothing about the story of Katarzyna going home due to family problems, he is just another pawn in a game of chess he doesn't even know he is in. He can sense someone is always one step ahead of him. How can that be? He looks at his phone, is he being tapped? It's all getting more like being in the field again.

He doesn't mind that, he is a good soldier and knows how to play the 'secret wars'.

The waiter returns just as Gary finishes his dinner. "This might help."

The waiter puts an address on the table with the bill. It's a London address. Gary writes down his mobile number on a serviette, pays the bill and puts £30 to the side of the bill and looks up at the waiter.

"I look forward to doing business with you."

Gary stands up and leaves the restaurant without saying another word. A few streets away is a payphone. He dials Jill's number. "Jill, I am in a payphone. Look, it's bad news, I think they have got to her."

"What do you mean?"

"She never showed and the waiter is a new guy who I think knows nothing. He has only just started working there, he said the Polish girl had to go home for family reasons! It's very disappointing, now we don't know what she wanted to say. I tried ringing her phone but it's a dead number. The whole thing really sucks."

"Shit. I think someone is shadowing us all the time."

"I was thinking the same in the restaurant and that's why I am in a payphone. Look, what time is it? It's 19.00. The last train to Newcastle is at 20.30. I am going to try and catch it and I will be back home tonight just after midnight. I am really exhausted. I'll get a good night's sleep and come round to yours in the morning and we can talk and catch up on all each other's news. Is that good for you?"

Gary hangs up and instinctively looks around the street, a habit from street patrols in the army. Nothing seems out of place but he feels exhausted, he feels as if he has been away from his home for years. He looks at the passing cars waiting for a cab to come along. Whilst he waits he texts Jill Professor Ashington's contact number in British Columbia that Gordon has just sent him so she can make the call.

A black cab passes by and Gary flags it down and gets in the back. He looks at the address the waiter has given him, "Driver, I want to go Hemingford Road, if you know where that is and incidentally how far that is from King's Cross?"

"I know where it is. That's actually about five minutes the other side of King's Cross, mate."

"Great."

The driver starts the meter.

"Did you watch the Magpies game at the weekend. Great performance."

The driver can tell Gary is from Newcastle by his Geordie accent and the Magpies are the main football team in Newcastle. As much as Gary is a keen fan he wants to think, not talk.

"I'm not a football fan, sorry."

The driver gets the message and stares ahead in silence.

After about twenty minutes, the driver interrupts Gary's thoughts, "That's King's Cross on the left, we will be there in a few minutes. What number do you want?"

"78, please," answers Gary, adding a few to the address number so as not to get out directly outside.

He has decided he is best walking the last part and playing safe, although he thinks the waiter is above board and the risk is low. The cab pulls up outside 78 as it starts to rain.

Gary walks down the fairly empty wet street past the address and discovers the number is in fact the basement flat. He checks the street one last time and walks down the steps to the front door where he pushes on the intercom.

"Hello?" The intercom crackles, with a European female voice.

"Is that Katarzyna?"

There is a pause. "No I am a flatmate, she does not live here anymore. She has gone home."

"I am a friend from the restaurant, I would like to have her address in Poland, can I come in please? It's raining."

There is another long and unnerving pause. Gary wonders if this is Katarzyna he is talking to when the intercom crackles to life again.

"OK. It's the first door on your right."

The door unlocks and Gary walks into an unlit corridor. He is looking for the light switch when a beam of light falls across his way from an opened door. A girl in her twenties, petite, shoulder length dark hair in bare feet, wearing jeans and a sweatshirt, greets Gary in the doorway, without letting him in.

"Do you work at the restaurant?"

"No, I met Katarzyna at the restaurant a few days ago. She was meant to meet me tonight at six but she never arrived. A new waiter told me she had gone home for family problems. He gave me this address. She had some information for me."

"What type of information?"

"Who are you?" answers Gary, trying to stop the questions.

"I am her flatmate, I have been here four months, Katarzyna arrived about two months ago."

Then, as though reassured that he is not going to hurt her, she swings the door wide open. "Come in."

It is a small basement flat with no real natural daylight. The girl invites him to take a seat in the living room. There is an open plan kitchen. The carpet and walls show signs of age. The kitchenette is small but tidy. Rents are high in London and this is definitely the lower end of the market.

"When and why did Katarzyna go and when will she be back?"

The girl hesitates. Gary can tell she is apprehensive. "Look, I went to the restaurant a few days ago and we got

146

talking and she gave me her mobile number and agreed to meet me tonight. She never showed up. I tried ringing her number but it's a dead number."

"What number did you ring?"

Gary gets out his mobile phone as the girl does likewise.

He reads out the number which the girl checks against her own mobile.

"You don't sound like you are from London."

"No, I am not. I am from Newcastle."

"What does she look like?"

Gary describes Katarzyna and the girl sits back in her chair.

"Why all the questions?"

"OK, you know her, I am cautious because, well, something seems to be wrong about the whole situation. A few days ago two guys arrived and said the landlord had asked them to pack up Katarzyna's stuff and send it back to Poland because she had rung the landlord and told him she had to go back in an emergency for family reasons, as you say."

"What's strange about that?"

"Why did she not ring me? She has only been here two months and we became good friends, we used to go clubbing together."

"Maybe she tried and could not get hold of you, maybe the family problems are very serious, or maybe – it's something else?"

"What else could it be?"

"Maybe she went away with a boyfriend at short notice and didn't want to give six months' notice on the rent so invented this story?"

"You mentioned she had some information for you, what information?"

Gary takes out his military ID to make the point, "Look I am a soldier and…"

"I know who you are, you're the guy she told me about."

"What did she tell you?"

"She told me she met a guy in the restaurant whose friend had been accused of drinking, I remember her telling me and Sophie about it."

"Who's Sophie?"

"She is another lodger, three of us live here. Sophie spends most of her time at her boyfriend's house. She keeps herself to herself."

"Did Katarzyna tell you more about why I wanted her help?"

"No, she started to tell us one morning, must have been the next day after you met her but I went away for a few days and was late. When I left she was telling Sophie. I told her to meet you anyway as she said you were cute! I have not seen her since. Would you like a drink?"

"I would love a cup of tea but I am in a bit of a rush. I have to get a train to Newcastle in 45 minutes. I also want to tell you why I needed to talk with Katarzyna so you understand what is going on. Do you have a toilet I could use?"

"Of course, it's the last door on the right over there. How do you like your tea?"

"White, two sugars, please. Thanks"

Gary takes the very short journey to the bathroom. It is obvious no men live here. The bathroom is tidy and has a large collection of perfumes and make up.

As Gary is washing his hands he notices different soaps and shampoos from a selection of hotels around Europe. He dries his hands and returns to the kitchen where the girl has made him a cup of tea.

"Thanks a lot, what's your name?"

"My name is Marta, I am also from Poland. What is your name?"

"My name is Gary. Your bathroom has so many different shampoos and soaps from so many hotels around Europe, do you travel a lot?"

"No, I am a doing Master's degree at University. Those are from Sophie – she is a stewardess."

Gary burns his mouth with hot tea and puts the cup down. Marta can see his body language has changed.

"Who does Sophie work for?"

Gary knows the answer before Marta utters it. "She works for a UK airline called JASP."

"And Katarzyna told Sophie about my visit to the restaurant after you left the other day?"

"That's what they were talking about when I left, you and whether she should agree to meet you."

"But you didn't hear why I wanted to meet her?"

"No more than I told you, something to do with a friend drinking."

"I see. Well, I think you'd better know the whole story. The reason I went to the restaurant was because the news reported that the crew of JASP flight 303 that crashed in Newcastle had allegedly been drinking in the restaurant where Katarzyna worked the night before the crash. To cut a long story short, I believed that the story that the restaurant owner gave to the media was not true. I told Katarzyna this and she said I might be right and hence I left her my mobile number for her to ring me. It was clear to me that she knew the story was not true. You see, my father died in the crash and a friend of mine, Jill, her sister also died in the crash and we want to know the truth."

Marta is seriously shocked.

"I never made the connection but now it's so clear. You were right. Katarzyna once told me she knew something she was not meant to know but never mentioned it again and said best I did not know. I think she was scared. I'll tell you something else now I know I can trust you. Wait here a moment."

Marta walks off to her room and returns a few minutes later with a HELLO! Magazine. She looks at Gary.

"I am scared. When those two men turned up and took all Katarzyna's stuff they were very organised and seemed too nice. They asked which was Katarzyna's room and said they were going to clear her stuff out for the landlord. I had the feeling if I asked too many questions it was going to be the wrong thing to do. I had lent Katarzyna an MP3 player to go jogging with and so I told them she had some of my stuff and could I get it back. They agreed and as they started to pack her stuff, I went to her drawer where she kept the MP3 player and took it back. I also took this."

Marta opens the magazine and drops a passport onto the work surface beside Gary's cup of tea.

Gary picks up the passport. It's a mauve European Community passport. He opens the passport and looks at the name and photograph of a smiling Katarzyna.

Marta is shuddering.

"You did the right thing to say nothing. You're also right that something is very wrong. When does Sophie get back?"

"She is away for at least a few more days. Why?"

Gary looks at his watch 20.20.

"Do you have to go?"

"Damn, I am going to miss my train. The next one is not until morning. Why? Because if Sophie informed JASP then it depends on how much Sophie is involved. She might have told one of her colleagues and word got around and she might not even realise the connection or implication or she might have become a player in all this. If so, you will be watched very carefully. Any behavioural change, anything that makes them think you might know something and you too will be... Shall we say, dealt with."

"What's going on?

"The JASP plane that crashed in Newcastle was most likely nothing to do with alcohol. It was, we believe, due to the crew breathing contaminated air. The contaminated air affected their thinking ability and their judgment without them even knowing and that caused the crash. The airline industry has known for over forty years about this problem, crews making mistakes, crews and passengers getting sick because of a design which is wrong."

Gary becomes more angry as he talks.

"The way they designed the way the air is taken from the engines and supplied to the passengers and crews is wrong. It will cost millions of dollars to resolve this problem so the aviation industry is covering it up. It's a fucking disgrace. It's corporate greed and the airlines and regulators don't give a shit!"

"This is amazing, how can it happen?"

"How can they fake pharmaceutical tests, sell cigarettes, pollute the environment, allow millions to starve every year? It's called money. The airline industry is no different. Money and profits will always be put before crew and passenger health or the impact on climate change."

"Are we safe?"

"If they think you are a risk you will be dealt with if they can. The secret is to make sure what you know is always shared with someone else, just in case you suddenly *disappear*, like Katarzyna.

You'll be safe tonight but if I was you I would get out of here before Sophie gets back unless you think you can stay 100% calm in her company. They will be watching you very carefully. There is a hearing coming up next week on this, I would go away until after the hearing. Then it will all be in the public domain. Then you will be safe."

"How do you know so much?"

"I am a paratrooper and do a lot of special forces type of stuff. Katarzyna's brother was a soldier, I think that is why she trusted me."

"Do you have anywhere to stay, do you want to stay here tonight? Have you eaten?"

"It's been a long day. I got up very early this morning and have been to Paris and back already investigating the plane crash. No, I haven't eaten more than a sandwich and some chocolate croissants this morning – even that seems like it was last week! Thanks, if I sleep on the sofa that would be great. I'll get up early and let myself out without troubling you."

"Let me cook you something to eat."

"Why did you not take the passport to the police?"

"Because if I did then I become part of all this. I also thought if Katarzyna came back suddenly I would give it to her. Now I know what is going on, what should I do?"

Gary's phone starts to ring. "Gary, it's Gordon Cooper. I have a meeting arranged for you tomorrow at 2000 in Warwickshire with two pilots at the..."

Gary cuts Gordon off.

"Gordon, Jill's place might have been broken into today. Her computer managed to walk out all by itself. Some other strange stuff is also going on. I fear we are being watched. I will ring you tomorrow afternoon from a payphone on your mobile number at exactly 1400. Can you be near a payphone just to be on the safe side? You can give me all the details then."

"Of course. I understand. I can tell you that you will be meeting two pilots currently flying the Boeing 757 for a UK airline. A man and a woman. We shall call them Patricia and Stephen. They will tell you what's going on today in the industry. Don't write anything down. They are very nervous but willing to talk off the record."

"OK Gordon, I'll be there. I am leaving London now and will be in touch."

Gary hangs up. "I've got to go – now."

Marta looks at him, clearly very scared.

"I don't like this. This is scaring me."

"That's why they do it. Look you have to trust me. I know how to play this game. I can't leave you here. It's not safe. You will have to come with me. I will take you with me to Newcastle and find you somewhere to stay until after the hearing. Then you will be safe."

"But what about my university course?"

"What about your life?"

Marta freezes in shock.

"Do you have any good friends on your course?"

Marta does not reply. Gary grabs her by each arm.

"Marta, this is a multi million dollar cover up. Everybody is expendable. Now listen to me. Do you have any good friends on your course?"

"Yes, yes I do."

"Ok text them now and say you are going away for a while with a new boyfriend and ask them to tell the university you are sick."

Marta does not respond.

"Marta, come on we need to go now. You must trust me."

Marta looks at Gary and then gets her mobile phone and starts texting.

Gary looks around the flat and puts his hands together, thinking of what to do next whilst Marta texts her friend.

"OK I have done it."

"Switch your phone off now and get a bag of clothes, your passport and Katarzyna's passport, credit cards and anything you need for a week or so."

"Why do I have to switch my phone off?"

"Why, because although it is unlikely, they may be following my moves through the phone company. If they wanted to they could know all the time where we were. I have

153

no idea how big this is. Better play safe. I am turning my phone off as well."

"Sorry, I will get my stuff. Give me 5 minutes. I trust you. What do we do now?"

"We will go straight to Heathrow airport and hire a car and get out of London."

Chapter 15

Late in the evening, Gary and Marta approach a car rental desk at Heathrow airport. The young representative greets them.

"Can I help you?"

"I would like to rent a car for a few days to drop off at Newcastle airport. Is that possible?"

"Certainly, but there will be an extra drop off charge as we will have to recover the car back to London. It will be quite expensive."

"That's fine. Family crisis, my grandmother is sick so that's what I will have to do. Here is my credit card and driving licence."

Marta indicates to Gary that while he is talking with the rental car representative that she will be back shortly and wonders off.

Whilst talking with the agent, Gary suddenly thinks that Marta has decided to run off, he turns and quickly looks at the ground. Her bag is there. His thought was unfounded and he continues to complete the paper work.

As the representative gives him the car keys, Marta returns with some hot drinks and a bag full of sandwiches. Walking to the rental car for the first time together, they temporarily forget about the scenario they find themselves in. Gary acknowledges the thoughtful gesture.

"Thanks for getting the sandwiches and drinks."

"Thanks for looking after me. I thought this stuff only happened in films!"

"I wish that was the case but we will be OK. I am either being extra cautious or paranoid, but better safe than sorry. Don't worry you'll be fine."

"Where are we going?" asks Marta.

"We are going to try and stay at the house of a friend of mine in the army. In fact my commanding officer, a guy called Paul Morrison, he lives in Oxfordshire. He sent me back to the UK when he saw I was pre-occupied with this contaminated air stuff. His wife should be at home as they have two lovely daughters, Sian and Sophie. I went to their wedding. She is like a second sister to me. She will let us stay."

At 0030, Gary and Marta walk towards the front door of a lovely Cotswold stone country house near Stonesfield in Oxfordshire. The infra red sensors trigger the outside floodlights to come on, illuminating both of them. Gary knocks hard on the front door. A short time later, a middle aged lady wearing a dressing gown unlocks and opens the front door after seeing who is there.

"Lizzie, I am very sorry to trouble you at such a ridiculous time of night."

"Gary, what on earth are you doing here at this time of the night and who is this girl?"

"Lizzie, this is Marta. I would not be here if I did not need your help. I don't know if you have spoken with Paul recently but he sent me back from Canada because he knew my mind was somewhere else."

Lizzie beckons them both to enter the house and relocks the front door.

Lizzie, Gary and Marta sit around the kitchen table in a large well appointed country house kitchen, with three empty cups of hot chocolate. The clock displays 0130, an hour has past since their arrival. Lizzie leans back into her chair and looks at Marta and then Gary.

"Bloody hell Gary, that is one hell of a story. I think if you went to the police with that one they would send you on a special holiday with the men in white coats! But after all you and

Paul have been through in the army, nothing would surprise me."

Marta agrees "Last week I was a student and now I am part of a multi million dollar conspiracy story, as a fugitive on the run. It just seems so crazy that all this is because the airline industry failed to filter the air passengers and crews breathe in the first place. Mind you if the pilot had never mentioned the dirty socks thing on the voice recorder and you had not experienced the smells on your flight to Canada and put it together with Jill, we would not be here now."

"Not quite" replies Gary. "It's only because of all the evidence that had been assembled for over forty years by others I was able to make the link. People have been complaining about this for fifty years!"

Lizzie stands up, "The two rooms in the annex are made up. Gary will show you where that is. Make yourself at home. I have to get up at 0700 to get the kids off to school. Sleep as long as you want."

"Lizzie, thanks for your help," replies Gary as he stands up.

Marta takes the cups to the sink and the gives Gary a hug.

"What you are doing with Jill is really good. It's great to be part of something so important."

"Thanks. Let me show you where the rooms are."

At 1400 Gordon Cooper's mobile phone starts to ring. He is standing in the high street in Storrington beside a telephone box.

He answers, "Gordon, it's Gary what number are you on?"

Gary writes down the number and calls the pay phone which Gordon quickly answers.

"Gary, how is it going?"

"Well, Gordon, part of me thinks perhaps it's all one string of coincidences and I am being paranoid. The other part knows what *could* be going on and assumes the worst case scenario."

"Best to play safe. It will become very clear soon one way of the other. Jill rang this morning asking if I knew where you were as you never arrived home. I told her I thought you would be back late tonight or early tomorrow morning and not to worry."

"Thanks Gordon, I forgot to tell her. That's great. So what's the deal for this evening?"

"Right, the two pilots will meet you in the Dog and Owl Pub in Snitterfield, Warwickshire at 19.00. The village of Snitterfield lies in the heart of Warwickshire and is situated between Warwick and Stratford-upon-Avon on the A46. The two pilots currently both fly the Boeing 757 for a UK operator but not JASP. They will give you a great insight into what is happening today in the industry. I know they are having problems as my contact said they were taking an active interest in the issue. They are in their 30s, I am told. She is about five foot eight and he is five foot ten. They both work for the same company. As I said last night, don't write anything down. Don't scare them off."

Gary looks across the street towards Marta in the car. She is looking at him and gives him an inquisitive thumbs up, to which he responds with a thumbs up sign. "Gordon, that's great. Thanks for organising that."

"You're welcome. I spent years of my life doing what you are doing. I am glad reinforcements finally arrived!"

Gary hangs up and walks back to the car.

Marta opens Gary's door for him.

"It's on for tonight at 19.00. We are meeting two pilots in a pub about 50 miles from here. Then we will drive up to Newcastle. That will be another 200 to 250 miles. That should get us in to Newcastle in the early hours but that's OK."

Gary pauses while he thinks for a while and carries on talking to Marta, "I don't think I will ring Jill just in case. What we should do is get to the pub by five and eat. That way we will blend in more. Is that OK with you?"

"Sure," replies Marta with a smile. "Why don't we go to the area now and have a drink somewhere to fill in time till five?"

"Why not?"

Gary looks at the road map for a few minutes and starts the engine in the small hatchback car for the drive to Snitterfield

Having finished their meal at the Dog and Owl Pub in Snitterfield, Gary and Marta survey the bar for the two pilots. At five to seven a couple walk into the busy pub, fitting the description given by Gordon on the phone. Gary gets up and walks over to them.

"Hi, are you Patricia and Stephen?"

Patricia, an attractive brunette, smiles "You must be Gary."

"That's right."

Gary shakes hands with Patricia and Stephen and invites them to join him and Marta.

"I have a table over here. I am with a girl called Marta. We arrived earlier and got something to eat."

All four sit at the table where Marta and Gary have been eating and Marta asks Patricia and Stephen what they would like to drink and goes to bar to get their order. Meanwhile Gary fills them in with all he knows on the issue. Marta has got another round of drinks in before Gary has completed telling them his story.

Stephen, a slightly overweight man with glasses, is taken aback by Gary's knowledge.

"For someone who only started investigating these matters recently you have covered a lot of ground. You have taught me a lot of things I never knew."

"Me, too," adds Patricia.

"Let us tell you what is going on in the industry today," volunteers Stephen, looking at Marta and Gary.

"As you correctly said, most crews don't report contaminated air events and even if we do, the airline don't take it seriously. Unless they see a problem with the engine during a visual inspection, engineers are simply instructed to tell us to *please report further* i.e. we are not interested. Our airline even issued a notice to all pilots saying not to report fumes and that they were normal! Did the regulators do anything? Of course not. The airlines and the regulator sleep in the same bed. Do the unions do anything? Well, the main pilot union does nothing. They see it as Pandora's box. Best not take the lid off it. The other union is more pro-active but their complaints fall on deaf ears at a governmental level. If you complain you get seriously hassled by the company. You can imagine I am sure, but let me give you two good examples."

Stephen takes a mouthful from his pint of Erdinger Weissbier before continuing. "One of our Captains complained about the fumes and was asked if he wanted to see the company doctor. Another pilot who complained was taken into the office and told if he complained the airline would get shut down and was that what he wanted, did he want his job, why was he the only person reporting and perhaps he was psychosomatic as most crews never complained. Complete bullshit as many others have complained but everyone gets the message to wind their necks in."

Patricia carries on while Stephen takes another mouthful of beer. Gary just listens.

"The airline tell us this bullshit that you can soak in a bath of oil and it's harmless, the CAA say its all OK, the government say it's OK and what happens is pilots fly around and make mistakes?"

Patricia looks at Stephen and pauses.

"Its OK Patricia tell them" says Stephen.

"Both of us on different flights have made serious errors which we can't tell anyone about. If we tell the airline we get fired. If we tell the CAA that's the same as telling the airline and if we do a confidential report well that's not secure and nothing gets done anyway. The type of mistakes we are making is like arriving at 1,500 feet on approach for landing and doing the landing checklist only to find we have still not lowered the under carriage and the flaps are still at 15, an intermediate flap setting. We use flap 30 for landing. Another mistake I made was to get too low without lowering the under carriage and getting a Ground Proximity Warning telling us we had screwed up, in a nutshell. So if we are making mistakes and sitting here and telling you, think of what else is going on. Think of what may have happened to JASP 303."

Stephen carries on from where Patricia left of. "These events, of course, don't happen on every flight but they are occurring. Many crews who have written up contaminated air events in any UK airline become totally despondent when they see that the regulator, the CAA, has the bloody cheek to say the events reported are not *safety of flight* issues! The CAA say we can't go to work with any alcohol in our blood but are happy for us to fly around being pumped full of contaminated air and the host of toxic chemicals we breath in every day at work. The books say we should use oxygen *if* we suspect the air is contaminated and we should, but if you do, you'll get a lot of hassle. They say things like, 'How did you know the air was contaminated?' or 'How do you know what you are breathing is hazardous?' It's so crazy. Yet, if you had some other technical defect such as an engine malfunction and shut the engine down, nobody would say a thing! Nobody would question you. The industry is shit scared of the contaminated air problem. Some say it's only the older aircraft like the BAe 146, MD80 or Boeing 757 that have the problem but I have found events occurring on every aircraft type, just some are worse than others."

Stephen takes out a large hard back reference manual entitled the Aviation Contaminated Air Reference Manual and turns to the appendices and carries on.

"Have you seen this newly published book?"

Gary recognises the title. "Yes briefly in Paris yesterday, I have been told to get hold of a copy."

"You should. This reference manual has all the facts to show anyone this is not fiction but fact. Not just fact, because really what the industry is doing is also 'criminal' in my opinion. It has been published by one of two girls who got the Australian Senate investigation going in 1999, Susan Michaelis. In the appendices there is a specific appendix with all the contaminated air events the editor had sourced in the UK, as well as others from other countries. In the UK, there are over a 1000 events. Anybody with half a brain who reads the data can see that the airlines and regulator are totally guilty of wilful misconduct."

For the next twenty minutes, Gary and Marta are mesmerised by the data in front of them. Pages and pages of events where crews were reporting contaminated air events and nothing much was done.

"I had no idea it was that big! I had found some events and I know the Australians investigated these things in their Senate but it's absurd nothing is done with all this data," says Gary looking at Stephen, Patricia and Marta.

Patricia leans forward and lowers her voice. "If I am really honest, what is really going on here is that many pilots are selfish and money driven and don't have the balls to stand up for what is right and their own health. Many pilots tell me how they go home with headaches, wake up with nausea, have heart palpitations, tingling in their arms or legs after the exposures and so forth but they still do nothing. They don't even tell their aviation doctor when they renew their medical certificate. We have to fill in a CAA form which asks us if we have had any injuries since our last medical or something like that. I always write down I have had exposures to contaminated air but the medical doctor (and don't forget they are CAA appointed) never asks me anything about these exposures. It's the taboo subject!"

Gary and Marta have sat quietly for some time listening to news from the front line. News of what is actually going on in the aviation industry.

"Your story seems to be the same the world over. It makes me so angry that the government who should look after the public always focus on industry better interests. As crews can't complain for fear of losing their jobs, what we really need to see happen is to have passengers complain every time they smell any form of contaminated air on an aircraft. They complain if they have no meal or if the flight is delayed. Now they need to complain that the air they breathe is hazardous when it is contaminated. This would force the airline industry to take full details of the event and explain what chemicals passengers have been exposed to. This would become such a nightmare for the airlines, only then would the airlines do what they should have done forty years ago and fit filters to protect crews and the travelling public. Not because they care but because its cheaper than the paperwork and aircraft down time created by complaining passengers."

Patricia and Stephen nod in acknowledgment to Gary's suggestion and strategy.

"Filters is the obvious solution especially as an engineer told me they are available today! If you can raise the issue and get justice at the JASP 303 hearing that would be a victory for all crews."

"I will try," replies Gary.

"I appreciate you coming along and being honest about the state of affairs of the airline industry. I will keep this all very confidential. When I hear you guys talking so openly and honestly it makes the fight even more worthwhile. My dad is dead and will never come back, but now I know that crews are being intimidated and are not free to report contaminated air events freely for fear of recrimination, then that makes me want to fight harder. What you told me tonight was the same story in Paris and in Australia. Hopefully, one day things will improve."

Marta who has been quiet most of the evening makes an interesting comment showing she has learnt a lot about the issue. "I am only a Master's student but surely you as crews are entitled to a safe working environment. Also even if you can't prove 100% which chemicals and in what concentrations are causing these effects, surely the precautionary principle should be applied."

Patricia agrees "You're totally correct but the CAA are the enforcing agency and as we said they are funded by the airlines so nothing gets enforced. The UK Department of Transport even got the so called 'independent' Committee on Toxicity to look at these issues. I applied to attend their meetings but was not allowed to attend. My investigations have revealed that their meetings are not open, you can't speak unless asked to speak, no media or filming is allowed and the minutes are not a transcript from an electronic recording of events but *their* version of what was said. The Government is not trying to protect crews and the public but to make sure industry interests are protected. We all know it's happening and it's real but it's just ignored and part of the job. Stephen and I have applications with other airlines on less problematic aircraft to get out of this nightmare. But why should we have to move house and change employer because the regulator doesn't do its job properly!"

"I hope one day this will be resolved," smiles Marta as she looks at Patricia.

Patricia and Stephen stand up. "It was great meeting you both. Have a safe drive to Newcastle and the very best of luck with your fight for justice."

Patricia and Stephen walk out to the car park with Marta and Gary. The sky is awash with stars. It's a very cold night and their breath can be seen.

Gary turns towards Patricia and Stephen, "If I was you guys I would make sure you document everything. Take pictures of the aircraft technical log books and have a good paper trail... Just in case."

Patricia and Stephen both agree the suggestion has merit.

Before they all go their own way, Patricia makes a final comment, "Do you know why I try to sort this out? It's not so much for my health but for the passengers who get exposed. They buy a ticket and they expect and deserve to be protected from these chemical exposures. It's only because they buy a ticket in the first place that I have a job! Anyway, take care and keep in touch."

Gary and Marta sit still in their car in the pub car park. Gary looks at Marta

"When you meet people like that it reminds me that this is really worth fighting for. Not like some of the places I go as a soldier for some hidden political agenda.

Marta who has been very quiet all night looks sideways at Gary.

"Come over here a minute."

Gary does not understand what she means.

She leans forward and kisses Gary on the cheek.

"I really admire you, Gary, for what you are doing."

Chapter 16

After ringing the door bell three times Jill pounds on Gary's door with both fists. It is enough to attract the neighbours' attention. The next door neighbour opens her lace curtains at the windows briefly to see what is going on. Shortly afterwards, an old man opens his front door and cranes his neck to catch a glimpse of who is raising the racket. Jill smiles and waves at him. The old man grumbles something and retreats back into his house. Eventually, Gary opens the door just wearing a pair of jeans. He is unshaven and his face is swollen with sleep.

"Rise and shine, soldier, it's another glorious day in the corps. Are you going to let me in, then, or start selling tickets to the neighbours?"

Gary half smiles. "What time is it?"

"It's nearly afternoon but not quite, it's five to twelve. Are you planning on leaving me out here to freeze until it's officially afternoon? Where the hell have you been for the last few days?"

Gary's puffy eyelids click open. "Wooh, I was sleeping like a log, guess it all caught up with me. Come in, make yourself at home. I'll be down sharpish."

Halfway up the stairs, he shouts down, "The kettle is in the kitchen."

"Yes, Sir!"

Still fighting off the sleep, Gary showers, shaves and gets dressed. Downstairs, Jill looks relaxed on the sofa, sipping a mugful of steaming tea, leafing through one of his car magazines, "Morning, soldier, is one awake now? I made you a cup of tea."

Gary looks at the table, where another mug of milky tea is beckoning. "Thanks a lot, Private!"

"I'll private you, Sergeant, what type of outfit do you think we are? Part time?"

Gary yawns. His brain is not quite in gear yet. He picks up the cup of tea and takes a slurp. He puts the mug back down on the table and attempts a smile. "I was so tired when I got home this morning. Absolutely dead beat. My mind was going a thousand miles an hour! I just walked up the stairs when I got home and was out like a light."

Jill's attention is caught by the sound of creaking timber under footsteps. Her lips part in disbelief as she watches a female stranger walk down the stairs.

"Jill, this is Marta. Marta, this is Jill."

Jill can't help noticing how at home the female stranger looks in Gary's home.

"It's so nice to meet you Jill, Gary has been telling me a lot about you" says Marta with a kind smile.

Jill is lost for words.

"Jill, there is so much to tell you. Marta shared a flat with the waitress in the restaurant. Anyway, we have all day to fill you in on what's been going on. You can trust Marta she knows the whole story."

Gary sits down. "Marta please take a seat. Jill was about to tell me all her news."

Jill has lost some of her excitement which Gary tries to rekindle.

"You seem very lively today. We have so much to tell you but let's hear all your news first. Did you get hold of Professor Ashington?"

Jill smiles knowingly but the light has gone from her face.

After hearing the realities of the problem last night, Gary needs to hear good news, "OK, let's hear it, that smile tells me I am going to like this bit. Let's hope it's better than what happened to me, last night!"

"Gary, I have so much great and absolutely fascinating news! As they say, are you sitting comfortably?"

Gary sits back in the chair with his cup of tea, "Hit me!"

Jill leans forward, her elbows on her knees. She is wary of Marta's stare. "First of all, night before last, after you rang me, Nicola Matthews from the cabin crew union called me and said I might want to talk with a girl in the USA called Judith Murawski. Now Judith is an Industrial Hygienist for the Association of Flight Attendants in the US. The Association of Flight Attendants have something like 100,000 members and unlike Carol's union they seem to be real fighters. Anyway, I get on the phone and she fills me in for over two hours on what has been happening in the US."

"She sounds like an amazing girl," injects Gary.

Jill continues, "After talking with Judith I rang Professor Ashington, last night. What a kind man, a real genius. Get this – when Gordon Cooper was getting unions and groups to fund the work back in 2005, Carol's union never took part, no surprises there but many unions did. Well they did it, they were able to take blood from a crew or passenger within a few weeks of flying on an aircraft suspected of being exposed to tricresyl phosphate and not only prove they were exposed – as Gordon outlined the other day – but also the time of exposure just as we were told. Accurate to more or less four hours. Before they could use the test they had to get it published in a peer reviewed journal which was very easy. However, and this is the best bit, during the review process it all got hijacked by oil manufacturer *friendlies*, shall we say. This meant the process got stalled so they tried to get it published in another journal and then the journals started fighting and time just ticked by. One peer review team claimed it was junk science and putting the name of the oil companies into bad light as there was no evidence to say the oils were toxic. Basically, all the usual spin like the UK Government,

CAA and others did when they used to focus solely on OPIDN as marker of toxicity."

Gary interrupts, "Just remind me of the OPIDN bit."

"No worries, it gets confusing but that is what they rely on to keep people in the dark. The CAA and Government agencies along with the oil companies considered that the only toxic effect of exposure to tricresyl phosphate is a medical condition called 'Organophosphate Induced Delayed Neuropathy' or 'OPIDN' for short. This was the medical condition diagnosed during the Ginger Jake epidemic in the USA during the Prohibition when they drank stuff that had been mixed with one of the tricresyl phosphate chemicals. OPIDN has a severe pathology. Now crews, doctors and scientists have been telling governments for years that OPIDN is not a suitable indicator of toxicity with the exposures being encountered on aircraft. Why? Because crews don't complain of OPIDN symptoms. Industry and the regulators always conveniently, or most likely deliberately, forget to mention or even discuss the other toxicological effects of exposure to tricresyl phosphate, not to mention the synergistic effects of breathing in the cocktail of chemicals present during these contaminated air events. Chemicals like phosphorous oxides, carbon monoxide and so forth. What is being seen in crews is different to OPIDN. For years, chronic exposure to organophosphates has been associated with a range of neurological and neuropsychological effects. Such symptoms have been defined as 'Chronic Organophosphate Neuropsychological Disorder' (COPIND) or 'Organophosphorus Ester-Induced Chronic Neurotoxicity' (OPICN), which leads to long term neurological and neurobehavioural deficits. In a nutshell, the airline industry focuses on OPIDN and nothing else. They totally ignore COPIND or OPICN. In simplistic terms, what they are saying is if you have no visual signs of damage then they don't care. The oil manufacturers used to feed the test chickens orally the engine

169

oils and look for OPIDN and assume that was a good and safe test. It's crazy, how can the chicken tell you it can't see straight or if its short term memory is being affected. Industry testing was little more than a paperwork exercise to fool the masses. How can you compare drinking the oil with inhaling the heated or pyrolised oil product in flight? Gary they never did any inhalation testing!"

"That's unreal."

"Anyway, I digress. So the oil companies influenced this chaotic peer review problem. Eventually, a judge rules that one of the publishers was free to publish, the blood test got through the peer review process and the test could be used, but that took a lot of time. By then it seems everyone moved on, left the industry like Gordon, ran out of money or forgot about it. The good news is the article got published last year, the test exists and Professor Ashington is going to do it on Carol's plasma!"

Gary is now fully awake and smiling. "That's fantastic, when? We are seriously running out of time. We need the results by Monday!"

Jill smiles and says nothing. It's just her and Gary again. Marta, for that moment, has ceased to exist.

"OK, let's have the next part!"

"Well, Professor Ashington is a wise old owl; after all the hassles of the peer review process he suggested what I needed to do was to take the plasma to a lawyer and get them to send it. This way he can send the results back to the lawyer and nobody can complain about the due process."

Gary interrupts again, keen to move things forward, "That's great, we need a lawyer in Newcastle, who shall we use?"

Jill smiles again and says nothing.

Gary sits back again and invites Jill to carry on, "There's that smile again, I better stop interrupting you."

Jill carries on, "Well, whilst soldier boy has been sightseeing for two days and catching up on his beauty sleep, GI Jill was on the case. I rang the lawyer, Mr Gloyer who dealt with my dad's death years back, he is a really nice guy and honest as a day is long in my eyes, a fantastic lawyer. I wasn't going to ring the union lawyers as they are clearly not interested, given how they have dealt with the crews we know about who have been affected in the past. I went around and saw Mr Gloyer and gave him a statement about how I got the blood. He said this is important so nobody can say I stole it, he wants to be able to argue that I was doing a public spirited thing, in the interests of public health and so forth. Professor Ashington also suggested and Mr Gloyer agreed, that he should send the unused blood back to ensure anyone can DNA test the blood to prove it was my sister's blood, very clever. We got a courier over at 10.30 and they took the box and the plasma. It's on its way to Canada. If all goes to plan the results will be back with the lawyers on Friday. Am I good or what?"

Gary stands up and goes over to Jill and gives her a big hug, "Jill you should have been in the army, you're a gem."

"Thanks, Gary, so are you. Anyway there's more."

He sits down beside Jill, "The lawyer said it would be a good idea to go to the media and see if they want to hear our side of the story for the weekend papers. What do you think?"

"It's a good idea but I can't because of my job but you should, Carol was your sister."

"We can only give it a try. Before we do that let's catch up on your news…"

Gary brings Jill up to speed with his trip to Paris, the restaurant, explains how Marta joined the story and their trip to Warwickshire the night before. His home phone starts to ring.

Gary answers. "Hey, Phil. What's the news?"

He holds up his crossed fingers for Jill and Marta to see.

"Gary, it's a no goer buddy, I am really sorry. The guys monitor all VHF and UHF frequencies using key words and random searches. After a week or so they dump the data because they should not be really doing it anyway, if you get my drift. It's really interesting how they do it. Obviously, words like 'explosives' or 'Semtex' will trigger a warning to listen to that communication but also other key words which would be out of place and used by terrorists. Anyway, the sad news is that they probably recorded anything that might have been said but don't have it anymore. The other thing that my contact said, was he was surprised nobody had come and asked before if they were doing a proper investigation. As for your other request that's a no goer either. Anyway sorry buddy, and good luck with the hearing. By the way, do you remember Eddie Brown from Brighton?"

"Yeah, how is he?"

"Apparently he was killed in a motorbike accident recently. Great shame."

Gary sounds very disappointed but grateful for the news, "I agree it's a terrible loss. OK, Phil, I appreciate what you have done. I really do. Sorry to have wasted your time. Cheers."

Gary hangs up and says nothing for a few seconds. Jill and Marta wait patiently. They see that Gary is in deep thought.

Gary looks up. "That was my army buddy. This is real serious shit. He just gave me a coded message that my phone might be tapped. We need to go and get new phones later today."

After they have had some very late breakfast, Jill starts ringing the papers on the list she has printed out previously.

Gary and Marta watch her as she goes through the numbers, "Hi this is Jill Parker. My sister was the co-pilot on flight JASP 303 that had the accident in Newcastle in January. I have some information which may show that it was not the crew error being reported but actually crew error due to technical problems with the aircraft... I see... OK. Thanks for your time."

Call after call has the same outcome. Nobody is interested. Some are rude and echo the same response: 'the airline industry would not try and cover something like that up, it's old news and you have no proof'.

Jill puts the phone down after her sixth call and looks at Gary. "They are not interested, more interested in the celebrity marriages than real news. I bet they don't want to upset those who advertise with them as well. Wait till we prove it and then they come crawling to us for the story."

"One step at a time. Look, we have been on the go for ages with contaminated air. The blood is on its way to Canada, it will be there soon so why don't we all go out for the rest of the afternoon and relax as best we can?"

Marta says, "I was thinking, I have a very good friend from my home town who works here in Newcastle. Why don't we find her and I can stay there with her and see the sights which I am sure you have seen a hundred times, you can get new phones and then you can contact me and catch up whenever it suits."

Gary looks at Jill, who seems happy at the thought of Marta not staying in Gary's house.

"You should have a look around. Let's find your friend and get new phones and have a laugh. Come on let's go. I'll drive."

"OK, just a second let me get my bag upstairs."

Jill whispers in Gary's ear and then winks at him, "I thought you only had one bed upstairs.

"Gary whispers back in Jill's ear with a grin, "You're right, but I also have a sleeping bag in my spare room that you know is my office!"

Marta comes back downstairs with her bag.

Jill grabs Gary by the hand to tug him along and drags him out of his house. Marta joins in the fun and takes Gary's other hand.

Chapter 17

Gary pulls apart the curtains in his bedroom and looks over the housing estate he lives in. It is certainly a pleasant morning with Spring trying to push its way into Newcastle but he knows it will not last. The weather can change very quickly in Northern England at this time of the year. Gary picks up his new mobile phone he bought the day before and his old mobile phone and sees that each has a new message.

One is from Jill and reads, 'Thanks for a great day out, after all we have been through it was nice to have a laugh again. Thanks a lot. Jill.'

After they had found Marta's friend and purchased new phones, Gary and Jill forgot for an evening all about the contaminated air issues which have become a daily part of their life. For an afternoon, they lived the life that most live, a life free from involvement in the evil aspects of corporate and governmental failings in the aviation industry and other corporate cover ups. They had even been out for an exquisite Italian meal together and enjoyed some Australian Rosemount wine. Gary then looks at the message on his old phone and this one is a surprise. It is from Dr Fedorova and simply reads, 'Hi Gary, I hope you are well. I have emailed you some good news (I hope), please ring me. Valentina x' Gary smiles, not just because of what the news could be but at the 'x' at the end of the message. He heads swiftly to his spare bedroom where his computer is running to check his e-mails and find out what the good news is.

He clicks on the message and starts to read. 'Hi Gary. I hope all is well in the life of a paratrooper. Since you walked into my office and told me about the contaminated air issues on commercial aircraft and the sadness of you losing your father in the aircraft crash, I have been unable to focus on anything else but this issue. I have been doing a lot of private research and I hope it will be helpful to you and to those researching these matters. Where shall I begin? Well, first of all, I looked for all the peer reviewed papers I could find which have been published to support the view that inhaling pyrolised or heated synthetic jet engine oils is safe and there aren't any! So how they can say it's safe is beyond me. Next, I looked for papers which support the view that drinking cold synthetic jet engine oils is safe and I found a few of these but they are all written by employees or contractors of the oil manufacturers and they all look at the wrong end point of exposure. They basically use hens to see how much needs to be drunk to cause OPIDN or neuropathy, a very serious clinical condition and then assume hens and humans are the nearly the same and that's it. It's complete nonsense. A hen cannot tell you if it has a headache or is having cognitive or respiratory problems and the papers don't even start to look at that. What is important in my view is to see what effect inhaling these heated oils would have on test animals or human gene expression in the brain and that's where I came up with some very interesting news. In 2007, research was done showing that exposure to very low levels of tricresyl phosphate would seriously affect gene expression in the brain. So when the oil manufacturers say all is well it's a bit like an alcohol manufacturer saying if person drinks 10 units and does not die it's not harmful, as we both know 10 units would impair most people and repeated drinking will also damage the body. It's all about using the correct end point or measure of impact or effect. The oil manufacturers use an end point which is totally irrelevant to then claim the product is safe. It's a shock to me that the regulatory agencies just turn a blind eye. Adaquate product safety testing has never been carried out so how can they say the product is safe without doing heated engine oil inhalation testing? Agencies like NIOSH in the US are well known to be under-funded and seem to naively to think that industry will always be honest. I guess they are kept under-funded by Government to ensure there is no one to properly police industry and detract from industry keeping their share holders happy.

The next piece of good news is that I sent one of my undergraduates off on a day out and she flew on four different aircraft types but not on a Boeing 757 and did swab tests of the passenger walls. She said she was sick of being a passenger by the end of the day but it was a very worthwhile exercise. Basically, she flew as a regular passenger and took some headset cleaning wipes that pilots use to clean their headsets and cleaned a 5 cm square patch of the passenger cabin wall on each flight and sealed it in a plastic container and brought it back to the lab were we had them all analysed the same day. The samples were sent for GC-MS analysis. Tricresyl phosphate was determined on all wipes. In addition, triphenylphosphate (TPP) was determined in all samples, while tributylphosphate was determined on all but two wipes. In basic terms it proves the walls of the commercial aircraft tested are contaminated with three different Organophosphates, tricresyl phosphate, triphenylphosphate and tributylphosphate. Tributylphosphate comes from hydraulic fluids used on commercial aircraft. We can't tell how much was in the air but we can tell the walls are contaminated and passengers are being exposed to known neurotoxins. When I searched the net I found that this work had previously been done in Boeing 757 and BAe146 cockpits and presented at a union conference in London in 2005 by a Professor Van Netten but it seems nobody did anything with the data which is really criminal in my view. Let me know who I should send the swab sample analysis information to and I will be happy to do so or I'll bring it over and take you up on your offer to show me around the sights of Newcastle! If you want to talk with me about the information then call me on my mobile number which is at the bottom of this email. Ring anytime. Take care. Valentina. x.'

Gary picks up his phone and rings Jill straight away,
"Morning Gary, thanks for yesterday. What's the news?"
"I have had an e-mail from Valentina."
"Valentina is it, used to be Dr Fedorova. Are you sure I got the full story? Let me guess she looks like a model and has the brains of a main frame computer?"

Gary is a bit embarrassed and a bit lost for words, "Well, she's very attractive and I guess she is fairly smart but let's stay focused. She emailed me with some really interesting data. They have found organophosphates on the walls of four different aircraft in Canada in the last few days. Look, rather than read it out, how about I print it out and come over to your place at tea time and maybe then we will hear from Professor Ashington?"

"That's a good idea. See you around five. Mum will be here as well to talk about Monday."

"OK, see you later."

Jill hangs up and her phone rings nearly instantaneously.

It is her mother. "Hello, Darling, is it still on for tea at yours later?"

"Hi Mum, of course it is, and Gary will be popping over as well. How are you today?"

"I am fine. I got a letter yesterday about the hearing on Monday. It starts at 10 and it tells you how the hearing day will proceed and how people can give any information should they wish to and so on. Shall I bring it round?"

Jill quickly thinks about Monday and realises she needs to know as soon as possible how the day will proceed, "That's a great idea Mum, yeah bring it with you. See you later."

Jill hangs up and rings Mr Gloyer, the solicitor, "Sorry to trouble you, my mum spoke with me today about the hearing on

Monday. She has received a letter explaining the procedures. If Professor Ashington was to find something or even if he doesn't, the whole Lebanese restaurant story needs to be brought up, do you need to contact anyone about the procedures of the day?"

Mr Gloyer reassures her. "I thought about this and we have obtained the information so don't worry, we can put forward any view or information we may have. This will not be like the other gagged government COT meetings I told you about where the public is not allowed to talk. As soon as you hear anything from Professor Ashington give me a call, you have my mobile number. Don't worry, I will make sure they listen to us."

"Thanks, Mr Gloyer – should have guessed you would be one step ahead. Of course, as soon as I hear from Professor Ashington I will call you."

Jill turns her attention to her new computer and types JASP 303 into a search engine to get an idea of how the media are covering the event. There is not a lot of coverage, mostly old news. Just like the media she contacted the day before they have moved on to new stories, new scandals but she knows that on Monday they will be there again. Hopefully, she will have something to focus their minds on. She is constantly thinking of what Professor Ashington will find to the point she is tired from lack of sleep and maybe the residual sides of drinking too much the night before. She closes the search engine but then opens it up again. Her mind has given her a new task to do, one she does with a naughty grin on her face. Into the search engine she types 'Dr Valentina Fedorova, Winnipeg'. The first link takes her to her biography page with a picture. Her smile fades. "pretty," she mutters to herself. She closes the browser and sits on the couch to rest some more. In a very short period of time she falls asleep.

Felicity opens Jill's door.
"Hello Gary, Jill is busy in the kitchen. Please come in."

"Hello Mrs Parker, nice to meet you again."

Gary takes his jacket off and Felicity sits down again in the living room where the TV is on in the background.

Gary walks into the kitchen, "Hi Jill, now that smells nice, what you up to?"

"Well, after we spoke I got some more sleep and then I decided to bake us all a chocolate cake to eat. Professor Ashington rang!"

Gary's eyes light up, "And?"

"He just rang to say the package had arrived, all OK and he was on the case. I pointed out that we needed to know as soon as possible and he said he would do what he could but realistically even if the sample is positive, he will then need to write a report. He said he would not be ready to send the results back until tomorrow. Now that means that they will not arrive till Monday morning."

Gary is looking very concerned, so she reassures him, "It's still OK, I rang Mr Gloyer who said that would be OK as all we needed was to present the findings at the hearing. Not ideal, but we have little choice. At least we will know what the results are before and if he finds nothing then it does not matter anyway."

Gary is looking more relaxed, "As you say, it's not ideal but the important thing is that we will know what the results are and Mr Gloyer, if the results are positive, can get things ready tactically in his mind. What happens if they don't arrive on Monday?"

"Well, that would not be good but the courier who I also rang said delivery was 99.9% certain for Monday. When he told me that, I started thinking about that Tom Hanks movie where the cargo plane crashes and he gets stuck on a deserted island with all sorts of useless packages. I also asked Mr Gloyer about just using the data that Professor Ashington could just email us. He said the coroner will not accept it unless it has an original signature and some of the blood comes back to prove that Professor Ashington actually tested Carol's blood."

Gary is inspecting the cooking, "OK, well at least as you say we will spend the weekend knowing what the results are. What if they are positive or negative? Have you been thinking about how you will feel?"

Jill does not reply. Gary puts his hand on her shoulder. "What about your mum – have you told her?"

Jill gives Gary a hug and then starts to cut the cake she baked earlier, "I have not told Mum anything as I thought it best to see what Professor Ashington says first. As for the positive or negative results, well, there is another question as well which I have been thinking about. How do we know it was Carol's plasma I actually sent? What if the person who got to her records was smarter than we thought and had already swapped the blood? What if it is Carol's plasma we sent but it's not usable for some reason? You see, there are so many questions that we have no control over. Let's just wait and see what Professor Ashington says. I know her blood group is A negative so let's hope the plasma we sent was hers. Anyway, tell me about the news your personal Doctor sent you?"

Gary blushes. "Jill, she is a nice girl and obviously has a big heart and high values of right and wrong to investigate these things for us at her expense, but I have only met her once. Anyway, let me show you what she e-mailed me."

He hands her the e-mail.

"Shall I take this all through to your mum in the living room?" asks Gary.

Jill takes a while to respond as she focuses on the e-mail. "Oh yes, thanks, Gary."

He takes the pot of tea, the cake and cups through to the living room on a big tray. Jill follows him whilst still reading. Gary sets the tray down in the living room on the table in front of the television.

"There you are, Mrs Parker, tea and cake."

Jill's mother smiles at Gary, "Jill knows that Napoleon was right, an army marches on its stomach and especially a young soldier like you."

Jill sits down and puts down the printed email Gary gave her and looks at him, "This information that your Doctor has sent you is priceless, she wants to know what to do with the data. I think I should ring Mr Gloyer and ask him, what do you think?"

"That's a great idea" replies Gary as he starts to eat some of the cake and sits back in a very relaxed manner.

"Jill, don't tell him about Marta, just in case.

"OK."

Jill stands up, "I will ring him straight away before he leaves the office and see what he thinks. Try and leave me some cake!"

She smiles and goes to the kitchen and dials Mr Gloyer's number, "Hi Mr Gloyer, it's Jill again. Sorry to trouble you."

"That's fine, Jill, do you have any news?"

"Nothing from Professor Ashington yet, Mr Gloyer, but a new development has occurred. My friend Gary Bamford who I told you about, well he met a scientist in Canada who has done some private research and found that the internal walls of four different passenger aircraft were all covered in neurotoxins from the engine oils and hydraulic fluids. She has asked Gary what she should do with the data and hence the call. What do you think?"

"Well, it depends on what Professor Ashington turns up, if he finds nothing then its fairly irrelevant to Monday but obviously massively relevant to the travelling public. If he finds something then in an ideal way if she gave evidence on Monday it would be very significant but if she lives in Canada I assume that would be unlikely. She could fax my office but it lacks the punch of delivering the data at the hearing personally. People like to see the person, ideally. For that matter, if Professor Ashington was there as well that would help but we know that is not going to be possible as his wife is poorly and he is taking her on a cruise for three weeks on Saturday. If Professor Ashington finds something there would be no harm in asking her to attend and my firm would happily sponsor her costs in Newcastle. Let's see what he finds."

"Mr Gloyer, that's very kind of you and your firm. I will tell Gary and call you as soon as I hear from Professor Ashington."

Gary is equally pleased with the outcome, "That is really generous of him, whether she would come or not is a different matter."

Jill looks at Gary and raises her eyebrows, "I am sure you would do your best for the cause to convince her to come over, would you not, Sergeant?"

Gary grins. "For the cause, of course!"

He winks at her. "This is fantastic cake, another quality I was unaware of, how many others are there?"

Felicity is quietly watching the evening news and enjoying the cake and tea. She does not ask any questions about their discussion and Gary and Jill do not try and explain things until they hear from Professor Ashington.

The TV programs come and go and they both notice each other frequently looking at their watches to see the time. At 20.17 the phone rings. "Yes, this is Jill."

"Hello, this is Professor Ashington, I need to know the time the blood was taken and the plasma spun out, do you have that data?"

"Professor Ashington can you hold on a minute, I have that written down."

Gary's eyes open wide, he knows how important this call is. Jill smiles at Gary and goes to the notes she made from the hospital records.

She finds her notes and then goes back to the phone, "Hello, Professor Ashington, the blood was taken at 08.20 and the plasma spun out at 10.00."

"Great, I hope to have some data for you in an hour or so."

"I will be waiting by the phone. Thanks for all your help. Bye."

Jill turns to Gary, "He needed the time the blood was taken and spun out for some reason. He will ring within the next few hours and let us know. I didn't ask him anything and he didn't volunteer anything. We have to be patient. Can I make you a sandwich?"

"No, you relax with your mum, how about I go out and get us a takeaway whilst we wait? How about Indian or Chinese? Does your mum like that type of food?"

"Mum loves Indian, that's very kind of you Gary. There is a good Indian at the end of Sharp Street, do you know it?"

Gary knows the place, "Yeah, I know the one you mean, near the petrol station?"

Gary knocks on Jill's door with two plastic bags full of Indian take away about forty-five minutes later. Jill opens the door and gives Gary a kiss on the lips.

"Thanks, Gary, you're great!"

Felicity walks up to Gary and smiles, "You're a good lad Gary. We are very proud of you."

Jill is smiling and Felicity has tears in her eyes. It dawns on him that the kiss on the lips and Felicity's comments are not simply related to his bringing them an Indian take away.

Jill says, "Gary, Carol never had a chance. Professor Ashington just rang, he did the biomarker test for tricresyl

184

phosphate exposure and it was the highest he had ever seen. He said she and the captain must have had a significant exposure of well over an hour and that combined with all the other chemicals they definitely would have been exposed to means they would have been significantly cognitively impaired in his opinion. He said they would have been intoxicated without actually realising it. They didn't stand a chance Gary. He is going to re run the tests, do a DNA fingerprint as well in case they want to compare her DNA with my DNA in the future and mail the remaining plasma and all the results by lunchtime tomorrow. Monday, when it arrives, they will not know what hit them!"

Gary is speechless, "That is awesome, justice at last."

Jill continues, "I have briefly explained to Mum how you read the report and investigated these matters. We are really grateful to you Gary."

"Don't forget my dad also died because of all this."

He has tears in his eyes as well. "It's a real disgrace this accident ever happened. The industry know crews were not taking contaminated air seriously, they know they quickly become de-sensitised when they smell the fumes, they know many of these neurotoxins have no smell and yet they did nothing. Sure, if they had used oxygen they might have been OK to land the aircraft but they didn't. The industry should have fitted contaminated air detection equipment years ago or filters. This corporate greed being put over crew and passenger welfare really pisses me off. At least on Monday they will get what they deserve. Sorry for going on Mrs Parker, it just really really annoys me."

"Gary I lost my daughter because of this corruption. I have tears every day. You have every right to vent your anger."

Gary puts the take away plastic bags on the kitchen work surface. "What a result Jill, I can't wait to see JASP management faces on Monday, that will be a priceless experience!"

"Think of Carol's work colleagues who would not help, think of what it's doing to their health. Think of the health of people who fly on aircraft who are being exposed. Gary this is so big. We have really kicked some arse, well on Monday we certainly will. Let's eat, I think I am going to enjoy this meal. Meal of justice, we can call it."

Jill gets out some plates and serves up the take away. They are all very excited. It is a massive weight off their shoulders. They eat their meal and then the excitement starts to pass. Jill starts to think about Carol and her mother is clearly upset again. The reality of how avoidable Carol's death and the death of the passengers and Gary's father starts to come home again.

The heavy silence of their thoughts is interrupted by a sharp beeping sound. Gary picks up his mobile. He is about to read the text aloud but his eyes have sped up ahead to the signature at the end of the message and he hopes that Jill cannot see him blush. *Guess where I am? Northumbria Hotel. Room 109.*

"Well, I'd better go," he says to Felicity, avoiding Jill's eyes.

"Is anything wrong?" asks Jill. "Who was that message from?" She knows she is being pushy the moment she has spoken.

"Oh, no one. A mate."

Jill you need to ring Mr Gloyer. I will keep an eye on Marta and... Let's keep in touch over the weekend and how about I come and collect you Monday morning and drive you to the hearing?"

"That's a great idea for Monday. Thanks, Gary."

As he walks to the door the years of training in the military awake an inner thought and he turns towards Jill, "Don't tell anyone about this, loose talk is not good. Keep it very quiet until after Monday."

Gary opens the front door and steps outside. It is raining and the wind is blowing stronger than it was a few hours ago. For a few seconds it reminds him of the windy crash morning but he puts the thought out of his mind, gets in his car and turns on the ignition, trying to work out the quickest route to the Northumbria Hotel.

"Are you all right, Pet?" asks Felicity. "You've gone all quiet, suddenly."

"Yes, Mum. Just tired."

There is a pang in Jill's stomach. She was happy with Gary, this evening. So happy. But she took her eye off the ball and allowed herself to hope that he could be more than a friend. She hates herself for that.

Chapter 18

It is another dull and overcast Monday morning in Newcastle as Gary drives towards Jill's house. The final item on the local 08.30 news on the radio is that the Coroner's public hearing for the crash of JASP flight 303 will take place that day. The radio reports that 'crew error is the expected verdict with the Coroner's Office even likely to rule that the crew acted negligently whilst flying in a state of alcohol intoxication'. The news is followed by the weather which paints a picture which will not encourage many to venture outside that day. 'Today the weather will be very cold with a northerly wind and heavy rain at times. The temperature will reach a maximum of 7 Celsius'.

Gary's phone rings, confirming arrangements he made for Marta over the weekend with an old school friend and army buddy, Mike.

"Gary, it's Mike. Just to let you know everything is sweet. I will drop Marta off at the hearing as agreed."

"Thanks, mate. Talk to you later."

After the news Gary listens to a couple of his old favourite songs which helps his mind relax away from what is going to be one of those days in life you never forget. First, Sting is singing 'Desert Rose' followed by Frank Sinatra singing 'My Way'. Gary pulls up outside Jill's house. He sits in the car for a few minutes with his eyes shut. He must not smile. He wonders if Jill will notice anything. If she will smell another woman on him. He can still smell her skin and her perfume. She said it was something called *Poison*.

Gary walks with Jill into the living room and is introduced to Mr Gloyer. He is an older man with dark hair streaked with grey but looks in good shape for his age.

He goes through the format of the proceedings. "As soon as the package arrives at my office it will be brought to the court and I will be advised that it is on its way. We expect it to arrive before noon, so we may miss that morning session but that's not a problem. There will be a lot of media and during the hearings you may hear things you don't like. This is not a trial but a public hearing day for any member of the public to give a view or to present any evidence which may be relevant to the accident investigation. You do not have to answer any question you may be asked. This is *not* a trial. We are there to give evidence. If something is said you don't agree with please stay calm. It's important to be seen to be as credible as possible. At the end of the day, we are going to win as we have all the aces. As they say, he who laughs last laughs longest! What we want is a complete ruling of any wrong doing by Carol. We know that will be difficult as she mentions dirty socks which shows an awareness that the air was contaminated and the crew should have gone onto emergency oxygen in line with the manufacturers and operators procedures."

Jill interrupts, "But we know crews don't take contaminated air seriously and the airlines did nothing to tackle this."

"I know, but the airline will try and blame the crew one way or another and we will fight the case well. Don't worry, I will give them a day they will not forget in a hurry."

She smiles, "Dad always said what a kind man you were."

Gary suddenly finds Jill irritating. His mind goes back to the weekend. He remembers his hand rubbing slowly along her inner thigh. He feels her breasts. He looks at his watch, 09.20. "I think we should head off shortly but before we do, we have a little surprise for you at the hearing."

Jill smiles. Mr Gloyer looks at Jill.

"Do you know about this?"

"Shall we say it's an extra ace – just to be sure – as they say!"

Mr Gloyer stands up, "As long as it's credible that's great. I agree we should head off now, I have arranged for a car to take us all in and it should be outside. Give me the details in the car."

He looks out of the window, "The car is here and luckily the weather has kept the media off your door. "

They make a dash for the car in the heavy down burst whilst Jill double locks her front door and then in turn rushes to the car.

During the short drive, Mr Gloyer calls his secretary to see if anything has arrived. Nothing yet. The car pulls up outside Rothbury house, a government building where the public hearing is to take place. It is an old grey stone building in the heart of Newcastle. Mr Gloyer, Gary, Jill and Felicity get out and make the short trip from the pavement to the entrance of the building.

A young girl with auburn hair approaches Mr Gloyer and he introduces her to his entourage, "This is Katherine White. Katherine is a junior lawyer who will be making notes during the meeting and will bring the evidence we are waiting for."

Everyone shakes hands with Katherine. She looks very enthusiastic. "The hearing is in room 101 on the first floor. We all need to sign in and go through security."

At that point, a journalist approaches the group clearly unaware of who they actually are, "Hi, Simon Donaldson from The Weekly in London, can you please tell me what brings you to the hearing today?"

Mr Gloyer takes charge, "Wait till the end of the day if you're a good journalist and you will find out."

The journalist stops dead in his tracks, his pen has nothing to write into his notebook. He was clearly not expecting such a sharp reply. The group walk up to security and register.

Mr Gloyer fills in the paperwork. 'Mr Gloyer + 4. Gloyer and Sons, Solicitors. Public Observers.' He knows the journalist will soon look at the names of the group and this will further confuse him. Mr Gloyer has been involved in many high profile cases and knows that discretion and confidentiality is the name of the game.

As they go through security, Captain Jones's wife walks into the building and four journalists descend on her. She is alone and clearly not enjoying the experience or the media attention. Jill looks back and sees her unease.

She goes back through security and takes on the media, "Do you mind, why don't you write your story when the day is over before jumping to conclusions like you always seem to do. Leave her alone!"

The media are used to hassling for a story but are a bit surprised to be taken on by Jill. Gary looks over and smiles, he is impressed with her courage. Mrs Jones signs in and Jill escorts her through security and invites her to join her group whom she then introduces to her.

Mr Gloyer shakes hands with Mrs Jones. "I would not worry unduly about the media, they have been very critical of your husband and Ms Armstrong but I am confident that today will see their names cleared. I would rather not go into the details now but I am sure you will leave the hearing significantly happier than when you arrived even though it will be a very sad day for us all."

Mrs Jones looks at Jill, obviously confused, "It's OK, Mrs Jones, let's say you have not been told the full story but we believe this will come out today. You will have to have faith in us. We are all on the same side. The side of justice and justice always prevails."

Jill smiles at Mrs Jones and puts her arm around her. As they walk towards the lift to the first floor Jill notices the media attention focus on a group of men and women all in suits with several personal assistants beside them. She recognises one of them from the settlement meeting they held at the Vermont Hotel. She is one of the human resources girls at JASP. The elevator doors open and they all walk in for the short trip up to the first floor.

Mr Gloyer and his group walk into room 101. It's a very large room with a top table of about nine places with six people present and three seats still to be filled. To the right of the table is another table with six other individuals who are administrative people, there to make notes, record the day's events and support the top table of nine. On the opposite side are ten places for what is obviously the media. Opposite the top table is a chair and microphone, obviously for those who wish to speak. The top table of nine and the administrative table places all have microphones in front of them.

The remaining part of the room has some one hundred and fifty chairs facing the top table with a gap between the first four rows and the rest of the seating. The first four rows are clearly reserved for key interested parties with reserved name places on the seats such as the JASP, Department of Transport, unions, Civil Aviation Authority, European Aircraft Safety Agency and so forth.

Of the one hundred and fifty places about eighty are taken. It is a big turnout. Also in the room is a selection of ushers. Mr Gloyer takes a seat about half way back on the side with Katherine White, who is on his right clearly sitting strategically to be able to quickly leave the room when she needs to. Jill sits to Mr Gloyer's left with Mrs Jones on her left and then Gary.

Mr Gloyer turns to Jill, "It's a big turn out, looks like a lot of the families are here."

Martin Stone, from one the pilot unions approaches Jill and Mrs Jones from the row behind, "Good morning, ladies, I am glad you have both been able to attend. I hope you have found that the union has been very helpful so far?"

Jill turns towards to Martin Stone, looks at him coldly and says, "Helpful? Helpful at what? Doing nothing and looking after the industry's better interests at the expense of crew health? Your members are getting sick and you do nothing. Got the message? Fuck off!"

Martin Stone is lost for words and obviously very embarrassed with those around him looking at him and retreats without passing any comment.

Whilst looking at the top table, Jill leans towards Mrs Jones and says, "You might think I was being very unfriendly but, like a good movie, just wait for the ending. Then you will see that in fact I was actually being very civil to the man."

Mrs Jones can clearly see that she will have to be patient and wait to find out what is going on. She offers no comment but a half smile and looks ahead at the organisation taking place at the top table.

More people enter the room over the next ten minutes and the top table and administrative support team start to get ready. Just before 10.00 Gary taps Jill on her left shoulder and uses his head to indicate to Jill to look at the entrance door to the room. It's Gordon Cooper.

Jill smiles at Gary and turns to Mr Gloyer, "That chap who just walked in, is Gordon Cooper. He knows a lot about the politics and facts around this issue. He got the blood test going in the first place! He resigned from doing the work for the union years ago when it became clear the union and the regulator had different priorities than crew health and welfare."

Gordon Cooper walks towards the back of the room and sits down.

Jill turns to Gary "Where is Marta?"

"I don't know. I spoke with her yesterday and arranged for her to get here. An army buddy was collecting her and dropping her off outside, he even rang me this morning and confirmed everything was OK!"

At 10.00 sharp the man in the middle of the top table stands up and starts the morning proceedings by talking into a wireless hand held microphone, "Ladies and Gentlemen, a very warm welcome to you all. My name is Mark Lamb and I represent the Newcastle Coroners Office. I will be overseeing this public hearing day. Before I introduce to you the people who are here in an official basis today I would like to outline clearly the purpose of this hearing. Since the tragic accident to JASP flight 303 which has affected many lives in Newcastle and elsewhere, the Air Accident Investigation Branch (AAIB), the airline, the manufacturer, the regulator, the Coroners Office, the Department of Transport, the Department of Health and union officials from both the pilot unions and cabin crew unions have been investigating the circumstances around the accident of JASP flight 303. It has been a formidable task and the Government have put a lot of resources at the disposal to all departments involved in the investigation to complete the investigation in as short a time period as possible, whilst leaving no stone unturned to better understand the causes and reasons for the accident. In fact investigations have been completed in record time. The AAIB issued an initial accident report and the final report will be completed in the near future. The purpose of this public hearing is to allow members of the public and interested parties to provide any new evidence or data which the investigators might not be aware of or to ask any questions of the accident investigation team. The Secretary of State for Transport from day one wanted the public to have this opportunity, especially as so many lives were touched by the tragedy. At the end of this hearing, I, on behalf of the Coroners Office, will give our findings. Because we only have a day we will not be able to provide answers to questions which can be answered by reading the initial accident report. I would also like to add that these can be very emotional times and we would urge that comments or questions be solely made on an informed and factual basis. We are not here to blame or debate these matters. This public hearing is an opportunity for anyone to provide new data or information under legislation which protects such an individual from any recrimination for speaking out on matters of public interest. There will be a thirty minute break at 13.00. We are scheduled to be in open session until about 17.00. At 17.30 I will give a view from the Coroner's Office. If you wish to speak, I would ask you to raise your hand and an usher will invite you to the front chair or you can speak from where you are seated and in this case an usher will give you a microphone. I would be grateful if you could give your name before speaking. All comments made here today will be minuted and put in the public domain as part of the open process called for by the Secretary of State for Transport. I would be grateful if you could please ensure your mobile phones are switched off or in silent mode and may I remind you that no photography is permitted. Media representatives are here but are not allowed to ask questions as this is not a press briefing and the media have other channels for asking questions through the various agency press offices. I think that covers the general aspects. If I may now introduce the eight members of the panel to you. First of all, on my left is Mrs Steel and Ms Richardson from the Department of Transport (DfT), Dr Pullen and Mr Forster from the Health and Safety Executive (HSE) on my right Mr Ash and Miss Prudhoe from the AAIB and then from the Civil Aviation Authority (CAA) we have Mr Evans and Mrs Mitchell."

Mr Lamb looks over at the administrative support table, "Have I missed anything?"

A man at the end of the table shakes his head to confirm Mr Lamb covered all the points he was required to cover before Mr Lamb completes his introductions, "Ladies and Gentlemen the hearing is now open."

Mr Lamb switches off his microphone and stows it in the mike holder in front of him before sitting down again.

One of the administrative support team is standing on the public end of the administrative table with a hand held mike and immediately takes the first question, "The lady at the back in the blue top. If you would like to approach the table. No..? That's fine a mike is being passed to you. Can you please state your name before asking the question."

One of the many ushers swiftly passes the lady a microphone. There is no shortage of ushers. The hearing is very well organised.

The middle aged lady in the blue top starts speaking into the microphone, "Yes. Thank you. My name is Captain Sally Muller, I would like to ask when the last braking action test was carried out by the airport and if this data will be published in the final report."

Mr Evans for the CAA answers, "There was no requirement to test the braking action as the runway was not covered in any contamination except for water. The flight crew from the aircraft who landed 10 minutes prior to JASP 303 were interviewed and reported braking action as satisfactory. Braking action in heavy rain may fluctuate depending on depth of water present but the runway meets all EASA regulations for drainage and braking action. Mechanical braking deficiencies have been ruled out as playing any significant part of the accident."

A slim lady in her forties asks for the microphone, "Does the CAA believe the aircraft was air worthy?"

Mrs Mitchell from the CAA replies, "Yes, it was."

Gary, looking down at his feet whilst texting Mike to see where Marta is, mutters, "That's a joke."

A man near the front puts his hand up and the ushers quickly give him a microphone, "The press have speculated since the initial accident report was released that the pilots were flying whilst under the influence of alcohol. Has this been confirmed?"

Mrs Mitchell from the CAA replies, "The investigation team were approached by a restaurant owner in London who provided an affidavit stating that Captain Jones and Ms Parker had been in her restaurant the night before and consumed a level of alcohol which would have resulted in them being on duty with a level of alcohol in their blood above the legal limit of zero. Full details will be in the final report."

For another forty-five minutes a selection of questions are asked and responded to on a selection of matters but the issues Gary and Jill are interested in have yet to be brought up or mentioned. Mr Gloyer sends Ms White outside to see what the news is on the delivery from Canada but she returns within a few minutes shaking her head. Still nothing. Gary taps his index finger on his leg, he is clearly frustrated and growing impatient waiting for the courier company and Marta to arrive.

Gary gets a text back from Mike which reads, 'Dropped Marta 100m from the front entrance at 0955. Been back to her friends and no one is home. I don't understand how she can not be there with you. Are you sure?'

Gary shows Jill the text, scans the room one more time and then texts back, 'Mike, we have a problem. She definitely never showed! Can you please try and find her.'

A man in his mid thirties stands up and is handed the mike, "Thank you. I am a local councillor. My question is for anyone to answer. In investigating this accident how many overseas independent, non industry experts were asked to assist with the investigation?"

Mr Ash replies in a very arrogant manner, "I think I can answer that question. The simple answer is that for this particular accident, we have all the expertise we need in the United Kingdom."

The councillor clearly not of the same political party as the Government replies sarcastically, "Seems like the Government always has its own so called 'independent' experts when they wish to control the outcome of any investigation. Thank you for confirming my suspicions."

Finally Gordon Cooper puts up his hand at the back of the room and then stands up

He walks to the front of the room with a selection of papers in his hand, calmly sits at the desk and talks into the microphone, "Thank you for the opportunity to address the investigation team. My name is Captain Gordon Cooper, I was a former Boeing 757 pilot and a member of the pilot union National Executive body. I have published and written on these matters. I have several questions. Would you prefer I asked them separately or together?"

Mark Lamb responds, "Individually would be easier."

"Very well. Can the AAIB offer an explanation as to what was meant by the comment made by the First Officer of 'there's the socks again'?"

Mr Evans replies for the CAA, "We believe this was a comment in relation to the windsock being full from the wind speed reported by the approach controller."

Gordon Cooper looks at the AAIB team, "The question was for the AAIB members."

Mr Ash looks uncomfortable with the question but replies, "We considered various options but concluded this was a comment as indicated by the CAA that this was in relation to wind speed."

"Can you please outline what the other options considered were?"

"I can't recall all the options but we believe the comment is related to wind speed."

Gordon Cooper does not suffer fools gladly and presses him further, "Is the AAIB aware that 'dirty socks' is an expression used by some pilots to describe the smell present when the bleed air supply is being contaminated by heated or pyrolised synthetic jet engine oils or hydraulic fluids?"

Mr Ash does not want to reply so Miss Prudhoe answers, "We are aware of the issue you raise but do not feel it has relevance in the investigation."

Gordon Cooper increases the pressure without compromising his calm demeanour. "How does the AAIB conclude that the comment made by the first officer was not in fact a reference to the fact that the air supply was contaminated? For the benefit of those present who perhaps do not understand the flow of what we are talking about, may I very briefly explain what we are talking about Mr Lamb?"

The journalists and many people in the room are taking a very keen interest in what Gordon Cooper is saying as they are keen to understand what he is getting at.

Mr Lamb seems keen to understand as well, "Mr Cooper please expand as I am a bit lost myself so I am certain we would all benefit from being better informed on the matters you raise."

Just as Gordon Cooper is about to reply, the door to the room opens and an usher points the person who has just walked into the room towards the vacant chairs at the back of the room. Most people do not notice the person entering but Gary's years of training have taught him to always be aware of who enters and leaves a room. Always assess the situation for any increased sign of hostility. In this case he already knows who has entered the room, before he even turns around. He feels his heart pound hard. Dr Valentina Fedorova is carrying a small attaché case and wearing a skirt suit and looks like a million dollars. He does not catch her attention and she appears not to notice him either.

Gordon Cooper replies to Mr Lamb, "Thank you, Mr Lamb. The air supply to the passenger cabin and cockpit on all commercial jet aircraft except for the Boeing 787 is supplied directly from the compressor section of the engines. The air which is taken from the engines and used as the air supply in the aircraft i.e. the air providing the life support system for all on board, is known as bleed air as it is bled off the engine. Like a scuba diver who relies on the air in the tank on his back to survive, passengers and crews rely totally on this bleed air for survival. The air in most commercial aircraft is made up of 50% new bleed air and 50% recirculated air. In the case of the Boeing 757 which was involved in JASP flight 303 the cockpit air is 100% bleed air. The bleed air should be as clean as the outside air but sometimes oils used to lubricate the engines contaminate the bleed air supply resulting in crews and passengers inhaling not only outside air but also pyrolised / heated engine oil chemicals. Now these engine oils are not like others oils such as car oils or mineral oils. The oils used are specialised synthetic (i.e. they are man made) which have had added to them some very specialised ingredients to make the oils perform better such as a flame retardants and anti wear additives. The anti wear additives are chemicals from the organophosphate family known as tricresyl phosphate. The organophosphate family also include the well known nerve agent sarin. The bleed air which sometimes is contaminated with these synthetic engine oils is not filtered in any way. This means that if the bleed air supply becomes contaminated then crews and passengers will inhale and be exposed to these neurotoxic chemicals. I should add that the toxicity of tricresyl phosphate present in many jet engine oils has been known since the 1930s. Some crews can smell the contaminated air and have described it as a dirty sock smell others call it a wet dog or a gymnasium smell, there are many different ways of describing contaminated air. In fact, in a 1997 Allied Signal report to Ansett Airlines on these matters, it was stated that, 'The higher-molecular-weight residue can be the cause of the 'dirty sock' odours that are sometimes encountered.' The reason why there are so many different descriptions is that the concentrations will vary and smell description will vary depending on concentration, also everyone has a different sense of smell if they have any smell at all. Contaminated air events have been reported on all aircraft types because it's an unwanted feature of the air conditioning / bleed air design found on aircraft. A design which manufacturers and airlines have failed to adequately rectify for over thirty years. With regards the Boeing 757 and the contaminated air events which have taken place on these aircraft over the years. These events are well known to the AAIB, the CAA, the manufacturer and the DfT. Therefore, I come back to my question of how does the AAIB conclude the comments were related to wind speed and not to contaminated air?"

The media are writing as fast as they can to keep up and look up to hear the response.

Miss Prudhoe of the AAIB responds, "If, as you suggest, the air was contaminated then the crew would have been on oxygen in accordance with procedures laid down for such circumstances, which they weren't; the crew would have reported the defect, which they didn't; the aircraft would have had a history of the problem, but the previous crew reported there were no problems, so obviously the aircraft was OK and finally the captain would have responded to the comment. For these reasons we concluded that the comment was in relation to the wind speed and we are happy with our conclusion."

Gordon Cooper is ready for the fight, "The issue of crew being complacent when confronted with contaminated air is not new. The Australian Senate Inquiry in 2000 acknowledged a strong evidence of a tendency of pilots to under-report incidents of this nature. British Aerospace issued a Service Bulletin in 2001 stating that, 'In the past oil leaks and cabin / flight deck smells and fumes may have come to be regarded as a nuisance rather than a potential flight safety issue. However, whilst investigations are being carried out to determine the nature of any agents that may be released into the cabin environment and to define any necessary corrective actions, oil leaks and cabin flight deck smells must be regarded as a potential threat to flight safety not just a nuisance.' I am sure you will recall that the AAIB in their 2004 report on the 'G-JEAK incident' from 2000 stated 'Other incidents have indicated that crews are not always fully alert to the possibility of air contamination on aircraft and have not always taken the most appropriate action.' Therefore, I do not think it unreasonable to assume that the crew dealt with contaminated air like most other crews and failed to take appropriate action. The UK AAIB are not alone in voicing concerns about crews not using oxygen when they should, the Australians highlighted this way back in 2000.

For the benefit of those of you who have perhaps not yet made the link between contaminated air and crew performance let me quote from a 1983 article entitled, 'Smoke / fumes in the cockpit' and published in the magazine 'Aviation, Space and Environmental Medicine' by Dr Rayman of the Aerospace Medical Association and another doctor. The article states, and I quote, 'Smoke & fumes in the cockpit is not a rare event and a clear threat to flight safety due to the acute long-term effects toxic effects oil and hydraulic fluid substances have.' If the air was contaminated with synthetic jet oil pyrolysis products these could easily have seriously impaired the crew in a manner they would not have been aware of, a bit like hypoxia and could easily have resulted in the tragedy which occurred. For the benefit of public members here today you might like to know that when an aircraft is first built and certificated it has to meet a large number design regulations. One of these is a 'Ventilation regulation' known as '25.831'. This regulation requires basically that the air being supplied to the crew should be, 'free from harmful or hazardous concentrations of gases or vapours' and that the air supplied should not cause any, 'undue discomfort or fatigue' on the crew. Now for an aircraft to remain 'airworthy' it must be maintained to ensure it continues to meet all the initial design requirements. Sadly, in respect to contaminated air events, the regulators around the world have failed to properly enforce this and turned a blind eye. Why? Because to have enforced the regulation would have been too costly to the industry. But in failing to do so they have compromised passenger and crew health as well as flight safety. Therefore, I am sure you will agree that deciding what the comment of 'there's the socks again' is actually key to the whole investigation. You have concluded that the crew comment was in relation to wind speed, I personally spent seven years researching these matters and would say your conclusion is wrong but I appreciate we have limited time so let me turn to my next question. Can the AAIB please advise why the cockpit voice recorder transcripts only shows time in hours and minutes and lack times in seconds as is usual practice?"

Miss Prudhoe of the AAIB responds, "I am not able to offer a reply at present I would need to seek input from the cockpit voice recorder analysis team. This may be simply a printing error. Is there a relevance?"

"If the crew are impaired this may show up by slow response times in their replies to air traffic control, so it might be very relevant?"

Ms Richardson from the DfT replies, "Captain Cooper you are implying that the crew errors reported may be due to exposure to contaminated air and this might show by slow response times on the cockpit voice recorder. Would you agree as a former Boeing 757 Captain that a crew flying in an intoxication state from perhaps alcohol might equally show as slow response times?"

Gordon Cooper is being cleverly backed into a corner, "It is very possible."

Ms Richardson pushes on, "So even if the time was available in seconds it would not add any further clarification to these matters as both exposure to contaminated air and alcohol would most likely show similar trends. I understand you have a big personal interest in these matters as you formerly investigated these matters for the union. Am I correct you are no longer a member of the union and resigned from the union national executive?"

Gordon knows where this is going, "That is correct."

Ms Richardson hammers another nail into the coffin, "So you are not here as a union representative today?"

Gordon fights back, "That's correct, but I thought as this was a public hearing you would appreciate the benefit of my many years of research and expertise on these matters, but obviously nothing has changed since I was in the union. The Government has still got its head buried in the sand. If the Government had listened and fitted filters and contaminated air detection systems we would not be here today. In my view, the Government has been seriously negligent. I would even say that this Government sacrificed the lives on JASP 303 in protecting the financial interests of the airline industry."

Gordon Cooper stands up and walks back to his seat. It is clear from the looks he gets and comments being made, that the exchange has really got people interested and engrossed in the issue.

Many hands go up but almost as if it had been rehearsed Martin Stone is given the microphone by an usher, "Mr Lamb and members of the committee, my name is Martin Stone and I am here as the pilot union representative speaker here today. I can state that the union is delighted to work with industry to progress these matters and can state that Gordon Cooper does not speak or give a view endorsed by the union executive. The union feels the investigation has been done in a constructive and open manner and we would like to thank the regulator and the AAIB for their hard work in researching the circumstances of this accident under difficult circumstances."

Jill turns to Mrs Jones and in a fairly raised voice says, "What a complete arsehole!"

Her comment is overheard by several seated near her.

Mr Lamb, from the Coroner's Office, responds initially looking at Mr Stone but then at the public in general, "Thank you, Mr Stone for your kind supportive words."

Gary stands up and takes Jill with him. They make their way to the back of the room to greet and speak to Dr Fedorova.

Mr Lamb gets the process going again, "Can we have the next question please."

A middle aged lady a third of the way back on the right is selected from the public and quickly given a microphone as Gary takes a seat beside Dr Fedorova.

"I cannot tell you how excited and pleased I am to see you, Doctor."

Dr Fedorova looks at Gary. Nothing in her tone or body language betrays her. "This issue is like asbestos, buried and covered up by an airline industry who made a huge error in using bleed air, an error they have tried to keep silent for many years. What I have discovered needs to be made public. I thought of writing to the investigation team as you suggested in your email but thought this is too important, too many people are being affected. I decided I needed to come over. I just booked the flight on Sunday morning and landed in London this morning and flew up to Newcastle on the first flight I could get on. That was an interesting flight. I smelt the contaminated air, it was not very strong but I was making a conscious effort to smell it and I did. I reckon millions of passengers would smell it if they made an effort to look for the smell. Anyway, here I am."

What a performance, thinks Gary.

Valentina smiles at Gary but before he replies the middle aged lady starts to address the investigation team, "My name is Dr Lynas, I am an occupational doctor and I lost my daughter in the accident. Can the regulator please clarify something for me. The speaker before talked about contaminated air and contaminated air detection systems. Can the regulator please tell me what type of contaminated air detection system was fitted on JASP flight 303?"

Mr Evans replies for the CAA, "There was no contaminated air detection system fitted as there is no requirement for such devices to be fitted to commercial aircraft either here in the UK or anywhere in the world and besides, as we stated previously we do not feel contaminated air played a part in this accident. We have an excellent safety record which is respected around the world."

Dr Lynas decides she would like to know more, "Mr Evans, if aircraft have no contaminated air detection systems, how do crews know the air is contaminated?"

Mr Evans looks very nervous, "If the air is contaminated then the crews will smell the contamination or see visible fumes and use oxygen as per the emergency checklists. The first item of the Boeing 757 contaminated air checklist is for crews to use oxygen. If the crew of JASP flight 303 thought the air was contaminated they would have used oxygen, they didn't so the air was not contaminated."

Dr Lynas does not like the responses she has received, "The gentleman who spoke before talked of crews seeing contaminated air as normal and not taking contaminated air seriously. Are you saying that 100% of all pilots use oxygen when they smell contaminated air?"

Mr Evans does not like these questions, "We do not know what percentage of crews use oxygen, how would we. We see crews as being professional and taking the steps they have been told to take in such circumstances."

Dr Lynas pushes Mr Evans further down this one way street of questions, "So Mr Evans, the regulator expects crews to use oxygen when the air is contaminated but does not know how many actually do, therefore let us assume that some crews do ignore the procedures as suggested by the previous speaker on the grounds that these fumes are seen as a nuisance, as the previous speaker highlighted. You mentioned that crews would *smell* contaminated air or see visible fumes and take action. Do all contaminated air events have a visible element?"

Mrs Mitchell from the CAA can see that Mr Evans is struggling and steps in, "As I understand it, most contaminated air events are extremely brief events with no visible clues. Crews are professional and if they smelt fumes for more than a few seconds I am sure they would use oxygen."

Dr Lynas takes on the new CAA spokesperson, "Thank you for clarifying that but what you are saying – if I understand it correctly – is that crews rely on their sense of smell to detect contaminated air and to judge if the smell has passed or not. I assume that crews are therefore required to have a good sense of smell?"

Mrs Mitchell, like Mr Evans, is also forced down the one way street of questioning and provides a brief reply, "Pilots under go strict medical testing to ensure they are fit to fly."

Dr Lynas makes her check move, "Therefore in their strict medical testing are pilots tested for their sense of smell?"

Mrs Mitchell knows she is beaten, her back against the wall, "Pilots are not tested for a sense of smell."

The media and public have followed the exchanges and are clearly unimpressed. Comments like 'that's outrageous' and 'our lives in their hands' echo out.

Mr Lamb takes control, "Ladies and Gentlemen please, this is a public meeting not a court trial. Dr Lynas have you finished?" Dr Lynas goes for the check mate move. "Mr Lamb, if I may just sum this up for my mind and ask the investigators to correct my thinking should I be in any way mistaken. The previous speaker talked about the possibility that the crew were exposed to contaminated air. There are no contaminated air detection systems on commercial aircraft except for a crew's ability to smell and yet crews are not tested or even required to have any sense of smell. I am totally shocked. Whether contaminated air did or didn't play a role in flight 303 I would suggest that such detection systems should be made a high priority. Contaminated air detectors exist on submarines, in propeller aircraft by way of carbon monoxide detectors, in mines, on spacecraft and even many homes have carbon monoxide detectors so why not on aircraft? What is there to hide?"

Dr Lynas hands the microphone back to the usher.

Dr Pullen from the HSE makes a comment, "We investigated the circumstances of flight JASP 303 in great depth and do not feel contaminated air played any part."

Dr Fedorova turns to Gary, "I never expected this to be such a heated meeting."

Gary leans towards her and the familiar scent of *Poison* wafts towards him, like an open invitation. "You missed the boring part. We have two aces to play. One we have temporarily lost but wait till you see the card we will be playing later. I am so pleased to see you. During the break I will introduce you to the people I was telling you about, I will go and tell them you are here. Thanks for being here."

Jill has said nothing.

Gary and Jill get up and go back to sit beside Mrs Jones. They wait for a quiet moment to brief Mr Gloyer.

Jill whispers in Gary's ear, "Where is Marta?"

Gary replies, "I don't understand it. She either got scared, talked out of it by her friend, lost or... Intercepted! Jill she only had 100m to walk from where Mike dropped her off. If she had changed her mind surely she would not have been there this morning when Mike collected her. That could mean someone was waiting for her outside!"

The usher gives the microphone to a man in his twenties near the front of the public area, "My name is Stewart Mainwaring, I am a pilot with JASP but I do not fly the Boeing 757. I am speaking under the HSE privilege rules."

The JASP representatives quickly look around. Obviously they were not expecting one of their own employees to be speaking.

Mr Mainwaring continues, "I would like to inform the investigation team that on the morning that JASP flight 303 left London I was attempting to contact my engineering department in relation to some aircraft defects on our engineering frequency of 131.7 MHz. A female pilot was finishing a conversation with engineering when I tuned into the frequency and advised engineering that she would write up the defect with the details they suggested in Newcastle. I do not know what the defect was and assumed it was not relevant as the initial accident report stated that the aircraft had no defects. I attended today because I work for JASP and live in Newcastle. After hearing the comments about contaminated air I thought I should bring it to the investigation committees' attention as it may be relevant."

Miss Prudhoe from the AAIB responds, "The aircraft operator advised us that the aircraft left London carrying no defects. The airline checked its records and confirmed it had no communication with the aircraft after it pushed back off the gate except for a communication about 'slot' times. Our initial investigations of the aircraft debris led us to conclude that the aircraft was fully serviceable at the time of the accident. Whilst we appreciate your input, it is hearsay and not supported by any records. It may well be that you confused the destination or the dates. We have not had any other such reports."

One of the JASP employees stares at Stewart Mainwaring; he can sense the person looking at him. He knows he cannot prove what he is saying and does not want to compromise his job anymore than he already has by being seen as a trouble maker. He hands the microphone back to the usher.

Mr Lamb then stands up and addresses the public, "Ladies and Gentlemen, this is a good time to adjourn for a short lunch break. It is 1.00, can we please recommence proceedings at 1.45 sharp."

The public stand up and start conversations and move towards the large area outside room 101.

Gary turns to Mrs Jones and Mr Gloyer, "Can I borrow you both for a minute? There is someone I would like to introduce you to. Mrs Jones, as Jill said, we have several cards to play this afternoon, you will have to trust us."

Chapter 19

Gary introduces Valentina. "May I introduce Dr Fedorova. Dr Fedorova has flown over from Canada yesterday and arrived this morning. She has come to personally give the accident committee the information about the swab testing on the walls of four commercial aircraft. This is how importantly she views the information."

Mr Gloyer is just about to respond when his assistant interrupts him. "I have just had a text message, there is a box for me to collect outside the building which the office has just sent over. It's from Canada. It's the package you have been waiting for."

Jill does not appear to have heard. Her eyes are shooting daggers at Valentina and Gary in turns.

"We have a key piece of evidence this afternoon which we feel will clear the crew's name from any wrong doing. We also have another witness who shared a flat with the waitress," says Gary. That is why Jill has her lawyer with her. It's probably easier for you to just watch the show rather than me try and explain it all in this short break."

Mr Gloyer says, "I think the morning session has opened up the issue well. Gordon Cooper clearly rattled them and the union and regulator have closed ranks. I think this afternoon it would be a good idea for you, Gary, to bring up the alcohol story at the Lebanese restaurant as well as presenting Marta. Is she here yet?"

"No, I am on the case."

Mr Gloyer continues his briefing, "I am mindful that without Marta we lack evidence. Perhaps Dr Fedorova could introduce her information and then we will release the final trump card towards the end. I suspect they have no idea what is about to hit them. I am going to call the office for a few minutes and get a coffee. I will see you back here in fifteen minutes."

Gary gestures he has to send a text message and Mrs Jones wanders off.

Left alone with Gary, Dr Fedorova and Jill resume their earlier conversation, "Gary never told me you were going to come. Last I knew was you had asked him what to do with the information."

Dr Fedorova senses Jill's unease but has no intention of reassuring her. "I got an email from Gary suggesting that as I could not be here in person if I could fax the investigation committee. I thought about it and decided that a fax might easily get lost or brushed off and in view of the seriousness of my findings I would make the journey. Besides, Gary had kindly offered to show me the sights when we met in Canada. So I flew in this morning."

Jill gives a tense little laugh. "I am sure Gary will give you a great tour, won't you Gary – if you haven't already. Sorry, I forgot you have only just arrived."

"It could be arranged," he replies clearly aware of the tension between Jill and Dr Fedorova. "We are both very grateful that you have come over today."

Gordon Cooper approaches Gary who greets him with a smile. "I bet they did not expect you to spoil their day?"

"I decided a few days ago I would come and tell them some home truths but sadly they don't seem to want to listen. The statement by the pilot about the lady pilot discussing a defect was very interesting. I definitely smell a rat and I am sure it is linked to the insurance story we discussed," replies Gordon.

Gary leans forward and whispers into Gordon Cooper's ear so no one can over hear the conversation, "Don't worry, the game has just started. You remember the blood test you got going, the biomarker of exposure?"

Gordon Cooper nods affirmatively. "Well the publishing case is all cleared up, and Professor Ashington analysed the blood, the results just arrived!"

Gordon Cooper turns to Gary, "And?"

Gary smiles knowingly and puts his index finger against his lips.

Gordon Cooper smiles back, "That's great. Poetic justice. I can't wait to see their faces. That's really great but also very sad. Why did they never listen? Look I will catch up with you later. I need to find the gents."

The afternoon session starts very punctually. Jill whispers in Gary's ear while he looks straight ahead

"Bit strange the doctor went to her hotel and checked in this morning at the expense of missing the start of the session, don't you think?"

Gary continues to look ahead, "I don't know what your on about. She is here that's what is important."

A man in his forties is first to ask the accident team a question, "Good afternoon by name is Mr Roberts, I am a former police officer. My brother died in the accident. We have heard about contaminated air but I would like to focus on the alcohol aspects of your investigation. The allegation – if I understand correctly, is that the two pilots consumed an excessive amount of alcohol which resulted in them operating the aircraft as operating crew above the legal limit of zero. I have two questions? When tested what levels were found in their blood and why was this not picked up. How could it have been possible for the crew to operate a commercial passenger aircraft in such a state?"

Ms Richardson from the DfT replies, "In view of the injuries sustained it appears that neither crew member was actually blood tested for alcohol levels. Some time into the investigation we were contacted by the owner of a Lebanese restaurant in London who advised us that each crew member had drunk a full bottle of wine late the evening before. We investigated the allegations and they were found to be substantiated. We do not know the level of alcohol present. Had we been able to ascertain this then we might have considered reconstructing the situation in a flight simulator and investigated what level of impairment such a level of alcohol would have caused but everybody is different and it might not have helped us understand any better what actually occurred."

Mrs Mitchell from the CAA adds to the response. "It is important to stress that this public hearing is part of the investigation process and we will await the coroner's view before attributing any causation to the accident. I would, however, like to highlight that the aviation regulations and law are very clear about these matters. As an operating crew member you must not report for duty with any level of alcohol in the blood."

George Mayman is given the microphone next by the usher. "Thank you for the opportunity to talk. I am a former member of parliament with the opposition party and find the investigation team's memory appears to be lacking Mr Lamb. Let me enlighten you. In February 1999 in the Commons, Mr. Tyler asked the Secretary of State for Defence, 'What organophosphate lubricants are used in the engines of military (a) fixed winged aircraft and (b) helicopters'. If I recall correctly Mr. Doug Henderson replied to the effect that 'The organic phosphate compound, tricresyl phosphate, is present in all lubricants used regularly in military aircraft engines and the inhalation of mist (containing tricresyl phosphate) which can be produced by high pressure systems, or direct contact with the skin, would be hazardous'. Therefore, I would agree with the gentleman who spoke earlier that contaminated air is very much part of this debate unless the military tricresyl phosphate is different to civilian tricresyl phosphate !"

There are several laughs at the sarcastic comment made by Mr Mayman.

Ms Richardson from the DfT replies with a face that does not find the comments amusing, "I believe the tricresyl phosphates are the same."

Gary is next to speak, "My name is Gary Bamford. My father died in the accident. I have been privately investigating the details of the accident of flight 303 for a few weeks. I have spoken with many experts and I, like Mr Cooper who spoke earlier, feel that the investigation team seem to be all too easily discounting any link to contaminated air. What I also find very surprising is how the story of the Lebanese restaurant only surfaced very recently just when some of us started asking a lot of awkward questions. This may seem like a conspiracy speech and that is because that is exactly what I am saying. This is a conspiracy. You quickly discount the information supplied by a JASP pilot that he may well have heard the co-pilot reporting a defect on the basis that it is hear say with no proof, yet accept the view of a restaurant owner on face value. You have no blood test to prove the crew were flying in an intoxicated state – just one witness. Do you have any photographic evidence to support they were even in the restaurant? I visited the Lebanese restaurant and met with one of its employees, a Polish waitress who indicated that this was perhaps indeed just a story. So what we are talking about is one story against another. Why is the investigation team so quick to discount the contaminated air possibilities? What proof would you want to prove the crew had been exposed to known neurotoxins?"

The media are extremely interested as are most of the people gathered in room 101.

Mr Lamb answers Gary, "Mr Bamford as I said before this is not a court but a public hearing so please keep to facts. The DfT and the London Metropolitan Police spoke with the

215

restaurant owner who confirmed by picture identification the crew had been in the restaurant and consumed a full bottle of wine each. You stated that a Polish waitress claims the story is false. This is an open public hearing so please introduce the waitress to the investigation team and we will be delighted to re-examine that aspect of the investigation. Is the lady here today Mr Bamford?"

Gary plays his ace card, "Mr Lamb I arranged to meet the Polish waitress in the restaurant one evening but she never turned up and I was then advised she had returned to Poland because family problems, but seems to have travelled without her passport! I went to where the waitress worked recently, her name was Katarzyna, you can check the details. A waiter gave me the address where she lived and there I met a flat mate of hers called Marta who is now in Newcastle and who has Katarzyna's passport. I hoped she would be here this morning as she was dropped off 100m from the entrance at 0955 but she has not yet arrived. She seems to have vanished. I hope she will arrive very soon. I know it sounds a bit far fetched but I am a soldier in the British Army and telling you the truth.

Mr Lamb attempts to calm the room, "Ladies and Gentlemen, please. Mr Bamford, your story seems to belong in a fiction novel. You seem to meet a lot of disappearing people."

There are many laughs from the room. Gary knows how it must all sound.

Mr Lamb keeps the proceedings moving, "Ladies and Gentlemen, please. Mr Bamford, such conspiracies stories are not what is needed at hearings such as these. I am sure you will agree that it would be unreasonable to accept what you are saying on face value without actually hearing from the waitress you mentioned and seeing the passport you claim she has. We can only work with facts. If you claim she has her passport, I suggest this is a police matter. You asked what proof would the investigation team need to show that the crew were affected by contaminated air. I would assume we would need a blood test to prove this but I am not aware that such tests exist. I understand blood tests were carried out on the first officer which showed toxins highly consistent with exposure to smoke from the accident but these are not relevant to the medical state of the crew in flight. I would agree that data from a contaminated air detection system might have added to the debate by being able to scientifically rule out contaminated air but we must work with the facts we have. I appreciate these are difficult times but we must deal with facts and not ridiculous conspiracy theories. These are difficult enough times without attempting to question the integrity of the investigation team. If I may have the next sensible question, please."

Gary sits down dejected and looks at his phone. A message from Marta, 'I am very sorry but I am too scared to risk my life and my family's life by getting more involved in this matter. I hope you understand.'

Gary passes Jill the phone and shows her the text message. Jill shakes her head and then tells Mr Gloyer.

Mr Lamb is starting to get annoyed with the tone of the comments being expressed. Gary looks at Jill who just shakes her head.

After a couple of other questions, Dr Fedorova puts her hand up and very swiftly is presented with a microphone.

"Members of the investigation team, my name is Dr Fedorova. I hold a PhD in analytical chemistry. I am not a UK resident but Canadian and have flown here to present data which I have only recently acquired which I feel is important to these investigations."

The two CAA representatives look at each other whilst one of the DfT representatives writes down her name on a notepad.

217

"The issue of the toxicological impact from exposure to heated or pyrolised synthetic jet engine oils has recently been brought to my attention. As we have heard today in this short session in matters relating to contaminated air these are complicated issues. I have reviewed numerous published papers on these matters and find that although swab testing was recommended by the United States National Research Council in 2002 it seems that no airline has actually done swab tests to see if the inside walls of their aircraft have the presence of any neurotoxins found in the engine oils or hydraulic fluids. I found that very surprising. The debate around the health issues of contaminated air seems to have been ongoing since at least 1977 if not 1953. Surely if the air supply is clean then the inside walls of the passenger cabin will also be clean, especially as smoking is now banned on passenger aircraft. I even found that a UK Research Establishment had done some air monitoring and reported that no data was obtained from flights where a contaminated air event occurred, although they were quick to argue the air was clean. The point I am making is – why did Research Establishments and airlines around the world not carry out the swab sampling recommended by the NRC? I then thought perhaps they might not have liked the answers, so I initiated a program myself. The data from this program is why I have travelled here from Canada. This is unpublished data but I feel it echoes the comments being made here today that in fact contaminated air may have played a part in the accident and that contaminated air is in fact a very serious public health and safety issue.

We took four swab samples on four different commercial aircraft in Canada last week and the wipes were individually extracted with a suitable organic solvent, and evaporated to dryness. The samples were redissolved in a small amount of organic solvent prior to GC-MS analysis. The organophosphate tricresyl phosphate was determined on all wipes (TmCp in all samples, and TpCP in three samples) in the µg mass range. This being the total mass on the wipes. In addition, triphenylphosphate (TPP) was confirmed present in all samples also in the µg concentration range, while tributylphosphate was determined on three wipes. The recovered amounts of organophosphates on the wipes cannot on a scientific basis be related to air concentrations in the planes alone, and only represent the amount of organophosphates present on the wipes from all sources possible, including deposition from air contamination in the plane. If this sounds too scientific or confusing, what I am saying is that we have found neurotoxins on the walls of all four commercial aircraft we analysed. This means the travelling public and crews are being exposed to neurotoxins. We do not know what the exact amounts are but the neurotoxins detected originate in engine oils and hydraulic fluids so we know these contaminated air events are occurring. These findings alone should result in immediate industry action in my opinion."

None of the investigation team step forward to comment.

Mr Lamb replies, "Dr Fedorova, I am sure the Secretary of State for Health would be interested in your findings when these are presented in a peer reviewed journal. As far as their relevance to the hearing we are having today can you please advise me if any of the aircraft sampled were Boeing 757 aircraft?"

"No, they were not but I might add that today when I flew up from London as a passenger on a Boeing 757, and I could on occasion smell the contaminated air smell that has been mentioned, especially when I first walked on to the aircraft."

Mr Lamb does not even acknowledge the importance of her comments, "Thank you Dr Fedorova for your comments. The UK COT Committee did not believe organophosphates were anything to worry about in these matters. May we have the next question?"

A very elderly man with a large beard takes the microphone, "Mr Lamb, as a scientist who worked on numerous Governmental Advisory Bodies, I would not trust the COT Committee as far as I could throw them. Go and ask the people at Camelford or the victims of pesticide exposures what they think."

Mr Lamb is becoming increasingly impatient, "Ladies and Gentlemen can we please keep to facts and to the matter in question and not personal comments or beliefs, please."

Jill looks at Mr Gloyer. His hand is raised. He turns to Jill and quietly says, "They may think they can get away with this but I think the public now understand the issue enough for our trump card to be played to maximum effect. Marta is obviously not going to arrive, we need to act."

Jill turns to Mrs Jones, "We are about to blow their minds. We are about to play our winning trump card."

Gary looks at Dr Fedorova as she sits down and gives her a discrete thumbs up whilst Mr Gloyer makes his way to the front of the public area and takes the public chair in front of the investigation team.

Mr Gloyer looks at all the members of the top table and then begins, "Members of the public and members of the investigation team. Thank you for giving me this opportunity to talk. I am a solicitor and my name is Mr Gloyer. I represent the interest of the Parker family. For those of you unaware, my clients' family included the first officer, Carol Parker. Carol was a twenty-four year old girl whose whole life dream had been to fly. Today and in recent times you have been led to believe that she would stupidly risk her career and the passengers on her flight to drink a bottle of wine the night before flying the next morning. You are led to believe that in an industry which would have fired her on the spot if she had reported for duty under the influence of alcohol, she still did so. I have been their family lawyer since Carol was a little girl. Her family have always been well respected and played an important part in the local community. Her sister Jill, who is also present here today with Carol's mother, has helped save many lives in the community as a nurse. What I am trying to make very clear here today is that the accusations against Carol are pure fabrication. Mr Lamb asks for proof and states that we can only deal with facts. I am a lawyer and I also only deal with facts so let us all today, here in this room deal with facts. I am not a great fan of the tactics used by the media and I feel they have not made life easy for my client but I am pleased they are here today, because today is judgement day for the airline industry and the Government. You have heard today accusations of conspiracies. These conspiracies are fact and Mr Lamb you have been misled as I will prove very shortly. When we walk out of this building today I ask the Coroner's Office to have the courage to stand up against a corrupt industry and exonerate my client and Captain Jones."

Felicity has tears running down her cheeks and Jill puts her arm around her. Dr Fedorova looks at Gary and raises her eyebrows.

Gary whispers in her ear, "You're going to like this part."

Dr Fedorova looks at Gary who smiles back.

Mr Gloyer takes a glass of water on the table, and then continues to address the investigation team, "We are led to believe the word of a Lebanese restaurant owner that Carol and Captain Jones flew under the influence of alcohol and the effects of the alcohol impaired the crew to a point which affected their ability to fly the aircraft during what was an approach in limiting conditions. Limiting because of the crosswind but also the low cloud base and heavy rain. It is exactly for situations of high work load as were found on the approach to Newcastle that sad morning that crews around the world cannot fly with any alcohol in their blood, as crews cannot have any form of impairment. I do not know who the parties are involved in the conspiracy that has been outlined but I can tell you that Carol's sister, Jill, inspected the medical records of her deceased sister and it appears in fact Carol was blood tested for alcohol but the results page was missing from her file. I would say it was not missing but had been removed because it proved Carol's innocence. However, as a lawyer, I accept that I cannot prove the allegations I am making anymore than the investigation team can prove she was blood tested and found positive. However, and I appreciate your patience Mr Lamb in allowing me to present my evidence, what I can prove is that, in fact, Carol was intoxicated. Intoxicated not from alcohol but from the air they breathed!"

The media again start writing as quickly as they can and a lot of people in room 101 exchange glances.

Mr Gloyer extends the suspense by taking another glass of water and then continues, "Yes, I can prove that Carol, and on the balance of probabilities Captain Jones as well, were in fact intoxicated unknowingly and as a result of being intoxicated never had the cognitive ability levels she ought to have had. In simplistic terms, the evidence I am about to reveal will show you that Carol and most probably Captain Jones were operating a commercial aircraft thinking they were cognitively OK but would have functioned like someone functioning under the influence of approximately six large scotches. Like a prize fighter fighting in the ring with one hand tied behind his back and not knowing it. In essence they never stood a chance of successfully completing the approach in such challenging conditions."

Mr Lamb is anxious to get to the proof, "Mr Gloyer, you have made some very serious allegations this afternoon, surprising for a man of your standing in society. You have also said you can prove your allegations. I am sure I speak for everyone present here today. Can we please see your proof?"

Mr Gloyer responds, "Mr Lamb, I am as we would say in the profession, setting the scene, but if the suspense is too much for you I will come to the point. We have heard today from various individuals that the issue of contaminated air could be the cause of the accident, but this has been dismissed by the investigation team in favour of the alcohol story. Ladies and Gentlemen, contaminated air *is* the reason for this accident and I will now prove it. I will now prove with absolute scientific fact that contaminated air was the sole reason for the accident. The representatives of the DfT may well shake their heads but I can prove it. Before I prove it I need a few minutes of your time, Mr Lamb, to explain how the proof works if that is acceptable to you?"

Mr Lamb nods, clearly intrigued as to what proof Mr Gloyer is going to present, "Please carry on."

"Dr Fedorova flew here today from Canada and told us how she had found a selection of organophosphate neurotoxins on the walls of commercial aircraft. She had not tested the Boeing 757 which was the type of aircraft used on flight 303 but nonetheless she had discovered neurotoxins on the walls of aircraft which had to originate from jet engine oils or hydraulic fluids. Of the three organophosphates she mentioned, one was tricresyl phosphate. Tricresyl phosphate makes up three percent of the engine oils and the oils used in the engines on flight 303. If the crew was inhaling contaminated air, air contaminated with heated or pyrolised engine oils, I am sure you would agree that in addition to the wide selection of chemicals released into the air supply such as phosphorous oxides, volatile organic compounds such as benzene and toluene and perhaps also carbon monoxide; as the oils contain tricresyl phosphate it would not be unreasonable to find tricresyl phosphate also in the air. Tricresyl phosphate is a semi volatile organic compound, heavier than volatile organic compounds which makes its journey into the aircraft cabin more difficult but nonetheless, if tricresyl phosphate is present, it would be sensible to conclude so were other oil pyrolysis products. So if we had been able to record what was in the air in flight 303 that morning we would have been able to clearly answer the question of whether the air was contaminated and if the comment made by Carol of 'there's the socks again' was in fact referring to contaminated air or the wind speed as the investigation team have concluded. Sadly, air monitoring on commercial aircraft does not exist, it seems absurd to me but as Mr Lamb has repeatedly stated we need to keep to the facts.

The coroner mentioned that Carol had been subject to a blood test which confirmed exposure to compounds released during a fire and in view of the fire it would not have been possible to do a swab test of the cockpit as Dr Fedorova's team did in Canada. So what we really need in the future is a blood test that could prove exposure to tricresyl phosphate. Something perhaps the aviation community could investigate further one day? If a blood test could prove a pilot was exposed to tricresyl phosphate then we would know they had been exposed not just to tricresyl phosphate but to a complex cocktail of compounds released when pyrolised oil contaminates the air supply or the bleed air as it is known. If such a blood test was developed in the future would that help to prove crew exposures? If you could prove exposure you would also be able to quantify levels of exposure and estimate what the toxicology effects of exposure would be. Mr Lamb, before I continue – and forgive me for digressing, would you as the Coroner's Office agree that if a biomarker of exposure to tricresyl phosphate blood tests was developed, if it even can be, in the future this would be a clear way of proving exposure to contaminated air, not just for crew but for passengers as well?"

Mr Lamb is clearly getting frustrated with the length of Mr Gloyer's speech, "Mr Gloyer, we have been very generous in giving you time to speak but despite your assurances you had some new proof to present today you appear to have taken us into future potential areas of medical research. We need to focus on the facts of JASP flight 303, can you please conclude your talk with new evidence or we will have to stop you."

Mr Gloyer responds very quickly, "Mr Lamb, please forgive me, I was seeking ways to solve these problems in the future. I will get back and very quickly conclude my input to the investigation team, but for the public record would you agree that a biomarker of exposure to tricresyl phosphate if developed in the future would be scientific proof of exposure which might assist in such matters in the future?"

Mr Lamb does not see the hole he is being very cleverly pushed towards and finally ends up exactly where Mr Gloyer wanted him to go. Mr Lamb forgot that Mr Gloyer is a formidable solicitor.

Mr Lamb responds, "Mr Gloyer, if a blood test could be designed to prove exposure to tricresyl phosphate and time of exposure, then this would be cast iron way of resolving areas of ambiguity in relation to contaminated air exposures. If you could now please get to the point, time is running out and we have several other people who wish to speak."

Jill leans towards Gary, "He is very clever, he has got the whole investigation team exactly where he wants them. Mr Gloyer knows he has now engineered the exact moment to give the *coup de grace* and turns towards his assistant Katherine and beckons her to the front.

Mr Gloyer stands to meet Katherine whilst addressing the investigation team, "Mr Lamb, thank you for your time, my assistant is bringing me the evidence I now wish to present to the investigation team."

Katherine hands Mr Gloyer a large box, about 50 cm square for which he thanks her. Katherine walks back to her seat.

Mr Gloyer turns still standing to face the investigation team, "Mr Lamb. In this box is the proof that Carol and Captain

Jones were intoxicated by contaminated air and this seriously reduced their cognitive ability to fly the aircraft without them being aware and resulted in the accident to flight JASP 303. You see what happened to JASP flight 303 was in fact an accident that has been waiting to happen for years, some say it has already taken place. In 2001, a Boeing 757 aircraft was approaching London Heathrow airport. The crew commented on contaminated air but like the crew of JASP 303 believed from years of industry misinformation they would be OK. In 2001, the crew forgot to slow their aircraft for landing, forgot to lower the under carriage or even put out the flaps for landing. On that day an air traffic controller saw that the aircraft had failed to slow down and ordered the crew to execute a missed approach which they eventually did, followed swiftly by using emergency oxygen. After using oxygen the crew finally realised that the contaminated air they had experienced on descent was seriously affecting their faculties. In 2001, they were lucky. This January luck ran out. In this box Mr Lamb is the future. A future that got lost in time but is here today. Mr Lamb you said a few minutes ago that if a blood test could be designed to prove exposure to tricresyl phosphate, then this would be a cast iron way of resolving areas of ambiguity in relation to contaminated air exposures. Such a blood test was designed some years ago. Mr Cooper, who spoke earlier, had the work commissioned even if his union did not want to support it. However, the work was commissioned and after some years wasted by the oil manufacturers influencing a publishing peer review process, the test was released but lost in time. The blood test was developed by a Professor Ashington in Canada, a genius of a genetics professor. He found that when you are exposed to tricresyl phosphate part of the molecule attaches to certain proteins in the blood."

A lot of intrigued and worried looks go around the investigation team whilst Mr Gloyer speaks. "Blood from any passenger or pilot can be taken and analysed for tricresyl phosphate biomarkers of exposure. Needless to say, the implications for the industry are very serious but I will focus on the implications for the investigation team. Three millilitres of Carol's frozen plasma was sent last week to the retired Professor Ashington who subjected the plasma to the tricresyl phosphate biomarkers of exposure test. He also carried out a DNA fingerprint of the blood so there can be no doubt that the blood tested was that of Carol's. Professor Ashington then sent back some remaining frozen plasma. The DNA test can be compared against Jill's blood if needed to scientifically prove that the blood he tested was Carol's and that the results are cast iron, as you put it, Mr Lamb. The package was sent to my office as her solicitor so I can sign an affidavit to the fact this package is as it was when it arrived in my office. Mr Lamb in this box is the future here today. In the box you will find four things. Firstly, a statement from Professor Ashington that the plasma he tested was sent to him from my office. Secondly, you will find a DNA fingerprint which will allow you to confirm that the blood was indeed Carol's. Thirdly, you will find some frozen plasma left over from his tests to prove the plasma sent was taken from Carol; and finally, and most importantly, you will find the results of the tricresyl phosphate biomarkers of exposure test which clearly show that Carol would have been seriously intoxicated from the exposure to contaminated air that morning such was the extent of her exposure. Professor Ashington actually stated the amounts found were the highest ever seen. I told you I had proof and I have. Before I give you the package for you to open do you have any questions?"

Mr Lamb looks at the investigation team members on his left and right, they are all silent, shocked at what they have heard.

Mr Lamb responds in a very calm manner, "Mr Gloyer, I was beginning to think that many speakers here today including yourself were simply trying to hijack theses proceedings to raise the issues of contaminated air which the investigation team had clearly dismissed. I was informed during the lunch break that in years gone by contaminated air has been the subject of much discussion but the Government has repeatedly concluded that contaminated air carries no risk to the travelling public. However, the evidence you are presenting is extremely significant. Before I open the package I would like to ask you if you could clarify a few points which I am sure the investigation team would like details on. Have the techniques used to carry out this tricresyl phosphate biomarkers of exposure blood test been published in a peer reviewed journal?"

Mr Gloyer answers, "Yes, it has, it was submitted for publication in 2005 and finally accepted in 2007 after a lengthy peer review legal process which I am advised the oil manufacturers manufactured, to delay publication."

Mr Lamb hesitates as he thinks and then asks, "Mr Gloyer, if the blood test proves exposure to TCP how do you know this did not occur as a consequence of the post accident fire?"

Mr Gloyer smiles and responds, "That is a very good question. Thankfully, and very importantly, the test proves time of exposure. You see proteins in the blood have different half life's so by taking a blood sample and knowing the time of the blood sample you can see the time of exposure and also the amount of exposure. All the scientific details are apparently contained in the report should you wish to have another opinion on their validity.

Mr Lamb continues, "Mr Gloyer where was the plasma obtained from?"

Mr Gloyer responds, "Carol's sister Jill obtained it from the hospital where her sister passed away."

Mr Lamb looks inquisitively at Mr Gloyer, "Was the plasma obtained with the hospitals knowledge and consent?"

"No, not directly Mr Lamb. The plasma was obtained by Carol's sister using a false name without the hospital knowing the purpose. Jill exercising her citizen rights of acting in the better interests of the public."

Mr Lamb raises his eyebrows and interrupts Mr Gloyer, "If you could now bring me the package I will open it."

Mr Gloyer gives the package to an usher who takes it to Mr Lamb.

"For the record, I am opening a package with courier markings indicating it was sent from Canada and is addressed to Mr Gloyer. The package is sealed and unopened."

Mr Lamb opens the package, "There is a polystyrene box within the package and a large envelope."

Jill smiles at Gary and Mrs Jones, they have been waiting for this moment. They are turning the airline industry upside down with this shattering proof. Something the airline industry has gone to extraordinary lengths to deny for over forty years.

Mr Lamb addresses the room, "I am opening the small polystyrene box. Inside I have found a cracked test tube which appears to have had some blood in it but there is nothing now and it has dried out from a lack of cooling."

Jill looks at Gary, "How did that happen?"

Gary is less concerned, "Don't worry about that, it's the results that really matter, the blood was just a nice touch. Obviously, the Professor did not pack it properly or the container got dropped maybe. I wouldn't worry about it. They can't argue with the blood tests results."

Jill responds, "That's OK, for a moment I was worried."

Mr Lamb continues, "I do have an envelope with statement and results printed on the cover which I will open. There are, let me see, about a dozen papers here, the first one is an affidavit signed by Professor Ashington, dated last Friday stating that the blood test results are included and that he received blood from Mr Gloyer for analysis last Thursday. Let me have a look at the others very quickly."

Jill smiles at Mrs Jones and takes her hand.

Mrs Jones says, "It's amazing what you have all done. I know you're right. My husband never used to be able to tell when I was wearing perfume unless I put tons of it on, he had a terrible sense of smell. This is real justice you have created here today. Well done. The industry will have to change."

"Have you told the investigation team that?" asks Jill.

"Nobody ever asked."

Mr Lamb continues, "I have here a page stating that a DNA test was carried out and the results are attached, which they are... They seem to be fairly clear... DNA results for Carol Armstrong... I have a large number of pages here about the biomarker of exposure test and a lot of in-depth scientific pages about the tests. There is a copy of the peer reviewed paper you referred to... Finally, I have a page which is headed 'Biomarker of exposure test... Results for Carol Armstrong...' It has the correct date of birth... The results state 'Negative for TCP exposure'."

Mr Lamb looks at Mr Gloyer, "Mr Gloyer, I am confused?"

The lawyer rushes quickly up to the top table and, like a man in a very serious panic, looks through the pages. He scans every page. The room is virtually silent in anticipation of what the next comment will be. He cannot find anything that supports a positive test result. He stops looking and slowly turns towards Jill and her mother and shakes his head. He looks very pale. Jill jumps up. Her chair falls back behind her. "You fucking bastards, you fucking stole the proof! You're all in it together! I spoke with Professor Ashington – he told me it was positive and she would not have stood a chance. You're all fucking bastards!"

Jill bursts into tears and Mr Gloyer's assistant helps her out of the room followed by Felicity.

Dr Fedorova calmly turns to Gary, "What is going on?"

"I am not sure. Either Jill has got it wrong or, we have been set up" replies Gary, motionless and facing the front of the room.

Mr Gloyer looks at Mr Lamb and speaks quietly to him, "Mr Lamb, my client had clearly indicated to me that the tests were positive. I do not understand what has happened here. Please forgive my client's outburst. I am sure you appreciate she and her family are under a lot of stress."

Mr Lamb replies, "Mr Gloyer, I can see that you are surprised and confused. You acted on the information provided to you by your client and in good faith, I have no doubts. I have to act on the facts as they are today. I am sure you can appreciate that?"

Mr Gloyer agrees and turns from the top table, too confused to be embarrassed, and walks back to his seat.

A young man mutters, "What a load of BS." As Mr Gloyer walks past.

Mr Lamb quickly regains control of proceedings, "Ladies and Gentlemen, if we can now continue with the questions."

A lady casually dressed at the back is handed the microphone, "My name is Elaine Johnson. Does the investigation team feel that Air Traffic Control were in any way to blame for the accident?"

Mrs Mitchell from the CAA responds, "Our investigation found that the air traffic controllers played no adverse part in the accident."

Another lady is given the microphone, "Yes, thank you, my name is Olwyn Matterson. At what point could the aircraft have carried out a missed approach?"

Mrs Mitchell from the CAA replies again, "The aircraft and the crew could have executed a missed approach procedure at anytime. The trace from the approach shows that the approach was unstable and the view of the investigation team is that this option should have been taken some time before the accident but wasn't."

For another thirty minutes the questions come and go both Gary and Mr Gloyer are speechless. Gary, his head lowered, has his chin in his hand as he thinks about what has happened. He thinks of going out to see Jill but feels he needs to listen to what is being said.

Gary turns to Mr Gloyer who is still in a state of disbelief, "This is seriously evil, Katarzyna and Marta both vanish and now this. On Friday evening, Jill told me when I got back from getting her and her mum a take away, that Professor Ashington had rung and told her the tests were positive and they never stood a chance. What is going on? How come the test tube was broken as well, that was the only plasma left. The test can never be redone."

He pauses for a second, "Hang on, isn't it a bit of a co-incidence that we can never do the test again and the results are negative?"

Mr Gloyer looks stern. "Gary, look at the facts. You got a text message from someone who could have been anybody asking you to meet in a Lebanese restaurant, Jill spoke with Professor Ashington and yet the results sent are not what Jill told you."

Gary looks blank, "Mr Gloyer, I am not following what you are saying."

"I am not sure what I am saying but perhaps Jill is suffering from serious shock and perhaps she only wants to see or hear what she wants. For all I know she texted you pretending to be the Polish waitress. Maybe she is not well. Her mother told me she has trouble sleeping, she is in such a state. Maybe it's a conspiracy. I don't know Gary. I would suggest we ring Professor Ashington but he apparently went on a three week cruise on Saturday with his sick wife. I don't know where or with whom, so we can't even start trying to find him. Besides, like a jury, the Coroner's Office will act on the information in front of them."

Gary looks at Mr Gloyer, "But what about Marta, am I imagining that as well?"

Mr Gloyer looks at Gary, "Where is she Gary? You are implying that this is a huge conspiracy. To be as big as you say it is, the Government would have to be part of it."

"Mr Gloyer, I know it sounds far fetched but Governments lying is nothing new. Governments simply lie to look after industry interests. What about the Gulf War Veterans, sick sheep dippers or weapons of mass destruction in the Middle East?"

Dr Fedorova puts her arm on Gary's thigh. "I am sorry, clearly something does not add up."

"I am not sure what is going on. Jill spoke with Professor Ashington, maybe she was mistaken. If she wasn't then this is more evil than I ever dreamed. Thanks for your support. Mr Gloyer is shocked. The media will not be kind to him. He acted on Jill's word without ever checking the facts and now Professor Ashington is on a cruise for three weeks. What a mess!"

Soon afterwards, the hearing open session comes to an end and Mr Lamb starts to sum up before giving a view from the Coroner's Office. Jill and her mother are still outside with Mr Gloyer's assistant. "Ladies and Gentlemen, today's public hearing was to allow for any new evidence to be presented to the investigation team and for the public to ask the investigation team questions in a frank and open manner. I am sure you will all agree the hearing has allowed for views to be spoken very openly and freely. Everyone who wished to address the investigation team has been accommodated. I would like to thank the ushers for their outstanding work and all the speakers for their comments. I would also like to thank the investigation team for answering all the questions in a frank and open manner. At the end of the day the Coroner's Office must act with the facts it has in front of it. To act on hearsay or unproven speculation would be unwise. We had scheduled a time window to allow for any new evidence to be considered but no new proven evidence has been provided. Therefore, I can conclude on behalf of the Coroner's Office that from a civil and non technical view point, the cause of the accident is most probably due to crew error. Crew error most likely caused by the crew flying in contravention of the regulations which require crews to exercise the privileges of their professional pilots licence whilst free of alcohol in their blood stream. The AAIB will issue a full technical report of the accident within the next four weeks. I thank you all for attending. The session is now closed."

Gary puts his head in his hands and remains seated as people start to leave the room talking amongst themselves.

Dr Fedorova turns to him, "I think you should go and join Jill and her mum."

Gary reacts quickly and stands up giving out a big sigh, "You're right, please come with me."

He turns to Mr Gloyer, "I thought you gave a great speech. Let's go and join Jill and her mum."

Mr Gloyer stands up, "I feel like I have lost the most important case of my life, a case I was certain to win. We can't talk with Professor Ashington for a few weeks so I think it's best to treat Jill gently for a while until we can get to the bottom of this."

Gary agrees and they leave room 101 defeated and confused.

Chapter 20

Beside Gary is Dr Fedorova and Mr Gloyer. Jill is sitting on a sofa with Mr Gloyer's assistant. The assistant sees Gary approaching and stands up to allow him to sit beside Jill. Jill has her head lowered looking at the floor. She is still crying.

Gary sits down beside her and puts his arm around her, "Jill the Coroner had to act on the facts he had and ruled that alcohol was the most likely reason for the crew making errors of judgment."

Jill says nothing.

Mr Gloyer sits besides Jill, "Look I know these have been hard times. Are you certain you understood Professor Ashington correctly on the phone?"

Jill stammers. "Those fucking bastards. They killed the Polish girl, didn't they? How did they gag Marta?"

Gary strokes her hair. "We don't know these things for a fact –"

"And they intercepted the blood sample test. How the hell did they know I'd sent it to Ashington? No one knew. Only Ashington, you and I, right? Oh – and Marta."

Felicity comes over and Gary stands up to allow her to sit beside her daughter, "Darling, I know you have been under a lot of stress since you sister died, we all have. Perhaps level of fatigue and anxiety made you misunderstand Professor Ashington. You mentioned to us that he had told you he was going to redo the tests to confirm the results. Maybe you got things confused, darling?"

Jill is now shaking. "Who else knew about the blood test results, Gary? Who else outside you, me and Ashington and Marta?"

Mr Gloyer turns to his assistant and asks her to get the car brought to the front of the Rothbury building where they are. Katherine steps away from the group and uses her mobile phone to carry out the instruction given.

She returns a moment later. "Mr Gloyer, the car is outside waiting already."

"Thank you, Katherine, that will be all for today. Thanks for your help. I will see you in the office tomorrow morning."

Mr Gloyer turns towards Jill and Mrs Parker, "I suggest we leave now and I will drop you back at your house. Perhaps we could get together next week and discuss the matter further?"

Felicity and Gary help Jill up from her chair and they all walk down the corridor. Mr Gloyer takes their passes and hands them in whilst Gary hands his and Dr Fedorova's pass in. They walk into the dry and dim day outside and the driver of Mr Gloyer's car gets out to open the doors for Mr Gloyer and his group.

Felicity gets in and Mr Gloyer turns to Gary and Dr Fedorova, "Dr Fedorova, can I drop you anywhere?"

Gary replies, "You head on, thanks. I'll walk Dr Fedorova back to her hotel."

Jill rolls down the window by her seat. "Gary, we have known each other since we were kids. You knew my sister. You're a professional soldier. We have investigated these matters together. I need to know what does your gut instinct tell you? Am I crazy or have we been screwed over?"

Gary looks down, "Jill, it's all over what does it matter? We can't do anything about it even if we wanted to."

Jill looks at Gary and wipes her left eye to clear the tears, "Gary It matters to me what you think. I value what you think. If I am crazy I would rather hear it from you. You're a trained soldier you must know if I am sane or if I have lost it. Two

236

people have vanished into thin air. Why are they always one step ahead?"

Gary does not reply. He is staring at Dr Fedorova. Mr Gloyer's car drives off. Inside, Felicity is trying to get her daughter away from the window. Jill is screaming. "Gary, don't do this to me!"

Standing alone on the pavement. Valentina turns to face Gary. She brings her face close to his and kisses him while running her fingers through his hair. He grabs her hand and pushes her away. "You knew."

Her eyes fix him coldly. "Knew what?"

Gary controls his anger from turning violent. "You knew about the blood test. You were the only other person who knew Jill had sent the blood sample to Professor Ashington. You were the only person who knew about Marta as well."

He hates the contempt in Valentina's eyes. "What the hell are you talking about?"

"You bitch. You used me. Whose side are you on? Who told you to fuck me to get information? Who?"

Valentina looks at Gary and raises the tone of her voice. "You'd better calm down, soldier. Your paranoia is starting to seriously screw up your thinking!"

"You fucking used me. You bitch."

"You are one screwed up soldier! "

She turns around and walks away. Gary wishes he could grab her and break her neck. How could he have been so stupid. He is powerless. Jill's tear ravaged face and screaming flash through his mind but he cannot bear to think of her. He cannot bear to think of anything. He stands rooted to the pavement as Valentina's figure grows smaller in the distance. It's his fault. He has fucked up and there's no fixing it now.

Chapter 21

Two older men dressed in suits sit in a large boardroom facing a third younger man dressed in jeans and sweatshirt with a Valentino label. The man in jeans is an extremely fit looking man in his thirties and is sitting with his legs crossed. He looks relaxed. In the middle of the table are three documents.

One of the older men looks at the younger man, "I think we walked a knife edge today and have been very fortunate to pull this off. I am sure the media will run with the story for a few days and then it will die away. Shall we say, I have been assured that will be the case."

The younger man smiles at the older men, "As they say – who dares wins."

The other older man replies, "We made our own luck or should I say, you made our luck. You and your Polish girl. Clever little thing she is. Three million to me to keep the airline alive is a small price to pay. You have clearly a lot of contacts and experience in the work you do. You were right. You were always one step ahead. Congratulations. The call to engineering was discussed today, it's just as well the tapes were removed and edited when you suggested from engineering. If ever they look they will only find the edited tape you put there. I had not considered that aspect. I will not ask how you managed to intercept the courier package or remove the blood test results from the hospital showing that the co-pilot tested negative for alcohol. Are we certain your contacts will be reliable and silent? You were very clever to engineer your contact being in the waitresses' flat."

The younger man uncrosses his legs, leans forward and smiles, "I can guarantee nobody will ever remember anything. Everything has been taken care off. It's a clean job all round, money has a way of changing peoples thinking. Marta is one of the best of the new generation of operatives I have seen for years."

He then picks up the three documents, stands up and walks over to a paper shredder, switches it on and starts to feed the three documents in, "I really am good value I feel. The Government never valued my services when I worked for big brother. One million for the negative alcohol blood test result, a million to edit the engineering tapes and a million to ensure the biomarker results read as we wanted and could not be done again."

The young man then switches off the paper shredder and turns towards the two businessmen, "It's a dirty business but I think you will not get away with it next time. It's important to know when your time is up. Like a good champion, you need to know when to quit. Just one thing – I am curious as to how you will lose three million in the books?"

The two men smile at each other and the man with the beard smiles, 'Let's say *interested parties* are being very supportive!"

The men in the suits stand up and walk to the boardroom door.

"Turn off the lights, will you?" they say to the young as they exit.

"Yes, Gentlemen, I will."

Alone in the office, the young man ponders for a moment, looking around. He listens for the footsteps to die down in the corridor outside. He then takes out a small tape recorder, rewinds a few minutes and listens briefly to the voices he has just recorded. He smiles. Just in case, he thinks. He then slides the recorder back into his breast pocket, turns off the lights and closes the door behind him as he leaves.